VATICAN
UNHOLY ALLIANCE

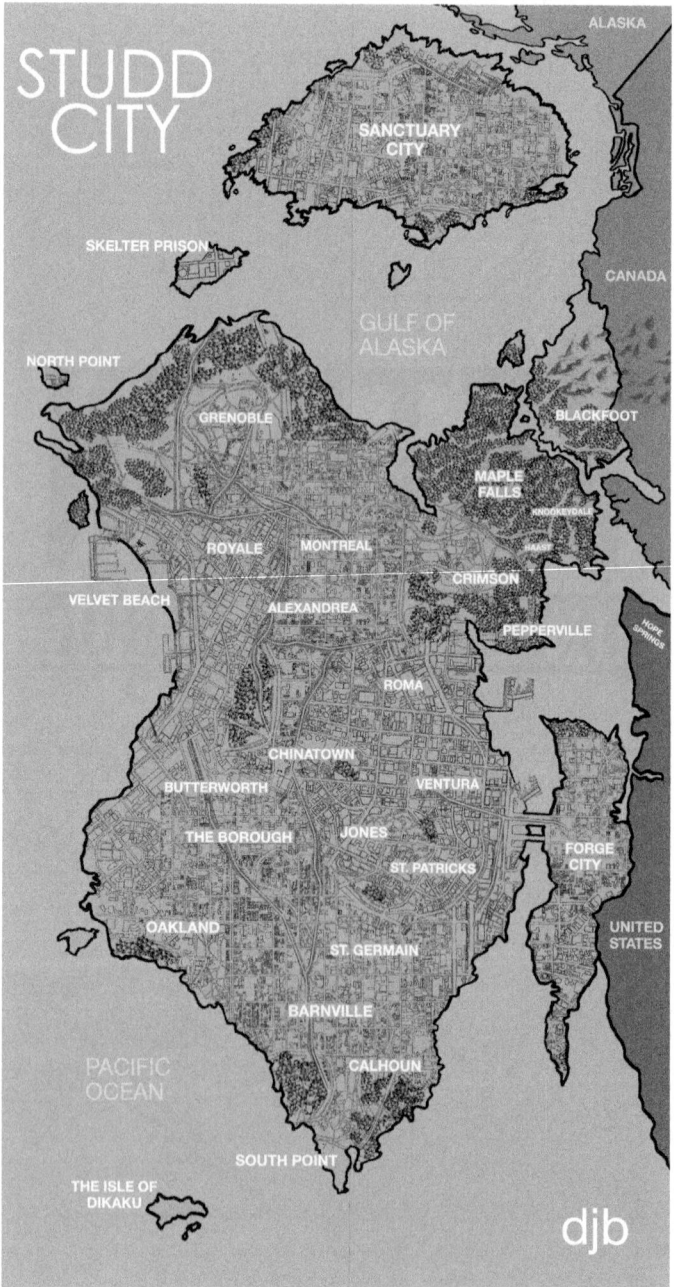

STUDD
CITY

ALASKA

SANCTUARY
CITY

SKELTER PRISON

CANADA

GULF OF
ALASKA

NORTH POINT

GRENOBLE

BLACKFOOT

MAPLE
FALLS

KNOOKEYDALE

ROYALE   MONTREAL

HAART

CRIMSON

VELVET BEACH

ALEXANDREA

PEPPERVILLE

HOPE
SPRINGS

ROMA

CHINATOWN

BUTTERWORTH

VENTURA

THE BOROUGH   JONES

ST. PATRICKS

FORGE
CITY

OAKLAND

UNITED
STATES

ST. GERMAIN

BARNVILLE

PACIFIC
OCEAN

CALHOUN

SOUTH POINT

THE ISLE OF
DIKAKU

djb

4

CHAPTER 1

Thomas Gabriel's voice carried through St Vincent's Church, his words spiralled around the cold stone pillars like some fast moving vine snake, before becoming lost somewhere in the arches high above.

When he first returned to Studd City, these words would have fallen on deaf ears, and empty pews. But a lot has changed since then, a short time on a calendar for Thomas Gabriel to make an impact, but just by the increasing congregation on this fine spring afternoon is enough to show just how much his presence has affected the city. The church no longer felt like the cold, unapproachable ruin that he had been, and Thomas was to thank for making it live again. He had been able to breathe life into a place that had been forgotten by many citizens of the city, many of whom would pass the gargantuan gothic structure on a daily basis but be unaware of its existence. It was a heart-warming feeling for Thomas to look out at the rows of pews and see them filled with the faces of his flock, a look of admiration and hope etched on their faces.

But, Thomas was modest and if you were to congratulate him for his hard work in accomplishing what was seen as impossible in some people's eyes, he would no doubt stop you in your tracks to remind you that he did not do this alone. None of it would have come to tuition without the support, guidance and passion of Burt Simmons. Neither of the crusades would have been manageable without him, not the struggle to convince the downtrodden people of the city that there was hope and somewhere for them to go that cares, and that secret battle being waged out on the streets, a dogfight for control of the city between the just and the corrupt. Granted neither crusade had concluded, but the strides that had been made in such a short period of time were enormous.

Burt Simmons sat at the woodworm infested organ, that was as weary and rickety as he felt himself. His eyes fixated on Thomas as he stood majestically at the altar addressing his flock. Burt's old bulbous lips quivered in mimicking mime, he had already read Thomas' Sunday sermon (as he did every week) and he whispered the words along with him unknowingly like a proud father that has learnt the words to his son's part in a school play. He was right there with him on that altar and he was so very proud, proud of his passion and dedication, and even prouder to have such a great person as his friend. He had told him this many times, and to Thomas it never got old, he needed to hear those words so very badly, he'd always needed to hear those words from that all important father figure in his life. Powerful sentiment that

6

sometimes made Thomas leave the room to dig something out from the corner of his eye.

Thomas spoke clear and loud, but with a smile on his face. His words and tone were neither doom nor gloom, like the flock had heard in the past, words that just kept them more fearful about their lives in this strange city. No, his words were words of positivity and hope and his ever increasing congregation listened intently to every single word.

Even in the twilight of his life, as Burt was he felt as giddy as a school boy, secretly wishing the time would pass quicker and he could pull the organ's stops to activate the secret passage and get onto more pressing matters.

Thomas smiled intently as he continued to talk, his eyes flitted from face to face, regular and newcomer gazed back at him. His mind had begun to waiver and flutter away as all manner of thoughts entered his subconscious. The sermon continued unaffected, he was used now to carrying on with such a simple task as a sermon to a room full of people while thinking of other things. Faces of the congregation changed to mirror his thoughts, Master Sato sat there and Thomas blinked, Sato's face disappeared and was replaced by local shopkeeper, Mr Brown.

Sato. It's been a while since I have been able to reach you. I miss you, Master. Your words were becoming sparse and nothing more than a whisper as though our connection had been severed. I have taken this as I no longer need your guidance and that I am following the right path. I hope this is true. But, with your words came a warning, a warning that replaced your words, The Black Crane.

Thomas' subconscious watched as a huge 8 feet tall black crane, scuttled from pillar to pillar at the back of the church, its burning red eyes seething in the darkness. Thomas smiled at the congregation and continued, there was no Black Crane. Not in the church anyway, in Thomas' head, well that was a different matter.

This blasted creature has haunted my dreams for the last year. I don't know what it means. I have regrettably seemed medical help to rid me of such heinous nightmares. I daren't tell Burt, I fear he would see that as weakness, as do I. Alprazolam is what the doctor prescribed, it does help me sleep, a dreamless sleep. I may have been guilty of taking too many lately. But, I have a hold on this, I don't have a problem. He realised he had stopped talking, he didn't know for how long and nervously he grinned at the congregation as he adjusted his glasses, moving them back into place on the bridge of his slender nose.

"My apologies!" He announced, "I must have lost my place there for a second."

He panned across the audience again, none of them looked annoyed or confused, so it may have only been seconds that he had spaced out for.

His eyes then met a familiar face standing at the rear of the church, and old man dressed in God's uniform had an ancient, worn face that seemed to hang off his skull. He stood grinning at him intently, white thinning hair slicked back from his head made him look like a vampire. Thomas smiled and nodded in the direction of the man, who stepped into the light and sat down on the last row of pews.

That's all I need. A visit from the superior.

He rubbed his dry tongue over the fresh laceration on his bottom lip and wondered how he would talk his way out of this fresh injury. Thomas always seemed to have some mysterious injury when his superiors paid a visit, usually he had a little warning that there would be visitors and Burt could apply some concealer to the said wound or bruise to make it not look as prominent, but today they did not have that luxury.

Busted lip. I'd best not show him my ribs then. After last night I look like I've been used as a human piñata.

His mind wondered again as he recollected the events that took place on what seems to be a normal Saturday night in Ventura for Thomas these days.

Chapter 2

Thomas remembered the tattooed knuckles of some thug connecting with force with his chin, his lip split immediately, with ease, as if his flesh were a packet of potato chips.

Lucky shot.

The thug smiled triumphantly, his mouth showing a crevice of broken and rowing shards. Blood seeped out of Vatican's bottom lip and trickled down his chin, dripping onto the pristine whiteness of his surcoat.

Burt isn't going to be happy. Do you know how difficult blood is to get out of white cotton?

Vatican grinned, his pearly whites now stained pinkish and peculiar. The thug's pierced eyebrows rose in shock, his opponent looked unfazed by the best right hand he had. Vatican whipped way the blood from his lip and chin, smearing it across his face and smiled again. The thug choked down his Adam's apple and started to shuffle back towards the wall of the dark alley.

"Hey, look Mister, I'm sorry." The thug begged, the heel of his foot stumbling over the unconscious body of one of his friends. He glanced around and realised he was the last of them, all his other gang mates lay in heaps deep in the land of nod.

"White vinegar." Vatican said quietly.

"Huh?" Grunted the thug, still backing off and looking for a way out of the situation.

"I said, white vinegar."

"What the hell are you talking about man!" The thug squealed as he backed into a gathering of trashcans. He fell over the cans and knocked them all over like they were skittles. The annoying clamour of crashing metal ricocheted off the alley walls as the rotting contents spilled out onto the floor.

"Please, man, I got a wife and kids to support." He cried as he flayed in the garbage.

Vatican stood over him rolling his eyes at the thug's feeble words to try and get out of this predicament.

"Well, if you're a family man, you'll have to tell your wife that piece of important information I just gave you." Vatican said as he stood over him.

"Tell her what?" He screamed in frustration, spittle flying out of his mouth and spraying Vatican's boots.

"White vinegar!" Vatican growled as he lunged forward and grabbed him by the collar of his white t-shirt and lifted him up out of the mess, pinning him hard up against the brick wall. The thug began to sob about not understanding what he meant. Vatican smiled again and released his grip on the thug's shirt and brushed out the crease for him.

"White vinegar, tell your wife, white vinegar."

"But what does that mean? I don't know what that means!"

"Best way to get blood out of cotton whites." Vatican grinned.

The looked at the blood droplets that had splattered Vatican's crusader surcoat.

"What are you gonna do? Get my wife to do your laundry?" The thug chuckled.

Vatican joined him in the laughter, and slapped him on the shoulder as if he had just told him the funnest joke ever. The thug seemed to relax and laughed more adding, "I got enough problem's trying to get the old broad to wash my clothes, let alone yours."

They laughed again and then Vatican's eyes dropped to look at the thug's t-shirt that was also white.

The thug mirrored the vigilante's gaze until he was looking down at his own shirt.

"I'll wash my own clothes." Said Vatican, as the switch of realisation had finally clicked on in the thug's head and he was met by two wide eyes like some startled deer that just saw headlights a second too late to do anything about it.

With the rapid striking reflexes of a viper, Vatican's palm connected with the thug's nose, the effect was like a water balloon being popped with a pin. It exploded. His eyes crossed and the thug looked as though he might pass out as blood cascaded down his shirt.

"Now, I'll ask again." Vatican said as he reached out and grabbed the thug, holding him up as he was semiconscious and at anytime could collapse to the floor of the alley to join his fallen friends.   "When are you guys going to learn, there's an easy way and a hard way to do anything!" The thug's eyes rolled up and down in his skull like a cherries in a slot machine. Vatican shook his head and sighed, "You guys always seemed to choose the hard way to do things."

He gently slapped at the thug's face, slowly he came round enough to where he could actually answer Vatican's question.

"Yeah..." He groaned.

"Okay, I'll ask one more time. I can see that you have been marked with a black widow tattoo, which indicates to me that you are part of 'The Webheads' gang, yes?"

The thug nodded.

"So that would mean that you are working for Spider?"

"Yeah."

"See how easy that was?" Vatican smiled letting go of the thug, and watching as he slid down the wall half conscious.

"But now for the question that no one seems to want to answer recently. Where is he? Where is Spider?" The thug shook his head.

"Don't tell me you don't know! I've shut down three of these little Stardust rackets this week and you Webheads don't seem to know where your boss is."

"I don't know where he is." The thug grunted, coughing and choking on his own blood.
Vatican grabbed him again and hoisted back up against the wall.

"I said…" Vatican growled with annoyance, but before he could finish his sentence the thug was wide awake now.

"No, no, it's true! Nobody knows where he's at!"

"So how are you getting the Stardust? Is it falling from the heavens into your filthy hands as if by magic?"
Vatican clenches a fist and recoils it back ready to unleash on the thug again.

"Wait! Please don't hit me again man. Nobody sees Spider. Nobody!" He sniffs as blood starts to clog around his nostrils like two ugly growths. "We only deal with Boris or Dallas. We meet in a different place each time and we don't contact them again until we sell all the dust."

"How do you contact them? I guess it would be too easy for you to hand over a cell number wouldn't it?"

"Don't use no cells man. None of us do these days. It's all old school. They use runners, that's how the info is passed." Vatican let go of the thug and he collapsed not the floor neck to the garbage.

"Where would I find a runner?"

"I don't know any of the runners, they usually use kids."

"Kids?"

"Yeah, homeless kids. They're so hard up they'll do anything for a couple of bucks. I guess if you can find a homeless kid they'll be able to help ya."

"I think I know just the kid." Vatican said under his breath as he looked deep in thought.

Vatican walked away from the fallen thug and headed to a decrypted looking van at the end of the alley, "Don't forget to tell your wife." He said, but the thug wasn't listening and had seen a broken bottle in the discarded entrails of a nearby trashcan and grabbed a hold of it.

"Remember, white vinegar." Vatican said turning to face the thug on last time, only to see him charging towards him with the broken bottle slicing its way through the air towards him. Vatican side-stepped the onrushing thug who hurled past him and into the rear of the van, knocking him silly again.

"And to think I was going to let you go. I actually felt sorry for your wife and kids. At least she won't have to do you laundry for a while, you'll be doing your own up at Skelter."

The thug swayed from side to side with the broken bottle still grasped in his hands, a goofy look on his face and Vatican gave him a gentle push to the chest and watched as he fell into another cluster of garbage cans. Another crashing cacophony stung Vatican's ears like a heavy metal drumming

15

thrashing at his cymbals.

Vatican stared into the back of the van, several packages of Stardust all wrapped up in neat piles, a table had been screwed down inside and scales sat on its top.

"They're all working mobile. He was telling the truth, Spider is selling franchises in the stuff."

Vatican activated his earpiece and in an instant the gravelly voice of his confidant, Burt was in his ear.

"Got a pick up for SCPD, Mr B." Vatican said.

"What we dealing with, V?"

"Six no names. Van full of Stardust, no plates. Looks like an old Pizza Wolf van. But tell them it's a rape scene."

"Why?"

"They'll get here quicker. Not because its more important to them, but some of them are corrupt and sordid and like the chance to be first on scene to catch a glimpse of the victims... flesh."

"The dirty..."

"I know, but if it gets them here sooner than later that's all I care about."

"Even if it's these vile corrupt members of the police department."

"I'm afraid so. The joke is on them, it'll dampen their harder when they are met by six unconscious apes, instead of a scantily clad rape victim."

"What is the location?"

"The rear of Brown & Crampton haberdashery on Momsen Lane."

"Roger, that V."

"Oh and Mr B?"

"Yeah?"

"You'd best have the white vinegar to hand."

There was a groan and a sigh from the other end, Vatican laughed and then flicked his tongue over his throbbing bottom lip.

Chapter 3

Thomas stood at the entrance of St Vincents Church, he smiled at his congregation as they spilled out, some of them wanted to shake his hand and thank him personally for his words and support. Thomas welcomed this feedback, he truly had started to make a difference to the city, which is what he had initially set out to do, in more ways than one.

As the last of his flock had left, Thomas glance back inside and noticed that his superior was currently chatting with Burt.

"Time to face the music." Thomas sighed, while sliding his tongue over the large bulbous welt that was still pulsing irritatingly. His superior caught his and smiled, beckoning him over with one wrinkled hand. Thomas smiled back and turned one last time to soak up that luscious sunshine that was forcing its way through the clouds. He felt like he didn't get to see the sun that much these days, he missed it and took his time in closing up the doors. Most of what he did now was either in the dim of the church itself or at night.

"Are you going to join us, Father Gabriel?" Came the echoing cackle of his superior.

"Yes." Thomas called pleasantly, "Just coming, Father Lamont."

The warming, wholesome sunshine disappeared as the large heavy doors closed, the sound rumbled through the hall, Thomas approached Father Lamont and Burt who stood near the font. The echoing rumble accompanied him as he made his way back up the aisle to join them, Thomas had the feeling that this was a foreshadowing of what was to come from his superior.

"Father Gabriel!" Lamont greeted him with and outstretched hand and wide smile.

"Father Lamont. This is an unexpected pleasure." Thomas said smiling through his anxious chattering teeth.

"Isn't it just." Replied Lamont.

"Well, It's nice to see you again. I hope you enjoyed the sermon?"

"Oh, yes!" Lamont nodded with enthusiasm and patted him on the shoulder, "Very good, very good indeed my boy!" Thomas was taken aback and shared a look of bewilderment with Burt.

"Thank you! Thank you very much Father!"

"You're the talk of the town Thomas." Lamont beamed again. Thomas reckoned that if that was the case and Thomas was being favoured by his superiors then Lamont was milking it for all its worth as he was technically Thomas' link between the bishop.

19

"Really?" Laughed a surprised Thomas.

"Of course!" Scoffed Lamont.

"I tell him all the time just how well he's doing, Father. But he doesn't seem to take any notice of an old codger like me." Burt added with a playful smile.

"You should listen to this man, Thomas. He knows what he's talking about alright." Announced Lamont as he started to walk down the aisle towards the exit.

Thomas breathed a sigh of relief, realising that the visit was almost over and for once was a positive report and he still had a job. Plus he hadn't mentioned his split bottom lip.

"It's only a flying visit. Busy man, you understand. Lots of places to be." Said Lamont.

"Of course Father." Thomas replied nodding vigorously.

"There was one thing that I wanted you to do for me."

"Yes Father?"

"I would like youth pay a visit to one of our other churches in the area."

"Oh, really?"

"Yes. Do you know St Joseph's up in Grenoble?"

"I've heard of it."

"Then you've heard of Father Harrison. St Joseph's is his jurisdiction."

"I can't say I have." Thomas shook his head.

"I've heard the man's a drunk." Burt scoffed and

then immediately wished he could take it back when Lamont span round to stare at him.

"My apologies Father." Said Burt "It's only what I've heard."

Lamont sighed and shook his head.

"And you'd be right, Burt. Unfortunately you'd be spot on. The man has fallen on hard times and needs some help to find a new direction back to the lord."

"Strange that I have never heard of him or his problems."

"We wanted to keep it hushed up. You know how it is if these things get out. The media would have a field day." Thomas and Burt both nodded.

"He just needs a little help I feel and that's where you come in my boy." Lamont stopped walking and smiled at him, the smile of a crocodile if ever there were one.

"Me?"

"Yes, Thomas!" Lamont patted him on the shoulder again. "You're the golden boy at the moment. What you have done here is extraordinary! We would like to see if you can rub some of that positivity off on Father Harrison."

"Well, yes, of course I shall try my best. I shall pay him a visit."

"That's all any of us can ever do, Thomas, our best." Lamont shook Thomas and Burt's hands and Thomas opened up the hefty doors for him.

"Oh, by the way, I should get that carpet fitted down more securely if I was you."

"Carpet?" Thomas' brow furrowed with confusion.

"Yes, Burt told me about your mishap last night." Thomas looked at Burt.

"What did you hit your head as well as 'bite your lip!' When you tripped up the stairs last night, Thomas!" Burt said through clenched teeth and raised eyebrows.

"Oh, yes!" Thomas cried "Of course, I'll get it seen to straight away."

"See as you do. I don't want my boy wonder hurting himself."

Lamont smiled and walked out of the church, leaving Burt and Thomas to deflate in mirroring sighs.

"Ha!" Burt laughed, the gravelled growl filled the church hall.

"What?" Thomas asked.

"Nothing 'Mister Golden Boy'!"

"Oh, give it a rest, Burt." Thomas laughed. "Good thinking about the carpet though."

"Good thing I was thinking. You looked like a dear in the headlights. You looked like you spaced out in your sermon too, everything alright with you?"

"Yeah." He lied, "Everthing is fine, was just thinking about last night that's all."

"You mentioned that The Webheads were using youngsters as go-betweens."

"Yeah, I think I have a good idea of who could help me."

"So you'll be looking into the homeless quarter I take it? Maybe Elliot could help out."

"Old 'eyes and ears'? I'm sure he could. But it's her I'm looking for."

"Her?"

"Yeah, there's a girl I've met a few times that may just fit the bill."

Chapter 4

Robert Devine rocked back and forth on his luxury leather office chair. The sunlight shone through the long slender windows, but Devine didn't care much for sunshine and stayed at his desk, hidden in the shade of a gigantic statue of what appeared to be an erect penis.

His designer penthouse office was uncharacteristically quiet, as he sat deep in thought. His wall of screens still flashed away with news from around the globe being shown, but they had been muted while Devine ponder over something he had read in the Studd City Gazette. He stopped rocking and scooped up the newspaper that lay on his generous desk, he grumbled and his scowled, he did not look happy.

"I need to put a stop to this immediately." He growled burning a hole in the headline that read 'AN ANGEL WATCHES OVER US', candid photograph of Vatican stood on some rooftop, beneath lay a mound of drug dealers piled up and surrounded by SCPD's finest.

"Bastard!" Devine snarled as he slammed the newspaper back down on the desk.

He jabbed at his phone that sat on the desk, which beeped loudly, alerting his secretary on the other side of the door that he wanted her assistance.

"Yes, Sir?" Came the immediate reply.

"Get Fame up here now." He barked.

"Yes, Sir! Right away." Came the reply with urgency in her voice.

"And Michelle?"

"Yes, Sir?"

"Bring me up a bottle of red while you're at it."

"Certainly, Sir, Anything in particular?"

"A Chateau Latour Pauillac would go down nicely."

"Very good, Sir!"

Devine sank back into his chair again and sighed as he awaited the arrival of his head of security.

"What can I do to rid myself of this fly in the ointment?" There was a knock on the door.

"Come." Devine barked.

The door opened and Famu stood out of breath, with a layer of sweat clinging to his forehead.

"You sent for me, Sir?" He gasped, trying to catch his breath.

"My word, Famu. That was fast! You must have leapt up those stairs."

"Michelle said it was urgent, Sir."

"If I call, it's always urgent." Devine replied. "Well, come in then! You're making a puddle in my doorway."

"Sir." Famu squeezed his enormous frame through the door and approached the desk, sweat patches had appeared through his beige suit, and his large flat feet squelched in his open toed sandals.

"Have you seen this?" Devine said, grabbed the newspaper and thrusting it towards him.

"The paper?"

"Yes, its a paper! What did you think it was?" Snapped Devine impatiently.

Famu's eyes skimmed across the page. He wasn't the smartest of people and he didn't have a clue what he was looking for, he was used to seeing Vatican headlines now that he thought it couldn't be that, so he tried to be clever and focus on something that he knew Devine Inc. was involved in.

"Hey, Chinatown is ready to open this month." Famu said excitedly, his little mouth smiling between two bulging cheeks. "Congratulations, Sir!"

"Not Chinatown you brainless boar!" Devine screamed slamming a fist down on the desk.

"Oh, Sorry." Famu gulped, and his pores began to leak again. "I just thought..."

"Thought? I doubt it!" Devine scoffed, "Yes, Chinatown is a huge deal for us, yes I have pumped an obscene amount of money to see that come to tuition and yes, I've already sold several establishments to a Mr Motou, who was very eager to spend a small fortune for his luxury Chinese restaurant, The Bronze Dragon, that will open soon.

But it's not just Chinatown, there is also the grand opening of Greta Geko's casino in a few days time in Regal. That deal alone has doubled my profit margin. Yes, that is all going swimmingly."

Famu smiled again.

"What I am referring to, is that asshole that keeps grabbing all the headlines!"

"Oh, Vatican!" The penny had finally dropped for Famu.

"Who else!"

Devine stood up and began pacing. Famu became unnerved and started to twiddle his bulbous thumbs rapidly, when Devine paced it never meant anything good for him.

"I want this guy's head on a silver platter, Famu."

Famu nodded, he had heard this more than once over the past year.

Devine strode over to a small marble table that homed a chess set, beautifully carved ivory pieces in red and white were positioned in the mid battle. Devine stood over the unfinished game silently assessed his next move. His slender fingers seized a red knight by its mane and removed a white pawn. He smiled and hoisted up the pawn and peered at it closely.

"This Vatican! This Angel of Justice!" He scowled while directing the pawn with his eyes, "Is one pawn that needs to be eradicated from the board."

Famu nodded.

"I spoke a while ago about forming an alliance to rid us of Vatican. But the collapse of The Doomsday Gang and the imprisonment of Valentine and his idiotic son has really left me in a bind. These smaller gangs that are sprouting up everywhere are not going to cut it. They have no guidance or leadership. They have no backbone and will be easily dismantled by this... Angel!"

"So what can we do?" Famu asked, hoping that he wasn't going to be sent on a wide goose chase again, staking out rooftops for a glimpse of this holy crusader. Granted he would love another shot at Vatican, for being humiliated by him in their last encounter, but a part of him knew that Vatican's skills were far superior to his own.

"That's where you come in, Famu." Devine smiled as he pointed the small ivory piece at him.

Famu's face fell.

"I want you to find..."

Here it comes.

"... The Webheads."

"The Webheads?" Famu croaked in surprise.

"Don't get too excited, Famu. I wouldn't ask you to tangle with him again, not alone anyway. We saw what happened the last time you did." Devine scoffed.

Famu sneered when his boss wasn't looking.

"Find these Webheads." Devine continued "There leader is called Spider I believe."

"Yes, Sir. That's right."

"Good. Hop to it then."

Famu turned to leave and then stopped, turning around again to query his mission.

"Sir?"

"Yes, Famu?" Devine sighed as he sat back at his chair, still playing with the pawn in his fingertips.

"Why would you want to bring these... thugs in on this with you?"

"Because there is safety in numbers. Because I don't have to get my hands dirty and because after the deed has been done they will be easy to make disappear."

"Disappear." Famu whispered a hint of a smile quivered on his thick lips, this was something that he did enjoy, making people 'disappear'.

"I thought that might perk you up." Chuckled Devine.

"What if they don't go for it?"

"They will. Money talks, just get them up here and I will soon have them eating out of the palm of my hand."

"Yes, Sir."

There was a gentle rapping at the door.

"Famu, get that on your way out will you."

"Of course, Sir."

Famu opened the door and Michelle sauntered in, carrying a bottle of the most expensive wine that Devine has at his disposal. She smiled at Famu and walked towards Devine's desk. Famu couldn't help but stare at her behind as it flicked from side to side.

"Your wine, Sir." Michelle said, offering him the bottle expertly so he could read the label.

"Excellent." Devine grinned triumphantly.

Michelle took the bottle to the bar and retrieved a long slender wine glass.

"Shall I pour, Sir?" Michelle asked.

Devine saw that Famu was still loitering at the doorway and he waved him away as he approached the bar.

"That's all, Famu, run along now."

Famu closed the door and heard the popping of a cork and Michelle giggling and sighed miserably.

Chapter 5

Detective Sidney Graham had pulled up to the entrance of The Oakland Institute ten minutes ago, but had yet to exit his tired old Ford County Squire. The engine ticked over as though the old nag was weary from its strenuous journey to the outskirts of Studd City.

He looked out the windshield at the eery looking building that stood before him and sighed, he didn't wish to leave the safety of his car and venture into such a place, but unfortunately he must. He slipped of the seat belt and was about to exit when his cell phone burst into life.

He let it ring.

Finally the annoying jingle stopped and he retrieved it from the inside pocket of his jacket, the screen displayed a cozy family portrait of himself huddled together on a snowy day with his wife Mae and their two boys. He exhaled in annoyance as the screen told him that he had eight missed calls from Mae.

"I best call her back." Graham sighed.

A gaunt looking man clad in a white lab coat appeared at the entrance to the institute, he adjusted his glasses and tilted his head to one side trying to figure out why the Detective was taking so long. Graham looked up, his cell phone cupped to his ear and the man caught Graham's glance.

"C'mon Detective, I'm on a tight schedule you know!" The man groaned tapping at his watch accompanied by an annoyed stare.

Graham held up a finger to the man and nodded.

"I know, Mae." He murmured, his tone was almost apologetic, "Yes, I understand that I haven't been home for three days, but..." *I've been busy fucking Valerie Nash's brains out.* "...really busy."

Graham sank back into the seat and let his wife gripe at him.

I know, Mae. Everything you are saying is the God's honest absolute truth. I have been neglecting the family, you, the boys... That one hurts. You may not think that someone in the midst of adultery could have such morals, but we do. I know I'm in the wrong, I know that I have been weak, I know that I have jeopardised everything I have ever loved for a what? An infatuation?

"Yes, Mae, I know, I will try to get back tonight. We have a lot going on at the moment, we have a big sting operation in effect at the moment and hopefully going to wrap it up in a few days, so things will get back to normal."

There was the sound of sarcastic laughter erupting from phone, Graham squinted and pulled it away from his ear for the moment.

"Yeah, get it out of your system, Mae. I don't know what normal is either." Graham smiled, it was genuine, there

32

hadn't been many genuine smiles over the passed few months.

"I know I got the tickets, they won't miss it, I promised I'd take them didn't I?"

More laughter from the other end of the phone and Graham rolled his eyes.

Yeah, promises, how would I know what a promise was, let alone how to keep one. I promised to love, honour and obey you until death us do part. Royally fucked that up didn't I?

"Look, I've got to go, I'm at Oakland now and I'm about to go and see Eric."

No, I don't think it's wise either.

"Unfortunately it's routine. No, Richard couldn't do it. Hayes wants me to do it. Says it will be good for me. Yeah, I know it's bullshit."

Graham noticed that the man in the lab coat was now pacing at the top of the steps that lead up to the institute shaking his head.

"Look, I've got to go." He hung up as Mae, started to say I love you. Graham exited the car and dropped his cell phone onto the seat.

Graham sauntered over the gravel towards the steps and casually climbed them, approaching the man in the white coat.

"I was beginning to think you were going to leave me waiting all day, Detective..."

"I'm very sorry about that. Graham, Detective Graham!" He said holding out a hand, "And you are Doctor?"

"Flint!" He replied coldly and shook his hand tightly.

"Careful Doc!" Graham teased clutching his hand, "That's my shooting hand."

Dr Flint smirked and then lead the way into the institute, "Shall we?"

Graham followed Flint as he lead the way, all manner of sights met Graham as they made their way through the large reception area, orderlies ushering poor souls around in wheelchairs, some patients just stood around looking into space. One even sat picking his nose and then talking to the mucus that now hung from the tip of his finger as if it was a pet. Graham's eyebrows rose as he then saw the patient stroking and kissing it.

"How many patients do you have here, Doc?" Graham asked.

"Do you really care?" Flint replied, not breaking his stride as he dodged the oncoming traffic of the afflicted.

"Sorry?" Graham was a little taken aback by Flint's sharpness.

"Well, do you? Or are you just trying to fill this time with idle chit chat."

"Well, I…"

"Precisely!" Flint snapped as he stopped at his office door at the end of the corridor. "These moments do not need to be filled." With that brashness he swung open the door and grinned falsely gesturing for Graham to enter.

"Charmed." Graham contorted his beard face into his own sarcastic fake smile.

"Now, take a seat, my time is incredibly precious, Detective."

Flint removed his white coat and hung it on then back of his chair and sat down swiftly. Graham sat down and relaxed back int the chair.

"So, what can we do for you?" Flint asked as he slid his elbows onto the desk and laced his fingers.

Graham slid a cigarette out of a scrunched up packet of Freebirds and slotted it between his lips.

"I'd like to talk with Eric Stone."

"There's no smoking in this facility, Detective."

"Of course." Graham nodded and put the cigarette back where it came from "I'm supposed to be quitting. My wife keeps telling me I should."

"Then your wife is a very astute individual. Maybe you'd be wise to listen to her."

"Yeah, you're probably right." He laughed under his breath as his mind flustered away to think about her and what a fool he had been. A part of him realised that the Doctor was right, he should listen to his wife, the other part of him conjured up visions of Valerie's writhing naked body kissed with droplets of sweat.

"But to answer your question the answer is no."

"What question?" Asked Graham, drifting back out of his erotic musing.

"Have you got something on your mind?" Dr Flint smiled leaning back in his chair staring at Graham with interest.

"What?" Graham looked up and met his eyes, his cheeks blushing. "I don't know what you mean."

"Of course you don't." Dr Flint laughed and rolled his eyes. "I'm a psychiatrist you know. It's my job to read people and I can read you like a copy of Good Housekeeping."

They stared at each other for the longest time. Graham could really benefit from talking to someone about his issues, but he wasn't there yet.

"What do you mean I can't see Eric?" Graham said, changing the direction of the conversation before Flint had him laid down in his long black leather couch poking his nose in parts of his brain.

Dr Flint smiled and rose "Exactly what I said, Detective." He walked over to the filling cabinet, flung open the middle draw and served swiftly through the files. "I can let you have a look at his file, and discuss his progress, but no you won't be allowed to see him I'm afraid."

"You do know that I am a police detective with the Studd City Police Department don't you?" Graham announced.

"I do." Flint said, retreating the file he was looking for and then turning to face Graham, "And you do know that I am Eric's psychiatrist and there is such thing as doctor-patient confidentiality. Now I'm being nice here and letting you peruse his file. I could say no to that as well if I wanted to Detective. I have that authority."

Graham sat back in his chair, he knew this was one battle he couldn't win.

"Now, do you want to have a look in the file or not?" Flint snapped.

"Yeah." Graham grumbled.

"Good!" Flint replied and slammed the drawer shut with enough ferocity to shake the framed awards that hung on the wall. Flint returned to his seat and slid the file over to Graham.

"Thanks." Graham said reluctantly and opened it up to reveal a photograph of Eric. The black and white picture didn't look like Eric, the friend he once knew. The eyes were dark and lifeless, his features gaunt.

"What have you done to him?" Graham whispered, he kept his head down, focussing on the file, so that Flint could not see the tears that were quivering along his eyelids.

"What we have done to him?" Flint scoffed and let out a cackle. "We are putting the poor soul back together again, well as best as we can."

"What drugs have you got him on? He looks like a fucking crack addict!" Graham growled, a tear dropped from his eye and laded on Eric's paperwork. Graham sun it quickly and hoped that the doctor didn't witness it.

"Nothing special really. Mainly Haloperidol on bad days."

"Bad days?" Graham said, composing himself and sifting through the file again.

"Eric's aggressive behaviour deems it necessary unfortunately."

"And he's definitely not fit to rejoin the inmates at Skelter Prison?"

"Oh God, no!" Flint shook his head vigorously, "That would be quite out of the question. He could cause harm to himself or other inmates and I can't have that only conscience."

"He'd already broken the wrists of two prison guards, and shattered another's jaw. Not to mention the fact that he gored three inmates with a sharpened toothbrush!" Flint looked at him unimpressed.

"Like I said, that place is no good for him, look what it did to him!"

Skelter isn't what turned him into this, Doc! Want to point the finger at anybody, point it at me. I didn't handle his situation properly. I should have been there for him when he was grieving the death of his wife and unborn child, not treating him like a leper!

"Eric is a lot better off in our care, Detective. We know exactly how to treat him. Skelter Prison for all the good it does, is no place for someone like Eric." Flint added staring inquisitively at Graham while he scanned Eric's file.

"I hear he had death threats from some inmates in there." Graham said looking up from the file and was a little taken aback to see Flint staring at him.

"What?"

"You intrigue me, Detective."

"Really, well..." Graham replied, shuffling uneasily in his seat "I'm not the one being discussed here."

"No, of course you're not." Flint smiled, "To answer your question about the death threats, yes I know. Eric has told me. That was one of the reason's that Skelter wanted shot of him. I guess they don't want that kind of publicity now do they."

Graham shook his head, but was eager to ask another question.

"So, Eric talks to you?"

"Oh yes!" Flint beamed "We have very good rapport. The death threats had come from some members of a gang called Doomsday? Have you heard of them?"

"Yeah, The Doomsday Gang was run by the Valentine family."

"Valentine, yes!" Flint nodded "Eric has mentioned that name too."

"Well, it's no real surprise that he had death threats from them, when he part of the guys who put them in there in the first place."

"Yes that is understandable. In their eyes he is still an officer of the law."

"And in mine." Graham said loudly, as if to inform himself more than Dr Flint of his views.

"Of course, Detective. Your views are your own and you are entitled to them of course. But, he has been through a traumatic time and it's going to take a long time for him to be the man you called friend." Flint leant over the desk, his face contorting with sympathy, "But he may never get there."

"Never?"

"We never say die, Detective. He has shown very positive progress since he has been under my wing, but it is very east to relapse. The mind is a delicate machine and one hint of mistrust and it could shut down all together. Or if something triggers this pain and aggression then we could be back to square one."

"That is why you won't let me see him I suppose. I would conjure up some painful memories."

"Yes, perhaps." Flint nodded in agreement, sitting back in his chair and starting to warm to Detective Graham slightly.

"Does he speak about that night. The night that Crystal died?"

"He has done. He had too!"

"Why put him through that?"

"I can understand your concern, Detective. But it was something he had to talk about if he wants to move forward. He occasionally speaks of her, each time it's less painful for him I think."

"Does he show remorse for taking the life of her killer?"

"Jones? Sylvester Jones?"

"Yes. Known on the streets as Sniff."

Flint nodded.

"We are working on that. As you can imagine it's a

very touchy subject. He flits from remorse and anger whenever we have that particular conversation."

Graham twiddled his thumbs nervously in his lap, he really wanted to ask one specific question, but couldn't bring himself to ask it, he was too scared to hear the answer.

"Does he..." Graham began but choked on the question. Flint's eyes narrowed behind his glasses as he could see that graham was bubbling up inside to ask something.

"Detective?"

"Does he..." Graham tried again, but again bailed out at the last minute, "What else does he talk about?"

"He discusses his past as an officer with the SCPD and about his promotion to the SWAT Team. He talks a lot about a future that he wanted to build with his wife and unborn child. Sadly that is a fantasy world, which can become unhealthy if he believes that these things are possible. I try to steer him clear of such thoughts and focus on where he is."

"Anything else?" Graham seems to plead with his eyes.

"He talks about how the system let him down. How his wife's name was dragged through the mud and nobody stood up to tell the world the true facts. And of course he still maintains his innocence that he only killed Sylvester Jones and was not responsible for the murders of those gang members or of course the murder of his wife and unborn child."

41

"But Elvis Valentine was the one sent down for the Doomsday Murders?"

"But wasn't there a time when the finger was being pointed at Eric for those crimes?"

"Yes." Graham sighed sadly.

"In his mind I guess he feels that he was being blamed for everything. And like Eric has sated in our sessions many times that the SCPD were just looking for somebody to pin it on."

"So he doesn't believe Elvis was responsible?"

"He doesn't know who was responsible, Detective. He just knows that it wasn't him."

"What do you believe?" Graham asked Flint.

"What do you believe, Detective?" Flint smiled, "He was your friend. I am coming at this from an entirely different angle. I'm a neutral you might say. But you, well, you must be very undecided about the whole affair. Am I right?"

Graham did not answer but held eye contact with the doctor.

"You were his friend, yes?"

Graham nodded.

"So that part of you doesn't believe he was capable of such heinous acts."

Graham nods again.

"But, the other side of the coin. Well, you're a police detective and you see things through a different pair of eyes don't you? Where there is a don't trust anyone attitude and a world where anything can happen and people are capable of anything."

Graham's eyelids flickered holding back tears and he finally looked away from Dr Flint.

Bingo was his name. You're correct across the board, Doc! Tell him what he's won, Johnny.

"I can see this is very hard for you, Detective. I feel that maybe your superiors would have sent someone who doesn't have an emotional attachment to Eric here, don't you?"

"Yeah, damn right."

"But to answer your question about what I think as a professional. Well, I don't believe he murdered all those gang members and I would stake my career and reputation on it that he didn't kill his pregnant wife."

"But how can you be so sure?"

"A guilty man will lie about everything, Detective. He will tell himself that it s all a mistake that he isn't to blame and will not take that step of admitting he did anything wrong."

"But isn't that what Eric is doing? Is he not accepting what he did?"

"No."

"No?"

"You're missing one vital point. He has denied everything that has been thrown at him, part from one thing."

"Murdering Sniff!" Graham whispered.

"Exactly! Not once has his story changed and he has never once said that he didn't kill Jones. So ergo I see him innocent of all other crimes that the authorities have deemed him guilty of apart from the murder of Sylvester Jones. Which obviously he has to pay for with a life sentence. But before he can serve such a sentence then he must be in the right frame of mind."

Graham sat for a while pondering all the information that Dr flint had just given him and then he stood up and smiled at him.

"Well, I won't take up any more of your time, Doc."

"Not a problem, Detective!" Replied Flint rising to meet him with a handshake. Flint looked into his eyes and asked "Are you sure there aren't any other questions you would like to get off your chest?"

Graham stared at him again.

Yes! There is so much I need to get off my chest, so much guilt. It's like I'm trying to bench press a mass amount of weight but I can't push hard enough to move it, I just keep holding it there. All my limbs shaking as I can't hang on much longer. That weight is going to fall and my life will fall with it. But again that's all about me. Ever the selfish piece of shit that you always are Sid! Thinking about your fucking self! This is about Eric. And there is one question that you need to know!

"Does he ever talk about me?" Graham finally managed. Flint looked at him, that sympathetic frown was back again.

"Has he ever even mentioned me?" Graham cried. Flint shook his head.

"He has never spoken your name, Detective."

Chapter 6

The sun slowly descended from its post and gently kissed the tranquil surface of the Hennig River. How beautiful the sunset appeared to onlookers, but little do they know what horrors lie beneath. 63 bodies were retrieved from its grim depths last year alone. It is unknown how many carcasses have taken the Hennig River as their final resting place and it is question that will probably never have an answer.

The dark shroud of the lenticular truss bridge hung over the river like long slender fingers reaching out to touch the shoreline. Its cold fingertips ticked the boats and yachts that sat forgotten in the tired docks of Ventura's docks.

A worn lobster boat sat moored at the docks, surrounded by many other useless crafts that were far from seaworthy. They looked like swaying gravestones as they gently moved from side to side. A light burst into life inside the lobster boat and figures moved around inside hastily, drawing the curtains of the small square windows.

Inside the three head members of The Webhead gang sat

around a table, the remains of a recent card game visible next to piles of wrinkled bank notes.

"Here have another drink." Dallas chuckled as he sat back down handing ice cold bottles of *Bobby's Light* to the losers of the last hand.

"You two have just gotta face facts." Dallas grinned sweeping his winnings towards him "That it isn't your game."

"Is he always like this when he wins?" Spider asks Boris as he effortlessly flicks the top from his bottle.

"Always!" Boris scowls picking up the cards and shuffling them, "The bastard!"

Dallas laughs loudly.

"You're just a sore loser, Boris my old pal."

Spider swigs almost half the battle in one go and then slams the bottle on the table, standing up and striding to the window.

"Something wrong, Spider?" Dallas asked.

Spider peeped out of the curtain and stared at the city that looked as inviting as an open treasure chest, with all its twinkling lights in the darkness.

"Everything, Dal!" Spider growled.

"Are we not playing any more?" Boris asked in mid deal. Dallas looked at him and shook his head.

Boris shrugged and sat back in his chair drinking his beer.

"When did everything go to shit?" Spider asked as he kept his bag to them, his long dreadlocks cascading down the middle of his back.

"I thought we were doing well. All things considered." Dallas shrugged.

Spider turned around quickly and sneered "Are you fucking serious!"

Spider glared at Dallas, the whites of his wide eyes flecked heavily with veins.

"I didn't mean..." Dallas tried to explain his comment, but with a hot tempered Spider there was no arguing with.

"Take a look around, Dal." Spider spat "Take a good fucking look around."

He slapped a hand across the table knocking bottles and money all over the floor.

There was silence in the boat for what seemed like the longest time as Boris and Dallas balanced on tenterhooks with where Spider was going to go next. His emotions were always up in the air.

Spider sighed heavily and leant on small window ledge. "We're hiding out in a shitty little fishing boat."

"It's a lobster boat." Boris intervened.

"A fucking what?" Spider growled.

"A lobster boat!"

"What's the fucking difference?" Spider screamed.

"It catches lobsters." Boris shrugged and casually went back to swigging his beer.

Dallas and Spider just looked at each other and shook their heads.

"I thought we'd rid ourselves of dumb-ass comments when Sniff bit the dust." Spider scoffed.

"Don't take any notice of him." Said Dallas as he waited for Spider to carry on with what he was saying.

"Hiding out in a damn 'lobster' boat!" He cried, looking sarcastically at Boris who tipped the neck of his bottle at him in some sort of casual salute. "My partnership with The Coyote is over and if he catches me he'll have my head as a hood ornament for his prized Chevrolet Impala!"

"That's kind of your fault there my man." Dallas says reluctantly, "You did screw the guy over on the Stardust deal." Spider sits back down on his chair and sniggers.

"Yeah, I did. Didn't I?"
They all laugh and slam their bottles together in toast.

"But still, I don't like all this lying low bullshit. I was supposed to be the cream of the crop when I overthrow the Valentines, but look at us! I'm going fucking stir crazy here!"

"It won't be for long. Just gotta sit tight." Dallas reassured him.

"Yeah, we got a network of those little bums ready to do all the hard work for a dollar and pretzel." Boris added.

"You see!" Dallas grinned "Couple more months of this and we'll be sitting pretty."

"Not if we don't collect the last Stardust drop we won't." Spider groaned.

"No problem! I will go and get it in a few days. We have plenty." Boris nodded confidently.

"Yeah, what's the worry?" Dallas added "We just carry on how we've been working, right?"

"Wrong." Spider shakes his head "This is the last pick up until The Vixen returns."

"You mean the circus is on the move?" Dallas asks.

"Yeah, she won't be back this way for another three or four months. So we've gotta make that shit last!"

"If worst comes to worst my comrade we can always, how you say..." Boris searched his brain for the correct English word "Die root?"

"You mean dilute it?" Dallas replied.

"That's it!" Boris nodded "Cut it with something else, flour, sugar, laundry detergent! Those bastards will be too fucked up to know any difference."

"For an ugly, dumb-ass Russian! I do love you!" Spider laughed and rose from his seat to plant a kiss on Boris greasy forehead.

"Fuck you!" Boris growled playfully, "I'm Ukrainian! Mother fucker."

They laughed again and Spider held aloft his bottle, "To Boris!" He called "The butt ugly Ukrainian with a big ass brain!"

"There is one good think out of all this though." Dallas said breaking up the merriment.

"What's that?" Spider asked.

"At least you got away with killing all those Doomsday generals."

Spider burst out laughing as he leapt from his chair and waved his bottle in the air triumphantly, beer showering Dallas and Boris.

"Damn straight!" Spider cried "I guess being stuck in those old boat with you two is better than being crammed into a Skelter cell."

"I still don't think they knew who did it." Boris said seriously.

Dallas and Spider looked at each other burst out laughing again.

"Shit!" Spider laughed as he shuck his head, "I'd got it all wrong. We are sitting pretty."

Spider flung an arm around his comrades and hugged them, all the while spilling beer all over them.

"Deal me in, Boris!" He cried collapsing back into his chair with a twinkling golden smile etched on his face.

Chapter 7

Thomas stared out of the window of the el train in contemplation as the huge carriage rattling loudly on the tracks. The city was bathed in a succulent vanilla sky that screamed spring was well and truly here. It made Thomas smile, all of Mother Nature's creations did. The journey from the Montreal area of Studd City to Grenoble was trying to say the least. The two hour journey had almost come to an end, but Thomas didn't seemed t mind, he had originally thought of catching up with his reading (a pass time that he no longer seemed to have time for now), instead he took in the delights that the city had to offer. Granted moving through certain parts like Solo, Alexandrea and Talbot were not picturesque in the least, but as a priest Thomas could take the troubles and strifes that the people below faced and keep him humble. His fight to save this city was far from over and the sights that he saw far below the elevated train track confirmed that. *There is still a lot of work to do here.*

The train shook violently from side to side as it turned a corner, the crunch of metal on metal was most unpleasant to Thomas' ear. He gazed around at the other travellers in the carriage who didn't seemed fazed by it in the slightest.

Veteran passengers I guess.

The train slowed and up ahead he could see the massive main building of the university campus. It stood strong, its white stone face and pillars reflected the sunlight, Thomas felt like he was in Rome again.

It seems like an age since I lived in Rome, learning the ropes of priesthood. He smiled to himself. *The food was to die for and I loved nothing more than sipping cappuccino at Mario's Café on a Sunday morning watching the world go by. Nights were different of course, it was then that I put in the hours to secretly hone my skills. Parkour in Rome and The Vatican City were highlights, but nothing beat racing along the top of the Coliseum. The most difficult part of training for this crusade was the room I stayed in, well it was more like a prison cell. But I made it work, even in such cramped conditions.*

He grinned again, a child's smile of reminiscing on simpler times.

"Ah, Rome." He sighed.

A long bell chimed which brought Thomas back from Rome and back into the rickety old carriage of Studd City's el train. A crackling robotic voice announced that the next stop was Grenoble and the SCU campus, the announcement sounded like someone chewing on glass.

Thomas rose from his seat and stood by the door, there were a few SCU students in front of him and when they noticed his collar they let him go first.

There's hope for the next generation yet.

Thomas thanked them and when the train staggered and stopped sharply, the students nearly lost their footing and almost fell, in fact everyone aboard almost did, all apart from Thomas, who was unfazed by such things. His Shaolin background was all about balance. The doors open and Thomas left the train.

He jogged down the steps to street level and looked around for the right direction, at the end of the street he could see a gothic shard cutting through the modern metropolis, the sharp steeple of St. Joseph's Church.

Now having a direction, Thomas strode on down the sidewalk, he took in the luscious warmth of the spring sunshine and again his mind began to wonder.

Maybe Father Harrison and I will be able to form a coalition with him and take on north side of the city, that would really help me out if he could come on board for something like that. Unfortunately, Father Lamont didn't paint an appealing picture. I really don't know what to expect. Burt tells me that he likes to hit the bottle, but there must be a reason, for every vice we adopt there is always a reason for it. Maybe I can help him? Lamont seems to think so, and the Bishop does too by all accounts, or else they wouldn't have sent me. It will be good to keep them on side though, if I am doing what is asked and making a positive impact during the day, then it leaves me uninterrupted during the night. At night when another battle is being waged.

St. Joseph's could be seen now, sat behind a broken iron fence and gate.

Thomas stopped and looked up at the once majestic church that had been neglected and was know hidden behind a layer of graffiti.

"This doesn't look very positive." Thomas sighed and approached the door.

The door was unlocked and Thomas struggled to move the door, it appeared to be blocked by something on the inside. As he muscled his way in he noticed it was a pile of garbage bags that was keeping him at bay.

"Hello!" He called out into the dark church hall, but the only response came from the cooing of pigeons that had taken the rafters for their own.

Thomas shuffled in calling out again. As he walked through the hall his feet connected with empty wine bottles that rolled haphazardly down the aisle towards the baron wasteland of what should be an altar, which should be uplifting and inviting, decorated with crucifixes, flowers and burning candles. St. Joseph's had none of this.

"Father Harrison!" He called, his tones disturbing the pigeons who flew around the ceiling, causing feathers to rain down around Thomas as the headed for the rafter nearest the entrance, an equally faeces stained beam as the one they had just left.

As Thomas reached the annex and peaked his head around the corner and was horrified by what he saw. Father Harrison lay wrapped in a dirty blanket on a mattress.

Thomas shook his head, wondering how anyone that was the same standing as himself could get in such a state and also more strangely how the superiors had allowed it to get this far. The air smelt stale, rotting food and urine attacked his nostrils, but the smell didn't seem to bother the unconscious Father Harrison that lay fast asleep.

"Father Harrison!" Thomas shouted, something scurried under the mass of food packets on the floor which made Thomas shudder.

"Harrison!" He shouted again, the sleeping priest stirred and grumbled.

"Well, at least you're not dead." Thomas said loudly, "I thought I might have to call the old meat wagon."
Harrison groaned, broke wind and rolled over.

"Come on now, Harrison. Time to get up!" Thomas said yanking the blanket off him, the mattress was filled with holes and splattered with wine and urine. Harrison lay in nothing but a pair of underpants that Thomas believe may one have been white, and a half full bottle of wine gripped in his mitt.

"Are you getting up?"
Two eyes slowly opened out of a mass of dark matted hair and a beard that had the remnants of potato chips perturbing from it.

"Fuck off." Harrison said and rolled over clutching his wine bottle like a child does a teddy bear.

"Come on now Harrison" Thomas sighed "I think it's time you got yourself up and motivated, don't you?"

Harrison turned around to face Thomas, his raw eyes blinked away mucus and a look of intrigue working its way along his mucky face.

"Who did you say you were?" He asked in a hoarse tone.

"I didn't." Thomas smiled.

"Ooh the intrigue." Harrison scoffed and sat up on the mattress, taking a swig of the red wine he was keeping so close to him.

"Father Gabriel." Thomas smiled holding out a hand to be shook "Thomas Gabriel."

Harrison looked at his hand and then back at his smiling face and with an unimpressed shrug of his shoulders he took another gulp of wine.

"St. Vincent's is my jurisdiction." Harrison smiled a strange drunken grin.

"Oh, you're their golden boy." He scoffed and looked him up and down "I expected you to have a halo."

"I'm waiting to have it fitted." Thomas laughed.

"Yeah, well you're welcome to it my friend." Harrison said stretching and rising from his pit, the leftovers of last night's midnight stack falling from him like a snow flurry. Harrison barged past Thomas and headed into the main hall, lips latched onto the ring of the bottle. He staggered almost losing his balance twice before collapsing on to a pew.

Thomas followed him in and sat down next to him.

"I've come to see if I can help you, Harrison."

57

"I know why they've fucking sent you!" Harrison growled, wine spilling from his mouth and dribbling into his dark matted beard. "They're always sticking their noses in! They can't just let me deal with things my way!"

"They're just looking out for your well-being, Harrison."

"Oh would you stop with the Harrison B-S! My name's John-Paul."

"Okay, John-Paul." Thomas smiled and nodded "I guess they think that you are failing them."

"Failing them!" Harrison roared, his voice echoing around the large hall and disturbing the pigeons again.

"Well, take a look around." Thomas said calmly "You haven't exactly looked after their church have you."

Harrison laughed and rose from the pew, he swayed on the spot a moment before launching the almost empty wine bottle at the pigeons high avoid him. The bottle misses them completely and drops to the floor and explodes, sending shards of glass sliding across the church.

"Dirty fucking pigeons!" He cried again.

Thomas stared at him.

"You said I'm failing them?"

"No. I said that's what they are thinking. These are not my words you understand."

"Yeah, those words would belong to Lamont, no doubt." Thomas nodded.

"It's those assholes that have failed me, Thomas!" Harrison collapsed on him and then rolled onto the pew

58

looking up at the ceiling, watching as feathers and fresh faeces fell around him.

"What do you mean?"

"You don't think I started off like this do you?" He scoffed and then laughed loudly, " I wasn't always a good for nothing but you know! I was once Lamont's golden boy like you are now. I just hope they're their for you when things get rough. Because they damn sure weren't there for me when I needed them."

"So is this revenge?" Thomas asked "They weren't there for you, so you drive their church into the ground?"

"I guess so." Harrison shrugged.

"What happened to you to allow it all to go this far?"

"I'd rather not talk about it. It's still painful."

"Is that why you drink?"

Harrison turned to Thomas, tears filled up in his tender eyes and he pulled himself up from the pew and started tottering around, lifting empty potato chip bags and pizza boxes in search gif something.

"Is it?" Thomas asked again "You drink to fill a void, to make the pain stop, yes?"

Harrison said nothing as he disappeared behind an overturned pew.

"I can help you John-Paul. If you let me I can help you get back on your feet."

Harrison appeared again with another bottle attached to his mouth, this time whiskey.

"I can help you and help St. Joseph's. It does need some TLC, doesn't it." Thomas smiled at him.

Harrison spat out the whiskey and started to laugh.

"Oh, you're just like all the others they've sent."

"The others?"

"I thought you might be different, but no, you're as lol the same!"

"What others, John-Paul?"

"What! You think that you're the only one of Lamont's cherubs that has been sent up here to 'help me'?" He chuckled to himself again and staggered towards Thomas. "You want to ask Lamont what I did to the last one they sent."

Thomas stared at him.

"I tell you it was a waste of a good bottle of plonk. Nearly half a bottle! But he had it coming."

Harrison laughed shaking his head.

"I take it you struck him?"

"Well, the bottle did!" He laughed again "I just swung the fucker! Eight stitches I hear. Righteous asshole!"

"Well, obviously they have failed to get through to you."

"Obviously!" Harrison laughed as he swayed from side to side head back towards his private quarters.

"Immaterial of their actions and how they have gone about the situation, I would still like to help you. Please let me." Thomas pleaded standing and following him.

Harrison span round on the spot and thrust the bottle in his face.

"Don't fucking bother!" He growled "You're just like all the others, filled with false promises, I don't need any more of that bullshit!

"I..." Thomas pleaded but was interrupted by a teary Harrison.

"Just leave it!"

"If you want to reach me for anything." Thomas said retrieving a card with his details on it "I'll leave my card on the..."

"Yeah, yeah!" He groaned walking into the gloom of his pit "You know where the door is, Father Gabriel!"

Thomas sighed and placed his card on the pew and left.

As the door closed, Harrison shuffled out of the dark cavern with his blanket wrapped around him, he picked up the card and looked at it, red bulging eyes filling with tears again.

Chapter 8

Eric Stone sat staring out of the barred windows at the sunshine, he smiled widely as tears danced in his eyes. He remembered the sunshine and the feeling that he got when he ran across the beach with Crystal, hand in hand and laughed as if they didn't have a care in the world. He remembered her enchanting smile and her mass of platinum hair that bounced around as they skipped through the surf together. Then he blinked away the tears and realised he was in discussion room number 32 of Oakland Institute. He could hear someone saying his name, it sounded so far away, as though he was being called through a long pipe of some kind. He looked at his hands and his wrists were shackled, a long chain connecting the cuffs to anklets, which were attached to sturdy fixture set into the floor, it's as if he was anchored there. Each time he moved and the chains jangled. Eric looked up and focussed.

"Dr Flint!" He said as if surprised to see him sitting across the small table from him.

"Yes, Eric, It's me." Flint smiled reassuringly and jotted something down with a pencil on his clipboard. "You left us there for a moment."

Eric nodded and looked around at the pristine white room, it made him squint.

"Yeah, I guess I did."

Two orderlies stood behind him, he could see them in the reflection of the mirror behind Flint. The orderlies were as wide across as they were tall, both equipped with hefty batons hanging from their belts.

"Those two are watching me again, Doctor." Eric sneered.

"I assure you that they're not, Eric."

He glared at them in the reflection, they stood looking off into space and paying no attention what so ever to Eric.

"I could fuck them both up you know."

"I know." Flint nodded.

One of the orderly's smirked, he obviously did not agree with Eric.

"Don't believe me do ya, big guy?" Eric asked, but the orderly did not reply. "You try me one day and I'll jam that baton down your throat."

"Okay, Eric that will be enough." Flint said sternly. Eric focused back on Flint and shrugged.

"Where did you go to just now?" Flint asked.

"The beach." Said Eric.

"The beach?"

"Yep."

Flint adjusted the small tape recorder that sat in front of him, moving it closer to pick up Eric's low tone.

"Who was there?"

"Just me and Crystal."

"Was it a nice memory?"

"Every memory of Crystal is a good one, Doctor."

"Indeed." Flint nodded.

Just then the door flung open and a cleaner barged in with reckless abandonment, her trolley that was filled to capacity with all manner of cleaning products and apparatus.

"Oh, sorry, Dr Flint!" She said loudly,, taken by surprise. "I thought your session was over."

"It's okay, Maggie. We'll be finished here soon." Flint smiled.

"Oh, okay." Maggie said hovering around on the spot.

"Is there something wrong, Maggie?"

"I really need to use the bathroom." She whispered with a hint of embarrassment, "Would it be okay if I left the trolley here while I went and spent a penny?"

"Of course." Flint nodded.

"Thank you, Doctor." Maggie said leaving the trolley near to the door and disappearing back out on to the corridor.

"Sorry about that, Eric." Flint apologised.

"No problem." He shrugged again.

"So, how do you think you are progressing since you've been with us?"

"You're the quack." Eric laughed "Aren't you supposed to
tell me?"

Flint smiled at him.

"An astute observation, Eric." He laughed, "But seriously, how do you feel?"

"I feel like I'm in limbo."

"How so?"

"A part of me feels okay, don't feel as aggressive or bitter."

"And the other part of you?"

"Feel like my heart's been ripped out of my chest and it's been stamped on."

Eric looked at Flint, tears filling up in his eyes again.

"The mental trauma that you have received was so very severe, Eric. It's going to take..."

"Time." Eric interrupted.

Flint nodded.

"Time I got." Eric scoffed, staring out of the window again.

"I think we will prescribe some antidepressants."

"I'm not depressed!" Eric snapped, a subtle glow of red flushing his cheeks, "Sorry, Doctor, I..."

"No need to apologise. It's actually a very positive sign that you recognised that you were about to have an aggressive episode."

"Yeah?" Eric looked at Flint with eyebrows raised.

"Very much so." Flint smiled again as he jotted down more notes on his clipboard. "The antidepressant medication will just be to calm you down a little. They'll just chill you out." Eric nodded and looked out the window again.

"Do you think I'll ever get to be out there again, Doctor?"

Flint's face contorted, trying to find words that weren't too negative, but Stone added to his question and made the answer easier for the doctor.

"I mean, I'm no schmuck. I know I'll never be free. For taking that machine gun and shredding Sniff inside out, I know I don't deserve freedom and to tell you the truth if I can't spend my days with Crystal, then I don't want to be free."

He lifted his cuffed hands, the chains rattled as though he had come to warn Ebenezer about visiting spirits. The orderlies reached for their batons eagerly. Flint shook his head and they begrudgingly returned to how they were.

"Just walking out in the fresh air." Eric said pointing towards the window, "To hear the birds singing, feel the warmth of the sun and smell the grass." He turned to Flint again, eyes welling heavily. "Do you think? One day?"

"Of course, Eric. Of course!" Flint smiled and nodded warmly. "I tell you what, if you can stay on this path and if we can go another week without incident I'll take you out on the grounds myself. What do you say to that?"

"You mean it, Doctor?" Eric gasped.

"Indeed I do."

"I'd like that very much." Eric smiled, his lip wobbling as he fought to hold his emotions in check.

"Well, that's just splendid." Flint said rising "That will be all for today. Thank you Eric."

"Thank you, Doctor."

"Oh before I go Eric I have something else I wanted to ask you?"

"Shoot."

"I had a visit from a friend of yours yesterday."

Eric's attention was pricked and he looked atheism confused.

"I didn't think I had any." He scoffed.

"A Detective Graham."

Eric turned back towards the window and said nothing.

"Does that name have any relevance to you?"

"Doesn't ring any bells." Eric said shaking his head.

"Not to worry." Said Flint and he exited the room leaving Eric alone with the orderlies.

"You boys want to go a few rounds?"

The orderlies laughed and one of them bent down to detach Stone from the floor.

"It's tempting, Stone. It really is. But if you end up with fresh bruises then there will be questions asked."

"Shame." Eric smiled.

The other orderly headed for door laughing, "Yeah, the doc wouldn't be too happy with us if we broke that pretty face of yours." As he reached the door the cleaner burst in again, causing the orderly to stagger back and fall over the trolley.

The orderly was sent tumbling onto the floor causing all the contents of the trolley to spill onto the floor.

"Oh I'm terribly sorry. I thought you would have left by now." Maggie cried.

"God damn it woman!" The fallen orders yelled as he tried to pull himself up.

Eric found much delight in this and let his feelings none with a fit of hysterical laughter.

"Shut the hell up!" Growled the orderly next to him that was now shackling the chain back into place before he head over to help clean up.

As they all clambered to pick everything up, Stone gazed at the bottles of cleaning solutions that lay on the floor next to him. His eyes rapidly scanned over them as if looking for something. He looked up at the orderlies and the cleaner groaning at each other as they quickly turned the trolley up right and were searching for the spilled items.

Eric smiled and reached out with is foot and placed it on a bottle of bleach. He kept his eye on them as he managed to pull it closer to him.

He was quick to move his foot when the orderlies turned around to check on him.

"Why are you so quiet all of a sudden?" One of them enquired suspiciously.

"You told me to shut the hell up, sir." Eric grinned mischievously.

"Yeah, well, don't you go trying anything stupid. You can't move you know?"

68

"Yeah, I know." He grinned again whilst the orderly continued with what he was doing.

Eric managed to drag the bleach bottle directly under the table and then slowly reached down and picked up the bottle. Quickly he tucked it down the front of his trousers, the elasticated waistband keeping the bottle I place.

Eric smiled, but it was almost wiped from his face as Flint burst into the room.

"What in heavens is going on in here?" He barked with authority.

"She came charging in here like a bull in a..." The orderly yelled.

"I saw you leave Doctor and thought you'd all finished..."

"Knocked me on my ass!"

Flint removed his glasses and rubbed his eyes, sighing heavily.

"Does it take three of you to clean it up?" Flint asked. They shook their heads and looked sheepish like naughty schoolchildren.

"Good! Then can one of you escort Mr Stone back to his room please!"

"But shouldn't we both..." One of them began.

"I've got to visit Ms Osbourne next so I will accompany you."

Flint looked over at Eric still sitting where he had been left, the sunlight beaming in through the windows, the only thing he was missing was a halo.

"You're not going to try anything, Are you, Eric?"

"No, sir." Eric shook his head smiling widely.

The orderly detached Eric and lead him into the corridor, they followed Dr Flint who strode out in front of them, still clutching his clipboard.

I'm just fine and dandy, Doctor Flint. Smelling the grass and breathing in the fresh air. Jesus Christ you must be all kinds of gullible to believe that horse shit. That orderly prods me in the back with that baton again and I'm gonna snap it in half and stick it up his ass. Crystal I miss you so much. Fucking Sniff! I hate that piece of shit! So Sid finally came to check up on me. Too bad you weren't there when I needed you. Yeah, too bad... They reached the rooms and Stone was bundled into his and carefully unshackled. As the solid metal door slammed behind him and the key crunched in the lock. Eric stood looking at the narrow padded cell, a small air block fitted into the wall let in shards of sunlight, but the room contained only a bed and a toilet to keep him company. The service hatch opened and Doctor Flint wished him a good day. Eric smiled and waited for the hatch to be closed and until he heard their footsteps move on down the corridor. He retrieved the bottle of bleach from the from of his trousers.

No, I'm fine and well doctor, there's nothing wrong with me.

Chapter 9

The Alexandrea section of the city swelled with downtrodden souls, the homeless congregated like colonies of penguins. An annoyed looking Famu barged his way through them muttering under his breath.

"I'm sick of looking for those brats. It's like looking for a needle in a haystack."

He looks around at all the frightened faces staring back at him under a layer of dirt and matted hair.

"I need some information!" Famu shouted, his booming voice ricochetted off the high walls of the abandoned buildings that sandwiched them. They cowered away from the sheer volume.

"I've been looking for some kids who I believe may have the information I desire."

He saw numerous wide eyes bulging through the muck at him.

I probably didn't word that right. They must think I'm some kind of child molester or something.

"These kids work for a gang. Anybody know any kids?" They shook their heads vigorously, some of them even manoeuvred themselves in front of their own children.

They're never going to give up the kids. I need to rethink my questioning.

"Okay, okay. I haven't come for your kids, relax!" He boomed.

They instinctively held their families tighter.

"I'm looking for someone that can help me track down this gang." Famu looked around, "Anybody?"

They remained silent.

Famu snarled with aggravation he was getting nowhere fast and did not appreciate the lack of cooperation.

"Okay. Listen up!" He growled, "For your own sake, one of you needs to point me in the direction of somebody that will be able to help me or I'm going have to start handing out broken noses."

There was swift fluttering of outstretched arms as the majority of them pointed towards a little crevice in a partly demolished building.

"Vermin." They murmured.

"I've heard of him." Famu nodded "The eyes and the ears. Am I right?"

They nodded vigorously.

"See! Wasn't so hard now was it?" He groaned and as he

trudged across a layer of broken bricks and mortar the entire population of vagrants disappeared from sight. Famu reared

72

the hole in the wall and turned around to see if they were watching him, he was taken aback to see that they had all vanished.

"Rats. Thats what you all are, nothing but rats!"
He entered and was met by a rat sitting on his hind legs staring up at the mammoth of man, his head tilting from side to side with inquisition.

"Nothing personal." Famu laughed looking at the rat. A light flickered at the end of a long narrow passage, made from fallen guilders and brick. He sidestepped through the narrow passage, struggling to squeeze his wide frame through it.
The rat scurried passed him and headed for the light, Famu's held on to a steel shard protruding from the man made wall. He pulled himself through it and in doing so disturbed some debris that fell down the wall gently.

"Is that you Kasper?" Came a voice from the clearing where the light was being generated from.

"Ah, there you are my friend." Came the voice again as Famu realised Kasper must have been the rat that had passed him a few moments ago.
Elliot Hayes sat in a corner of the clearing, sitting up on his pull out bed and relatively new sleeping bag and blankets. Cardboard boxes sat filled to the brim with tinned and packeted foods. An electric lantern sat on a crate in the middle of the clearing brightening up the cavern, there was even a selection of paperbacks piled up next to his bed. It didn't look like your average homeless person's abode, in fact

it was probably seen as paradise for some.

Kasper scuttled straight up to Elliot and onto his lap, his nose wiggling vigorously, whiskers twitching as if he were trying to communicate something to his human friend.

"Something the matter Kasper?" Elliot asked and he looked tor's the entrance, he saw nothing.

"You're just jumping at shadows again my little friend." He smiled an unattractive smile, his cleft palate and severe scaring all over his face was not pleasant but there was warmth there as he stroked and fussed his pet rat.

Elliot rose from his cot and stretched out his weary old limbs, the hair that was allowed to grow on his heavily disfigured head was long, grey and greasy.

"Now I think we have some cheese around here some place." He said searching in a shopping cart that was parked in the corner of the cavern. It was overflowing with random things that he had found on his travels.

More debris fell around the entrance, Elliot's gaze automatically moved towards the sound and was shocked to see the enormous Hawaiian mastodon entering his home.

"What? Who are you?" Elliot cried.

He immediately pulled up his hood as to conceal his ideas features from this uninvited guest.

"Aren't you going ask me in?" Famu scoffed, as he rose to his full height and smiled menacingly at Elliot.

"What do you want?" Elliot snapped and backed up against the wall, Kasper ran up his body and hid in the chest pocket of his disheveled overcoat.

Famu looked around seemingly impressed by what he saw.

"You're doing okay here aren't ya, Vermin."

"Thats not my name!" He growled, his teeth shape and jagged like that of a rodent's shone in the light of the lantern.

"That's what they said." Famu shrugged as pointed back towards to passageway.

"Just get the hell out of here! You're not wanted here."

"Now look... What's your name?"

"Screw you!" Elliot shouted.

Famu lunged forward with such swiftness and agility that it caught Elliot completely off guard that someone so large could move with such speed and finesse. He wrapped his huge mitt around Elliot's throat and drove him back into the wall. Debris fell all around them and they both looked up at the obviously unsafe makeshift roof.

"Now you'd better tell me your name. It wouldn't take much to bring an end to your bachelor pad now would it?" He smiled looking up at the ceiling. He heard debris falling around the entrance again and wondered if his huge frame was the catalyst for an imminent collapse.

"Elliot." He squeaked.

"Good!" Famu smiled and released his grip.

Elliot coughed and spluttered and then asked through bruised larynx "What do you want?"

75

Famu started to rummage around in Elliot's shopping trolley.

"What have we got here?" He asked pulling out a Studd City Sharks football jersey, the number 32 embroidered on the front of back. Famu whistled. "Dee Zee Reed's final Shark's jersey! How the hell did you get your grubby little hands on this?"

"I acquire things."

"I bet you do." He sniggered, "Do you know how much you could get for that on the collector's market?"

"I don't care. Down on the streets it's worth food and water and that's all I care about."

Elliot bravely approached Famu and snatched the jersey from his grip and placed it back not his trolley.

"Okay, I will let you keep the jersey if you play ball." Famu smiled but then he grabbed Elliot's hood and pulled him in close. "But, if you ever snatch anything away from me again, I will rearrange your face!"

Famu was relishing being in control and using his strength to over power someone that was weaker than him, in many ways he was doing this to make himself feel like a man, as although he wouldn't like to admit it he was usually the one in the clutches of a powerful hand.

Elliot managed to push him away.

"You'll have your work cut out for you there my friend."

Elliot laughed as his hood fell down to reveal a face that would be perfectly at home in a freak show tent.

76

"Jesus!" Famu gasped.

"Tell me what you want to know. If I can help you I will."   "That's the spirit!"

More debris fell around the entrance.

Elliot made his way over to his bed and retrieved a bottle of water and drank from it, hoping to soothe his throat.

"I've heard of you, they call you 'The eyes and the ears of Studd City' right?"

Elliot nodded and then he took another swig of water.

"So if I wanted some information on the whereabouts of someone, you would be able to point me in the right direction."

"Depends who it was."

Famu laughed, moving ever closer to Elliot.

"The Web-Heads."

"No can do." Elliot shook his head.

"It's the top dog Spider really need to find."

"Sorry, from what I hear he's gone into hiding. He's made a lot of enemies. One of them being the Coyote and he's out for his blood."

"Well, if you don't know where they are then you must at least know some of the brats they've been using as runners." More debris fell from the entrance way.

"No!" Elliot shouted, "No way am I going to rat out children to you."

Famu slammed a large fist into Elliot's face, he immediately hit the deck.

"You stupid old bastard!" Famu growled and began driving lefts and right into Elliot's already disguised face like two piston powered meat tenderisers.

Blood erupted from his nose and mouth as it seeped into the his scars, giving the effect that his face had been cracked.

Famu came up for air, his vast chest breathing in and out quickly and he panted heavily.

"It would be easier on you if you give something to go on."

Elliot spat blood out over Famu's flamboyant tropical shirt and Famu slammed another unforgiving hammer into his face.

Elliot's head rocked back and forth and his eyelids fluttered trying to stay conscious.

"Look." Famu said his breath short and his chest struggling "I've been over this city looking for one of these kids and you know how many I've found?" He stopped to catch his breath again. "Zero! So where are all the fucking kids?"

Elliot smiled an uneven smile, blood staining his broken incisors.

"Go to hell." He murmured, gargling on his own blood. Famu pulled back to land another blow when Kasper bravely broke out from the safety of Elliott's pocket and ran up Famu's arm to bite at his thick neck. Famu howled in pain and grabbed at the rat, as he pulled him off flesh tore from his neck and hung in Kasper's mouth.

"You little bastard!" He yelled and threw the poor rat into the corner of the room, where he hit the wall and then the floor and scurried off though a small hole to safety.

"Oh that's it!" Famu growled clutching at his bleeding neck. "I'm going to kill you for that!"

"Wait!" Came a voice and Famu spun around to see a small hooded figure at the entrance.

"Please leave him alone."

"Who the hell are you?"

The figure removed the hood to reveal a teenage Asian girl, her long dark hair secured in two ponytails either side of her head. She looked at him with pleading eyes and she edged towards them.

"Look, I'll tell you where they are, just leave him alone." Famu smiled.

Chapter 10

Dr Flint sat on a chair in the corridor outside the room of patient, Nicholas Smith. His legs crossed casually and balancing his clipboard on his knees the service hatch had been opened and Smith's deranged face was pressed up to the opening, a smile from ear to ear as his wide bloodshot eyes flitted from side to side.

"I can't hear it anymore, Doctor." He moved away from the hatched and the pressed his ear to it "Still nothing."

"You can't hear it anymore because the circus has moved on Nicholas."

"Such as shame." He sighed and his face returned, gaunt with sharp pointed features.

"Did you like the music?"

"I did. I did." He nodded vigorously, banging his head on the door with each nod. "*Hey! That's fun to do!*" He cried and started head butting the metal door.

"That's enough Nicholas! You'll hurt yourself."

"**Fine.**" Smith sighed and stopped, "**you never let him have any fun Flint!**" He growled, his face contorting horrifyingly.

"I was wondering when you were going to join us." Flint said, his attention focussed on his scribbling pencil, he wasn't fazed at all by the change of voice of attitude from Nicholas Smith in the slightest. In fact he was expecting it.

"**Nothing but a troublemaker you are Flint.**" Smith spat, saliva dribbling down his pointy chin.

"Well, that's the pot calling the kettle black now isn't it?" Flint chuckled and finally looked up to see that horrendous face that looked like some goblin.

"**Why don't you let us out of here? We won't do any harm ?**"

"You know I can't do that Nicholas. You are a danger to yourself and anyone that you come in contact with."

"Go away and let me talk to the doctor!" Smith whimpered his expression changing again to that of a frightened child's.

"**Oh, shut up!**" He growled "**Well at least let me out !**" He pushed his face up against the hatch forcefully as if he were trying to squeeze through the small gap. "**you can leave Smith here. What do you say ?**" He smiled with a frenzied expression.

"So you have finally denounced Smith?" Flint asked.

"What's that mean? What is he doing to me?" Smith whimpered.

"He is saying that he is recognising that you are both separate entities."

"Of course I fucking am! Dont think I'm a useless wet lettuce like Smith do you ?" He began to cackle, the sound escaped down the hatch and danced around the corridor, it was enough to make skin crawl.

"Do you have a name?" Flint enquired.

Smith didn't answer and his face changed to that of worry and he stepped away from the hatch.

"If you are not Nicholas Smith, then who are you?" Still no answer.

"You must have a name?" Flint continued.

"STOP!" Smith cried as he angrily grabbed at his wild greasy hair and yanked at it.

"Okay, Nicholas. It's okay now." Flint said in a reassuring tone. "Has he gone now?"

Smith nodded, but he looked in pain.

"He's gone now, but he stabs at my head doctor. Stabs at it like an ice pick!" He squealed and fell to a heap on the padded flooring.

Flint stood up and approached the hatch, an act he wouldn't dare do if Smith had have been upright. Smith suffered from severe schizophrenia which has gradually become worse over time as the inner voice battles to takeover the host. Smith is becoming weaker and giving into the voice. He will never be released from Oakland Institute.

"Are you okay now, Nicholas?" Flint asked as Smith rolled onto his back and stretched out his limbs and started making snow angels.

"Yes, Doctor, I'm fine." He looked at him strangely "Why?"

It was if he had no memory of what had just happened.

Flint took the time to look around Smith's room. Some of the pads had be shredded and the inner foam was piled up in various places. The had no bedsheet and stuck to wall with tape were newspaper cuttings of Vatican sightings. Blurry, candid photographs that had been captured of Studd City's own vigilante standing on rooftops or bounding across them, they were not the best images to say the least but it was all the tabloids had been able to get at this time.

"I see you still have your newspaper cuttings, Nicholas."

"Oh yes!" Smith cried with excitement and jumped to his feet.

Flint backed up a few steps, so he was out of Smith's reach if he were to turn nasty.

Smith bounced up and down on his bed looking at all the paper cuttings.

"He's my favourite, he is. Vatican is my hero you know?"

"Yes, I know Nicholas." Flint smiled.

Smith suddenly looked spooked and his eyes flitted from side to side as if he was being watched.

"Something wrong Nicholas?"

Smith put his finger to his lips as if to shush the doctor and stood on the edge of the bed looking from one corner of the room to the other.

"Nicholas?" Flint lowered his voice. "Is he coming back?"

"No." Smith suddenly cried and bounced towards the hatch again.

"Do you want me to show you something?" Smith whispered.

"Oh yes Nicholas, I would like that very much." Flint nodded.

"You can't tell anyone though not even him."

"I promise." Flint said crossing his heart.

Smith laughed, dropped to the ground and scuttled under the bed. Flint gambled and stepped closer watching Smith's bare feet dangling out from underneath the bed.

"What have you go under there Nicholas?"

"I'm coming!" He yelled as he shimmied out from under the bed with what looked like torn white bedsheets in his hands. "Now close your eyes." Smith asked.

Flint stepped back a few spaces and then closed his eyes.

"No peeking!" He squealed started to ready his surprise.

"Okay you can look now Doctor Flint."

Flint opened his eyes and was met by Smith with home made cape and bandit mask, his hands on his hips in his best super hero pose.

"How do I look?" He grinned, mask dropping over his eyes.

"You look just like Vatican!" Flint gasped, "If I didn't know any better I would have thought that it was the real Angel of Justice standing before me."

Smith's face changed again, that sneer replacing the smile.

"Don't be ridiculous Flint!" Smith growled angrily "He looks nothing like him and you know it! Tell him the truth go on!"

Flint sighed and scratched down some more notes.

He looked back up to see a rejected looking Smith sitting on the bed with his head in his hands.

"He doesn't even wear a cape you moron!"

"He's right isn't he? He doesn't wear one does he?" Smith whimpered.

"But maybe you are better than the Vatican."

"Really?"

"Sure! I mean real super heroes wear capes, don't they?"

85

"They do, they do!"

Flint watched on as Smith had the entire conversation with himself.

"Yes, I think you'll make one hell of a super hero, Nicholas."

"You really think so?"

"Oh yes!"

Flint sighed with defeat and wrote down something else as an orderly arrived.

"Yes, Derek?" Flint asked.

"It's Vicks, Sir. He's refusing to take his medication again."

Flint nodded.

"I think we are done here anyway." He said closing the hatch and leaving Smith to carry on with his conversation.

"Something wrong, Sir?" Derek asked, seeing that Flint was deep in thought and starting at his clipboard.

"Lost cause I'm afraid, Derek." Flint sighed and then moved his chair next to the wall out of the way.

"Most of them are." Derek shrugged.

"Oh no, don't say that, Derek." Flint groaned "I really take it personally when I can't make a difference."

"You can't help them all, Sir."

"No." He nodded "You are right of course. But I can put things in place so that they have a more comfortable journey. But this one I'm afraid has backfired."

"The Vatican thing not work?"

"I thought it was, that Smith would focus on being another entity and gradually move away from that inner voice."

"And I take it not all has gone to plan?"

"No, the voice is actually egging him on to become Vatican, which means he is taking control. It won't be long now until he has been completely consumed."

In the next room Eric Stone stood with his ear to the hatch of his door listening to everything Flint was saying.

"I suggest we run a sweep of his room tomorrow, remove all the Vatican paraphernalia and there are some pads that are in need of repair."

"Yes, Sir." Derek nodded.

"Oh and he'll need some fresh sheets too."

Stone heard them start to walk away, their footsteps echoed around the narrow corridor, making it sound like they were in the room with him.

"It might be worth doing a sweep of all the rooms tomorrow." Flint said. "Give us chance to check all the rooms over and make sure they are safe."

Stone remained with his ear pressed up agains the cold metal hatch until he heard nothing but the cries of his neighbour Smith.

Stone approached his bed and lifted up the mattress underneath it in hollowed out pockets were several bottles of cleaning solutions.

"I guess tonight's the night then." He smiled "Lets get the hell out of here."

Chapter ll

The secret cellar of St. Vincent's church was uncharacteristically warm, usually Burt would be sat at the control centre with a crocheted blanket around his shoulders and a hot water bottle in his lap, as the cold wind swept its way through the crevices of Studd City's sewer system. Tonight he had no need for either, just the constant stream of hot coffee would suffice. The abundance of coffee on offer had led to Thomas installing a portable toilet in cellar, being Vatican's wingman could be a long, arduous task and it was a big ask of an elderly man to go without a bathroom break. Burt took a sip from his new 'Best Sidekick Ever' mug that Thomas had purchased him for his birthday, the hot steam sweeping into his face. He looked for a place to place the mug down on felt covered card table and realised that his work station was becoming too small to accommodate all of the paraphernalia needs for keeping tracks on a vigilante.

"Hmm!" Burt grumbled looking to try and move something from the surface to make way for his mug.
A new desktop computer had replaced the ancient laptop he had been using which took up double the amount of room as

well as the old CB radio which blasted out constant chatter from the SCPD's frequency. Not to mention a pot for his pens, a pile of notepads, a cell phone and two flasks (one containing coffee, the other tomato soup for his supper).

"I guess the radio could be moved." He pondered, "I mean I don't need to have that to hand, just to listen too."
He started to rise from the swivelling office chair that ladder with cushions incase Burt's haemorrhoids flared up again. The computer started to let out a piercing sound to alert him of something.

"Ah, he's on the move." He said and sat back down, dragging the mouse across the felt top, the cursor on the screen expanded a map of the city and a red blip flashed on the screen as it moved rapidly.

"Well, would you take a look at that." Burt laughed, he shook his head in disbelief "The son' bitch actually works!"
The tracker that he had purchased from the internet was currently in the heel of Vatican's left boot and his exact whereabouts were now being displayed on Burt's computer scree. The internet and technology was all new to Burt and he was quite often astonished by what was capable these days.

"What will they think of next?" He chuckled.
He took another sip of coffee and then frowned at the screen.

"If I'm not mistaken, Thomas," He said, "You're on your way home."

The first thing that seeped into Burt's brain was that he was hurt and he was coming home. He controlled his emotions and tried to let his worry consume him, he knew from his time in Vietnam that that only leads to panic and in these situations a cool head is always needed.

He pushed himself away from the table, the chair's wheels screeching across the flat stone and settled in front of an old military trunk. He lifted up the old rusted lid, it was crammed with first aid equipment and medical supplies. Burt reached in and grabbed bandages, a syringe, antiseptic cream, forceps and anaesthetic.

Burt rose from the chair and placed the equipment on a table next to the training area, pulling the chair out from underneath it and readying it encase Thomas was in urgent need of sitting. Burt glanced at the screen and noticed that he would soon be back and was moving quickly through the sewers.

"He's moving quick enough." Burt said to himself, "Can't be anything too serious, physically."

He waddled over to the foot of the stairs where and small refrigerator was located and grabbed a fresh bottle of water from it. He moved back towards the table and swept a towel that was hung on Thomas' wooden training dummy and placed them both on the table and waited. He glanced towards the door and he could hear the rubber soles of Thomas' boots colliding with the moist concrete.

Burt made one last trot back to the refrigerator and retrieved and icepack from the freezer compartment. As the

91

refrigerator door closed behind him, the entrance to the sewer opened and Vatican stood in the door way, wheezing heavily.

"Is everything okay, Thomas?" Burt blurted, trying not to sound too concerned.

Thomas was doubled over with his hands on his thighs as he tried to catch his breath. He indicated to Burt by the wave of a finger that he would be with him in a second.

"Can I get you anything?" Burt asked as he approached, Thomas shook his head.

"Are you hurt?" Burt continued, scanning Thomas for any wounds or signs that would help him decipher what was wrong.

"I'm okay, Burt." Thomas managed to utter before standing upright again, "Just need to catch my breath that's all."

"Here sit down, have a drink."

Burt ushered him to the fair he had arranged by the table. Thomas grabbed the bottle of water and drank eagerly.

"Okay now?" Burt asked, looking confused as to why he had returned so early into a patrol.

Thomas nodded and then perused the table at what Burt had laid out.

"Is all this for me?" Thomas smiled.

"Well..." Burt shrugged, almost embarrassed, "I knew you were coming back and I didn't know what time to expect you."

92

"Bless you, Burt." Thomas smiled again, "I really should have called."

"It's okay. Just best to be prepared. It was a good test for the tracker anyway."

Thomas nodded and drank some more water his breathing pattern was returning to normal now.

"I may actually need some of this stuff when I head back out anyway."

"Well, are you going to keep me on tenterhooks all night?"

Thomas laughed.

"I paid Elliot a visit and he is not in good shape."

"What happened?"

"Somebody really did a number on him. Cut his face up pretty good."

"Oh dear!" Burt croaked with concern, "But why?"

"I haven't been able to get anything out of him yet, he can be a stubborn old mule sometimes, and he obviously won't let me take him to a hospital so it looks like it's left to me to patch him up as best as I can."

"Think you can manage it?"

"I think you've taught me enough to make a decent job of it. Probably going to need a needle and thread and some superglue too."

Burt nodded and returned to the trunk again and retrieved the items he had asked for.

"Thanks, Burt." Thomas said wiping the sweat from his brow. "I mean Elliot is in no way a looker, he's never going to win any beauty contests but I've got to do my best for the guy." Thomas attempted to stand, but Burt placed a hand on his shoulder and pushed him gently back into the seat.

"Get your breath back first and finish your water first. You'll be no good to him if you're all fatigued when you get back to him."

"You're right." Thomas nodded and then laughed "But then you usually are."

Burt started to pack all the items he may need into a separated utility pocket that Thomas could attached to his existing unity belt.

"You didn't tell me how you got on with your visit to see Father Harrison."

"Not well at all!"

"I didn't think you would to be honest." Burt scoffed "I've heard some terrible things about the man. I know its not my place to tattle..."

"I sense a 'but' coming." Thomas laughed.

"But!" Burt chuckled, "I hear that he would be drunk during his sermons, he has assaulted other members of the clergy on numerous occasions and he was even involved in a murder case."

"Murder?" Thomas gasped, eyes wide.

"That's what I hear. Apparently stabbed a girl, wasn't enough evidence to have a case on him."

"Why wasn't he fired?"

"He threatened to sue if they terminated his position, because technically he was seen as innocent in the eyes of the law."

Thomas nodded and seemed to be somewhere else. His mind's eye conjured up flashes of his past, his father beating his mother in a drunken rage, while he cowered in the corner of the room as a child crying. His father's face splattered in blood, grasping a bloodied bottle opener in his hand, the haunting sound of it tearing through the flesh of the poor defenceless care worker that was sent to collect him when his mother took her own life.

"Are you okay Thomas?"

"Yeah." He smiled, "Just brings back some painful memories, Burt."

Burt looked at him solemnly and nodded.

"The thing that sticks with me though, Burt is that why
did he start drinking in the first place? I mean we shouldn't judge, we all have our vices."

"Yes, we do." Burt laughed and then slapped Thomas on the shoulder "All part from you, Thomas! You're as righteous as The Pope himself!"

Thomas didn't look at Burt, he couldn't, nor could he answer him. He was thinking about the bottle of Alprazolam that he had hidden on the top of the bathroom cabinet.

"I wonder what drove him to make the decisions he has?" Thomas said quickly to break the silence before it became uncomfortable.

"Who knows!" Burt shrugs "I doubt you'll ever get to the truth of the matter."

"You may be right there. I doubt he'll want to speak to me or anyone else for that matter."
Finally rested and refreshed, Thomas stood and took the pouch from Burt and clipped it onto his utility belt.

"I better get going, got lots of ground to cover tonight."   "Anything particular?"

"I really need to see Detective Graham."

"Really?"

"Yes, I can't keep putting it off. I can't see an innocent man incarcerated for a crime he didn't commit."

"I wouldn't call Elvis Valentine innocent." Burt scoffed.

"Even still, he shouldn't be serving a life sentence for The Doomsday Murders. I alone know that it was Spider that was responsible and I need to pass that information onto Graham, even if it's for my own conscience and sanity."

"Would you be willing to take the witness stand?" Burt asked.
Thomas was silent for a moment as he pondered the ramifications of doing such a thing.

"I would."

"Even if it could possibly jeopardise your crusade" Burt asked.

"I..." Thomas thought long and hard, "If it came down to that then I would have too, Burt. It's the right thing to do."

96

"You're a better man than me, Thomas."

Burt looked at him beaming with pride as if he were his own son.   "You're right of course." Burt nodded "He probably deserves to rot in Skelter for God only knows what heinous crimes. But as you say, not this one."

"Exactly." Thomas smiled "I've also got to try and track down that girl, I believe she is the key to me finding Spider and his goons."

"Well, what are you waiting for?" Burt barked with a smile on his face, "Get going!"

Thomas smiled, sarcastically saluted and left hastily through the door to the sewers.

"Go get'em soldier." Burt smirked closing the heavy metal door behind him.

Chapter 12

The Oakland Institute was relatively quiet, only the odd scream or ludicrous babbling broke the silence that had settled in the corridors. The inmates were safely locked away for the evening and the presence of orders would be sparse, hourly in fact, the few that were on duty would no doubt be settling down for a game of cards in their little staff room. Stone knew this, that is why he put his plan in to action slowly over the last few hours. He had retrieved everything he needed from his hidden stash that he had assembled over the past few weeks.

It's amazing how easy it is to steal things from under people's noses when they think you're mad. Although they watch you closely, they are watching for what they think you'll do. If you're looking lethargic they ease up thinking that you're not going to get aggressive. And while they're talking about last night's Sharks and Warriors game, I make my move.

Stone smiled strangely as he sat on the edge of his bed.

It feels good to know that that fat bastard Derek will be

looking for his matches right about now to light up a fresh Freebird.

He'll be out of luck.

Stone placed a pack of matches on the bed next to him as started to tear away at his bed sheet, that looked as though it had already been torn up for something else.

The room had reeked earlier on in the evening of human faeces, but now it was replaced by an overpowering smell of bleach. Stone's eyes were red and runny as the potent fumes dominated the small 8 by 6 room.

Stone dropped the torn piece of sheet next to the box of matches. He stood up and checked the door, pressing his ear up against the hatch, he felt a cool breeze seep through the gap and caressed his face, he looked out the small vent like holes, he saw nothing.

"It's time." He whispered to himself.

Stone stood for a while longer at the hatch refreshing his sore eyes with the soft breeze.

I still can't believe I have been put in this predicament. Three months ago my life was perfect. If I close my eyes tightly I can still see her face, I can still smell her, I can feel her. It was a warm, soothing feeling. All that has gone now. There are no warm, soothing feelings anymore, the only things I feel now are cold. Ice cold.

Stone walks over to the toilet in the corner of the room, he leans over to make sure everything is in order, the burning fumes rose up and made him wince, attacking his eyes and nostrils. He mistakingly exhaled it, his throat was on fire now and a coughing fit ensued.

He moved back over to the bed again and tore another piece from his bedsheets, he tied it around his not and mouth and returned to the toilet looking like some outlaw about to hold up a stagecoach.

He peered into the toilet. His pillow had been stuffed down into the bowl as far as it would go to soak up any excess water. He had drenched the whole thing with numerous cleaning products he had acquired over the past few weeks.

Ammonia, bleach, hydrazine are just a number of things you can find with everyday household cleaning products and when they're mixed together... well...

Stone stood staring at the toilet bowl, his train of thought and wondered away again, his mind had become a little intoxicated by the fumes.

...A dangerous mix anyway.

Stone walked back over to the bed and delved underneath it to retrieve something.

And the finale piece of the puzzle. I'm not proud of this, but my hands were forced and I had to move tonight, so this is the outcome.

Stone held in the palm of his hand a piece of his own waste. A strip of bedsheet dangled out of it, acting as wick, the faeces had been moulded around it.

I was hoping to use porridge for this particular part of my plan, but alas this morning they served that granola shit, and that's just not malleable enough.

He playfully threw the round ball of faeces up and down a few times as if he were a pitcher for the Studd City Jays, standing on the mound ready let rip a knuckle-curve pitch.

"It's go time!" He said placing the tacky ball of waste and the matches on the floor next to the door. He looked through the holes in the hatch again, nothing but silence. He upended the bed and dragged it in front of the door, then he crouched down behind it grasping the faeces in his hand. He looked over the bed and closed one eye to focus on the angle and distance to the toilet bowl.

"Now I may have gone a little bit crazy after what I have been through, I mean Hey, who wouldn't? You loose your wife, your unborn child, get accused of being a serial killer by your so called friends and have your best friend turn their back on you and see how sane you feel!" He growled, through gritted teeth. That anger had bubbled up inside him, but Stone managed to cut it off before he reached boiling point, he had a task to complete. When he was out of this nuthouse he could be as angry as he liked at least direct it at the people that need to feel its wrath.

Chapter 13

Nicholas Smith's eyelids were getting heavily, they fell closed several times but the voice that had sent up permanent residence in his head kept informing him that he wasn't tired. He was. He was in fact extremely tired, the mental anguish that comes with carrying around another individual (even if it was technically a figment of his own reality) could be very tiring indeed. He yawned and tried to nestle himself in a comforting position around his pillow.

"Stop yawning! you're not tired!" Snapped that voice again.

"But I am!" Nicholas whimpered, "I am so very tired. Let me sleep please."

Tears seeped from between his clenched lids.

"Will you quit your whimpering and your constant whining! Honesty it's like babysitting some days! Do you Remember that time we babysat your little brother?"

"Stop it!" Nicholas snivelled and then sat up focusing on something completely different.

"What was that noise?" He asked himself as he stared into the gloom of his room. The only light from the corridor streaming in through the air holes in the doors hatch.

The voice didn't answer him. He sat up and listened, his mouth hung open as he listened intently, his feature were sharp, he looked almost malnourished.

There was a ruckus from next door, the sound carrying through the corridor.

"There it is again!" Nicholas whined "What in God's name is it?" He cried and hid under the blanket.

"Could be a ghoul." The voice mocked.

"Stop it! You know I hate ghouls."

"The Vatican wouldn't be scared of a little ghoul, would he ?"

"No, I guess not." Nicholas pulled back the blanket again and looked into the darkness, the toilet had started to make strange heaving noises as though it needed to throw up.

"There is one in the toilet too." He whispered.

"Maybe you should investigate, Nicholas."

"No!" He squealed and beneath the blanket once more. "That's what happens in the movies..." He peered over the blanket, clutching it tightly to his face, his bloodshot eyes bright in dark sunken sockets. "...And in the movies they always die in the movies."

103

"yes they do." The voice agreed, "But they aren't super heroes are they?"

"No, no they're not!"

"And you, why aren't you The Vatican?" Gasped the voice in surprised.

"Yes!" Nicholas appeared from underneath the blanket once more, expanding his scrawny chest.

"Then you must investigate. It is your duty."

"Yes, it is!" He beamed proudly, throwing back the blanket and jumping out of bed, he bare feet slapping on the cold linoleum.

"Only you can keep the people of studd City safe from these ghouls. Nicholas!"

Nicholas nodded and grabbed his homemade cape, and applied his mask.

"I Nicholas Smith am Vatican!"

The wall exploded in a flash of amber and a deafening burst, the wall erupted and the sheer force sent Nicholas tumbling backwards onto the bed. From out of the smoke the toilet sprang from its fittings, launching it into the air and wedging into the padded ceiling.

"Ghouls?" He stuttered.

"Ghouls." The voice replied.

Nicholas left the safety of his bed and walked towards the vicinity of the explosion, thick smoke consumed the room and soft pieces of foam fell like plump flakes of snow all around him.

"What do I do?" Nicholas asked. The voice said nothing.

"WHAT DO I DO?" Her erupted, becoming incredibly vexed at the whole situation.

"*Oh, now you want me to talk!*" The voice scoffed "*Normally you are telling me to shut up, or go away. Now you need me, you snivel like a wounded dog!*"

Nicholas began to cry. "Please tell me what to do."

"*You accept me?*"

"Yes, yes, just tell me what to do!"

Nicholas' face contorted and seemed to morph into something ugly

"*Finally!*" He grinned.

The smoke cleared and a jagged hole appeared in the wall before him.

"Is that outside?"

"*Yes. Nicholas it is. Shall we go and have an adventure.*"

"Yes, lets!"

Nicholas smiled, the look of excitement like that of a child walking into a theme park, but again the face changed it was though his face was a reflection in water, changing with each ripple. Nicholas Smith was no longer in charge.

105

Chapter 14

It was very late and it had been a while since Valerie Nash had turned over and gone to sleep, her naked body immersed in the thick goose down duvet. Sidney Graham was still wide awake, It was normally him that was rolling over and hugging the bedcovers after a vigorous session of love making, but tonight he had things on his mind. He was now carrying around so much guilt with him that he was afraid that if he boarded a plane he would have exceeded his baggage allowance. He sighed heavily and looked around at Valerie's modest one bed room apartment, the lights from Studd City's lively streets forced its way into the apartment, illuminating it int fluorescent pinks and purples. This was life living in Roma opposites a gentleman's club known as The Cat's Whiskers.

He turned to look at Valerie, she looked content and peaceful, comfortable. Graham smiled, but he felt none of these things. He rose from the bed and slipped into a pair of trousers that lay strewn on the floor, along with several other pieces of clothing, evidence that they had consumed each other in a primal moment of lust.

Retrieving a half used pack of Freebird cigarettes and lighter that sat on the bedside table, and his shirt he made his way towards the window that homed a fire escape. As quietly as he could he hoist up the window, it scraped against the frame and he stopped suddenly turning to see Valerie stirring. He waited for her to settle and then crept out of the window, his bare feet recoiling on the cold metal grill of the fire escape. He closed the window behind him to keep out the shrill of the street.

He lit up a cigarette and inhaled deeply as if sighing, he thought it would make everything better, take away all that guilt. He exhaled and didn't feel any different.

He leant on the railing and looked down at the vibrant night life f Studd City's red light district.

The smoke from his cigarette danced around him, like a comfort blanket, keeping him warm and protecting him from anxieties of the outside world.

"What the hell are you doing, Sid?" He asked himself, shaking his head. The rest of his conversation was obviously not meant for neighbours that may be eavesdropping, so he kept it to himself.

Fuck it, Sid! Your an adulterous pig nothing more! Poor Mae, why have you done this to her? How could you! And the kids... What are they going to think of you?

"I know, I know." He murmured.

Not to mention how you have dealt with the whole Eric affair. He needed you at a time when he was at his lowest and you turned away from him. That chain of guilt that you wear around your neck is justified!

He sighed again and let the smoke drift away into the night, he watched as it cascaded to a building adjacent with a mirroring

fire escape when he noticed a figure perched on the railing in the darkness no more than ten feet away.

He squinted to see if he could make out what it was, then the neon sign from the Cat's Whiskers flashed and the figure was bathed in cerise, revealing Vatican. He remained motionless, almost cat-like in his presence as the light illuminated the crimson colour of his face mask and the crucifix emblazoned on his templar type attire.

Graham's tired eyes doubled in size and he dropped his cigarette, which fell through the grate and drifted in a trail of smoke to the alleyway below.

"You're supposed to be quitting anyway." Vatican said, his tone level and unflustered by being exposed.

"You!" Graham exhaled as he instinctively reached for his firearm that was usually safety nestled under his left armpit, but it wasn't there now.

"It's under your mattress, Sidney." Vatican said, his words causing Graham's jaw to drop, "Isn't that where you keep it?"

"H-How did you know?" He stuttered.

"I make it my business to find out things."

Graham suddenly snapped out of his astonishment and tried to shift gears into authoritative detective mode.

"Now you just stay right where you are!" He barked as he tried to open up the window again without taking his eyes of Vatican.

Vatican didn't move a muscle just sat on the railing almost smirking at him.

"Come on, Sidney, there's no need to be silly."

"What the hell do you mean, 'silly'! You're a wanted criminal! And I'm taking you in."

Vatican laughed, the sound echoed between the buildings.

"What is it that I am wanted for?"

Graham having being caught with his pants down and on the spot was flustered, and had no answer for him.

"Exactly!" Vatican said, "If you don't realise that we are both on the same side by now, you'll never know."

Graham stared at him.

"Look, we are soldiers in the same war here, Sidney."

"Who are you?"

"Not yet." Vatican smiles, "Maybe one day, after this war

is over."

"Then what do you want from me?" Graham asked.

"I trust you."

"Trust me!" Graham laughed, "You don't even know me, pal."

Vatican smiled, "I know more about you than you think. I know that you are noble, reliable and proficient."

Graham's eyes widened, lost for words again.

"Of course this is all based on your professional career and not your personal life." He said with a hint of sarcasm.

"Keep your fucking nose out of my personal life!" Graham growled, pointing an accusing finger at him.

"Sorry, Sidney." Vatican said holding aloft the palm of his hand in an apologetic gesture, "I didn't mean to offend you, but..."

"No." Graham interrupted and then sighed lowering his head slightly, "You're completely right in your assumption. But if you're looking for someone to put your trust in then maybe I'm not the right guy."

"Yes, you are." Vatican nodded, "You're a good cop, Sidney and a good guy. You've just lost your way. We can all loose our way sometimes."

"What? And you're here to put me on the right path again?"

"No, that's not for me to do, that is something you'll have to do yourself if that's what you decide to do."

"Then why are you here?"

"I have some information for you."

"About what?"

Vatican remained quiet for a moment or two.

"I have kept this information to myself for a while and I realise now that it was wrong to do so."

"What information?"

"Elvis Valentine was not responsible for the Doomsday Murders."

"What are you talking about? We caught him red handed."

"No, he was set up."

"But, how do you..."

"I was there that night at the warehouse." Vatican interrupted, "I saw who was responsible."

"Then if it wasn't Elvis, the who was it?"
Graham swallowed hard the same thought played on a loop in his head *Please don't say Eric, please don't say Eric.*

"It was Webb. Joseph Webb, I think you know him as Spider."

"But, how? Isn't he..."

"Dead?" Vatican smirked, "That's exactly what he wanted you all to think. He framed Elvis so that he could take the mantle of Doomsday leader."

"Fuck!" Graham moaned.

"He's also behind the Stardust surge in Studd too." Graham ran his hands through his hair as if trying to process all this new information. "I thought that this information could be usual for your friend too who is currently confined in Oakland. I understand that your superior thought that he was to blame for the killings, this new information may help his sentence in some way." Vatican shrugged, "Well, I hoped to could help."

"This is huge!" Graham exhaled and pondered.

"It is. No matter what kind of human being Elvis Valentine is, he shouldn't have to pay for another man's crimes."

"If I can bring Spider in..." Graham started eagerly, but was interrupted.

"We."

Graham smiled and nodded.

"Will you take the stand and help put that son of a bitch away?"

"Yes." Vatican nodded.

Graham laughed and clapped his hands together.

"There is one thing, Sidney."

"Please call me, Sid." He laughed, "Hell, if we nail this bastard you can call me your Daddy!"

"If we are going to work together, you'll have to let up on the profanity." Vatican said smiling.

Graham laughed at the top of his lungs, and suddenly the lights in the apartment burst into life, which turned his attention to the apartment and he could see Valerie waddling towards him, wrapped in the duvet.

"Oh busted!" Graham whispered and turned around to say farewell to Vatican, but he had already gone.

"What the..." He gasped and looked down at the empty alleyway.

The window rose up in a yelp of wood on wood and Valerie's sleep head poked out, eyes squinting from the bright neon.

"Who are you talking to?" She yawned.

"Just my guardian angel." He smiled.

"Huh?"

"It doesn't matter." Graham said and he climbed back

into the apartment where they embraced kissing passionately and as the duvet feel to the ground, he swept her naked body into his arms and took her over to the bed.

Chapter 15

Nicholas Smith gazed down with confusion at the blood that was seeping from fresh wounds on his fingers. The blood congregating in his palms like two shallow pools.

"It's just a little scratch." The voice scoffed, "I don't see what all the fuss is about!"

"But, the pain..." Nicholas whined, clenching his fingers causing the blood to drip down rapidly onto the dirty track beneath this bare feet.

The moon shone through a gap in the trees above, bathing him its cool beam, other lights circled around the trees, bright and yellow, searching the trees as a horrible whining alarm sounded.

"It was inevitable that climbing a fence topped with razor sharp wire would end in some kind of injury."

"But it hurts..."

"Enough!" The voice roared, "It's the least of your worries, you need to get out of here, they're coming."

The sound of dogs barking and grumbling joined the constant shrilling of the alarm and Nicholas hopped nervously from one foot the other, his feet crunching on old dead leaves and cracking twigs.

"What do we do?" He snivelled.

"Pull yourself together!"

Nicholas stopped immediately and looked around at his environment, his world for so long had consisted of four padded walls, now had replaced by rows upon rows of all manner of trees, he could feel the dirt between his toes and smell the cool night air. It was almost blissful, but he did not have time to bask in his newly found freedom or else he would find himself back in one of those padded rooms again.

"you're a super hero, Nicholas !"

"Yes, I am! I am The Vatican!"

"Exactly! And The Vatican can easily find a way out of this."

He gazed up at the moon, "I shall follow the moon." He whispered, and hearing no reply from the voice he took that for this is a good idea and started to trudge quickly through the over grown foliage of the woods.

He took cover behind a thick tree trunk as he heard the sound of several footfalls crunching down heavily not to far away, he stopped and waited for them to pass. He looked down at his bleeding palms again.

"My hands bleed, like Jesus." He gasped. "Am I the messiah?"

"Maybe one day that's how you will be looked upon. But if you don't make it out of this you won't be remembered for shit."

Nicholas wiped the palms of his bleed hand down the front of his white shirt, smearing it in a line of crimson. Then taking his other had he wiped it horizontally across his chest. His shirt now adorned with a vibrant red cross, it glistened in the moonlight making it look almost alive. Nicholas looked around the trunk of the tree, his pursers were nowhere to be seen, so he moved on again, his torn white cape streaming behind him, to an onlooker he may have appeared to be some ghostly apparition fleeing into the night.

"Quickly, quickly Nicholas!" The voice spurred him on, his unprotected feet being lacerated with each stride by the irregular terrain. His trailing foot caught the fallen trunk of a tree as he tried to hurdle it and fell unceremoniously into a mass of shrubbery.

"Get up you idiot!" The voice growled.

Nicholas' scrawny face looked almost ghostlike as he pulled himself up out of his predicament. His bloodshot eyes bulged in their dark sockets almost trancelike, he reached out with a boney hand that was stained with his own blood and gasped.

"The stars!" He whimpered, "Look at all of those pretty stars!"

A star hung from a branch above his head, it glittered almost magically in the moonlight, as it slowly rotated in the cool breeze. As he rose he noticed that the whole area was filled with them, dozens of ceramic stars of all colours hung from random branches above him.

"They're beautiful."

Follow them."

Nicholas drags himself off the ground and shuffles down a dirt path, his head tilted as he looked lovingly at the stars above.

"Nicholas! Look!"

Nicholas changed his gaze and stared at the old hollowed out tree that rose out of the ground in a crooked V shape.

"V..." Nicholas pondered, "V for..."

"Vatican!"

"Yes, V for Vatican!"

He moved towards it and saw that t was completely hollowed out a large package sat inside it.

"What is it?" He whispered.

"I don't know." The voice replied **"But whatever it is, it belongs to you."**

"It does?"

"Yes V for Vatican, remember?"

Nicholas nodded and leant into the tree and scooped up the package.

"What do I do with it?"

"Open it."

Nicholas tore open the packaging to reveal a white substance wrapped in a thick layer of shrink wrap. Nicholas tore into it and the white substance within erupted in a twinkling explosion. It fell all-around him on the floor.

"What is this stuff?" Nicholas asked in confusion, it stuck to the blood on his hands as the rest of it poured onto the floor around him like sand in an hourglass.

"Try some."

Nicholas licked the Stardust that has stuck to his sticky finger and his eyes sparkled in euphoric ecstasy.

"This is... power!" Nicholas screamed and cackled loudly. His hand dived into the every decreasing bundle and then wiped it across his face, breathing it in and tasting it again on his tongue. He roared with intensity, the cords on his neck tightened with intensity and he shrieked again, "The power!" Again he though that he heard the footsteps of his pursuers, the searchlights danced rapidly all around and the stars sang to him. He clutched what was left of the package of Stardust and then headed off through the trees once again.

He was breathing heavy and his lungs felt as though they were about to burst out of his ribcage, but his head was spinning, in his head it felt like he was still moving, still running at full pace, unbeknownst to him that he had stopped. He felt gravel underfoot and looked down at it, trying to focus, but his eyes played tricks on him, the large pieces of gravel started to move as if they were little creatures scuttling around.

He looked at his package and it was almost half empty now, anyone that was close on his trail could have easily followed the line of cocaine to find his whereabouts. He Grabbed another handful and splashed it across his face. As he looked up he noticed an old manor house stand in front of him, one light illuminating a long slender downstairs window.

"Is that home?"

IF you WanT iT To be, Nicholas."

"Home."

With his gaunt face smothered in blood and glittering cocaine it contorted into a hideous smile, and he danced towards the large manor house.

The gravel crunched beneath his bare feet that were now covered in dirt and dozens of lacerations that he couldn't even feel, the amount of Stardust that he had consumed meant that pain was a distant memory.

With each step, Nicholas jumped in the air fearful that he was crushing the small creatures that were scuttling around his feet, he apologised profusely not realising that they were just inanimate stones. Finally he reached the front door and examined it, the humungous hefty door knocker loomed forward as if it wanted to kiss him, before floating around his head and finding its place on the door again.

"It's all so magical!" Nicholas whispered, reaching out to grasp the moving knocker in his hand to no avail. Finally his blood red eyes managed to focus and he grabbed the knocker and vigorously hammered it against the door.

Nicholas smiled and continued to use the door knocker to beat it against the poor door.

"IsnT This fun ?" He laughed.

He suddenly stopped when he heard the distant sound of a

dog's yapping. He looked around the vast gravelled drive and then his paranoid eyes flitted towards the woods. It wasn't the sound of police dogs it was closer and more high pitched than a German Shepard's call. It was coming from behind the door, he place his ear gently to the door and he stumbling as the door swung open. He wobbled on the spot, grabbing tightly his package in his arms and stared at an ugly patterned, maroon carpet that looked up at him, the patterns seemingly changing ever few seconds like the shapes within a kaleidoscope.

"And who the devil are you?" Bellowed a haughty English accent.

Nicholas swayed from side to side and finally found a pair of worn slippers looking up at him.

"Hello!" Nicholas wheezed smiling at the slippers.

"I asked you a bloody question!" Came the impatient reply.

Nicholas' eyes dashed across the moving carpet and was met by a small dog, A pug dog babbling at him fiercely.

"I'm sorry little dog, are you talking to me?"

"Up here man!" The voice growled in annoyance. Nicholas' could see the words bursting from the pug's mouth.

"A talking dog!" Nicholas murmured.

"I said up her you bloody babbling buffoon!" The voice roared and slowly Nicholas' eyes left the carpet and the dog and headed north only to be met by a vast black hole.

"Hello?" Nicholas asked the black hole and his voice echoed around it as if it were the entrance to a tunnel.

"Where does this tunnel lead I wonder?" Nicholas gasped in wonderment.

"I'm going to ask one more bloody time or you'll be picking your brain up off the gravel!" The voice seemed to come from behind the dark tunnel and Nicholas stepped back a few shaking steps to focus the tunnel was in fact the huge barrel of an old Flintlock Blunderbuss. Holding it was an old gentlemen, a bushy white moustache hanging over a grimace.

Nicholas looked him up and down and took in his slippers, socks heist up by sock suspenders and draped in an elegant silk dressing gown and giggled.

"Oh, hello!" Nicholas grinned, his red eyes spinning. "I'm Nicholas..."

"No, I'm The Vatican!"

The old man lowered the gargantuan rifle and stared at him in bewilderment, a thick white eyebrow contorting around a monocle.

The pug continued to bark until the old man said, "Oh, knock it off Worthington II!" The pug immediately stopped and sat down, his head cocked to onside as he tried to work out their late night visitor.

"You seem to be struggling there, my old chum." The man asked, "Are you from the institute by any chance?"

Nicholas nodded.

"I see." He looked down at Worthington II and shook his head, "Poor sod."

Worthington II yapped in response.

"And what is that you've got there?" He asked pointing at

the broken package in his hands.

"That's...Power!"

"Is it now." The man said, knowing exactly what he had, He leaned past Nicholas to survey his vast driveway, it was deserted, "It looks a ton of bloody powder to me chum. Why don't you come in my boy and rest a while?" The old man said grinning under a mass of moustache as he ushered him in and closed the door behind them.

The old man slotted the large rifle into a bulbous elephant foot umbrellas stand that sat next to the front door.

"Now then!" He said enthusiastically clapping his hands together and then rubbing them together vigorously, "How about a little drink, ay?"

Nicholas smiled, swayed on the spot and then collapsed head face first to the floor.

Chapter 16

"FOR FUCK'S SAKE!" Spider screamed launching his cell phone across the small one roomed boat. It collided with the door frame and exploded. Dallas and Boris looked on in nervous angst as Spider looked as though he was about implode.

Spider, swiped at the tabled, knocking down the empty beer bottles like they were skittles at a bowling alley.

Spider stood with his back to his fellow Webheads and stared out of the window at the flickering lights of Studd City.

Several moments ago, Boris and Dallas were the unfortunate bearers of bad news. They had travelled to Oakland Wood to retrieve the latest supply of Stardust, only to find that it had already been removed. Spider had spent the last couple of minutes uncharacteristically grovelling to his supplier, Elizabeth Martle AKA 'The Vixen' who happened to be the only person capable of supplying the very popular versions of cocaine. He had obviously had no luck in convincing her that none of this was his fault and just like that she had severed the ties that held their relationship together.

Boris and Dallas passed glances, each trying to urge the other to speak first and put an end to uncomfortable silence. Boris pushed Dallas spurring him to be the one, Dallas shock his head and pushed the large Ukrainian as hard as he could, Boris jabbed Dallas playfully in the ribcage and made Dallas yelp. The sound dint go unnoticed and Dallas knew now that he had to speak.

"So, erm..." Dallas said reluctantly, "She's not willing to give you a second chance, huh?"

"Second chance!" Spider growled, "A second fucking chance!" He dropped his fists down hard on the window ledge and then said nothing.

Dallas looked at Boris and they both shrugged.

"Forget her, boss." Boris scoffed, "We don't need her."

Spider turned around slowly to face them contorted grimace etched on his face.

"What the fuck are you on Boris?"

Boris stared back at him as if he didn't understand.

"Of course we needed her! Where'd o you think the Stardust comes from? Little Russian pixies!" He growled mimicking a terrible imitation of a Russian accent.

"No, boss!" Boris shook his head, "Also I am not Russian, I am Ukrainian." He shrugged.

"I fucking now you're not Russian, Boris! You tell us every Goddamn day!" Spider yelled and then collapsed in heap on a chair.

Dallas and Boris joined him at the table.

"We'll get passed this, Spider. We always bounce back."

Spider shook his head.

"Not this time, Dal." Spider answered his voice calmer
now, "Without The Vixen we have now Stardust, she doesn't hand out second chances so we are fucked. So now we're hiding out in this shit heap, wanted by the SCPD and The Coyote, I don't see a way out of this."

"Maybe it's time we leave town." Dallas says reaching fro the playing cards left discarded on the table and starts to shuffle them, like some Vegas veteran. "Besides, I reckon that's what most people think we've done anyway."

"No!" Spider growls, slamming his fist down on the table again. "I ain't no fucking coward and I ain't running!"

"Then what do we do?" Boris asks, "We don't have many options left now."

"If I could just get my hands on the bastard that stole my dust, I'd cut him a new asshole!"

Spider seemed to ponder this thought a moment.

"Wait, you said that there was a trail of the stuff in the woods."

"Yeah," Dallas shrugged, "But I mean that place is going to be swarming with cops, we'd never get..."

"I don't mean go searching the woods." Spider intervenes, "Besides, whoever took the stuff would be long gone by now."

"Then what?" Dallas asked.

"He's got to get sell that shit hasn't he?" Spider smiled, "I want you two hitting the streets and find him."

"Where do we start?" Boris scoffs.

"Anybody who buys the shit! Anybody who has brought any Stardust recently from someone else. We find the seller we find our guy. Then we rip him a new one!"

"It's going to be risky showing our faces on the streets." Dallas warned.

"What other choice do we have? Without the Stardust gig we don't have anything else that's going to bring that kind of bread in."

The boat suddenly rocks too and fro as if it has just taken on some excess weight.

"I wouldn't say that." Comes a voice from the boat's entrance.

Blocking the doorway is Famu, casually standing with his hands in his pockets, a little smile on his massive face.

The Webheads instinctively draw their handguns and aim them at Famu.

"Who the fuck are you?" Spider roars. Famu remains unfazed and still smiling at them.

"I'm Famu." He says pleasantly.

"Oh yeah?" Spider marches over to him and points his gun up at his face, "Well, now that we are acquainted, you want to tell me what your fat ass is doing here before I blow one of those chins away."

"Take it easy Spider." Famu chuckles. "You're in no danger."

"Are you with The Coyote?" Spider anxiously asks, "TELL ME!"

The others join Spider, their guns also staring at Famu's rotund face.

"No need to worry, I'm not with The Coyote or the SCPD or anybody else that's out to get you. Now just lower your guns so I can tell you why I'm here."

Dallas and Boris lower their guns but Spider remains exactly as he is.

"No fucking way!" Spider says, "For we know, you're the guy that just stole our three month supply of Stardust!"

Spider prods the gun into Famu's face and his smile finally leaves.

"Get that gun out of my face, or things are going to get unpleasant." Famu whispers.

Dallas and Boris' guns are back and pointing at Famu again.

"Tell us what the fuck you want!" Spider growls.

"I have a proposition for you that's all. A quick way to make a lot of money, but if you pussy's aren't up to it, then perhaps I'll have to look elsewhere."

Spider lowers his gun.

"Go on then, talk!"

"I can't divulge all the information here, that's not my place, that's up to my boss."

"And who's your boss?" Dallas asks.

"Robert Devine."

"Who the fuck is Robert Devine?" Spider yells, hand

gun aimed back in Famu's face. "I ain't heard of now Robert Devine."

"Sure you have." Scoffed Famu.

"He's that billionaire property guy right?" Dallas asked intrigued.

Famu nodded.

"Billionaire?" Spider asked slowly lowering his gun.

Dallas nods grinning greedily.

"That's right." Famu starts, "It's strange that you don't know who he is, yet you see him everyday."

They look at Famu confused, Famu moves out of the entrance way and puts to the skyline of Studd City lit up brightly, the red neon sign displaying the words DEVINE INC. flashing back at them from the highest building in the city.

"Shit." Spider murmurs.

"What does he want with us?" Boris asks.

"He may have some work for you. He asked for you personally and I have to tell you, you guys weren't easy to find." Famu laughs.

"And he's a billionaire?" Spider asks again.

"Yeah." Famu nods, "Whatever he wants you to do, it won't be for peanuts."

"A mother fucking billionaire!" Erupts into laughter.

"I'll take that as a yes." Famu smiled and then left the boat, stepping off onto the harbour and approaching his long streamlined limousine. "I'll pick you up tomorrow around 10. Don't be late, Mr Devine detests tardiness."

Chapter 17

The central precinct of the SCPD was alive with a hum of commotion as Detective Graham sauntered in with his early morning coffee in his hand. He looked around confused by the melee that was taking place around him. He ignored whatever was going on around him, it couldn't be bigger than the information that he had to disclose and he swiftly made a beeline for Commissioner Hayes' office.

Graham arrived the door, knocked and waited. He could see the Commissioner's silhouette striding back and forth behind the frosted glass door. There was no cry of 'Come in' to greet him so he waited.

"What the hell is going on around here?" He asked himself, sipping his coffee from one of Perfect Java's polystyrene cups, as he continued to watch officers rushing around in front of him.

He tried the door again and this time it opened, Hayes was on the phone pacing around his office, a serious look carved into his old wrinkled face. He gestured for Graham to come in and sit down. He did as he was asked and waited patiently still sipping away at his coffee. He understood from the onside of the conversation that Hayes was discussing something of great importance with the Mayor, but only hearing one side of it, he had no idea what it was about.

Finally Hayes cradled the receiver back in place and collapsed into his luxury leather chair, sighing heavily and rubbing at his eyes.

"Is everything okay, Commissioner?" Graham asked.

"Ha!" Hayes scoffed sarcastically, "Where have you been?"

Graham didn't wish to tell him that he had been cavorting with Sergeant Nash under her bedsheets about an hour ago.

"I just got in, Sir."

Hayes glared at him as if he was holding Graham personal to blame for whatever was going on.

Graham sensed that Hayes was about to break into one of his verbal onslaughts so he cut him off before he could begin.

"I have had some very important information fall into my lap, Sir" Graham blurted out, "And it needs your immediate attention."

"Oh, does it!" Hayes chuckled, taken aback by Graham's bluntness.

"We need to reopen The Doomsday Murder case."

Hayes' eyes widened, his face becoming taut and for once void of wrinkles.

"Now why would we want to do such a pointless exercise?" He sighed, "As far as I'm concerned that case is closed. We have murderer safely locked up in Skelter Prison, and besides..."

"We got the wrong guy." Graham interrupted.

Hayes stared at him, his face glowing, he did not appreciate being interrupted.

"Elvis Valentine wasn't the killer." Graham continued.

"Oh really?" Hayes growled, "And what makes you say that?"

"I have received some new evidence, an eye witness who claims that he saw everything and he heard Spider, erm Joseph Webb admit to the whole thing." He took a sip of coffee trying his best not to make eye contact with the fuming Commissioner. "He is willing to take the stand. We have to reopen the case and put out a nationwide search and find Webb."

Haye stared at him for what seemed like the longest time, until it was beginning to make Graham feel uncomfortable.

"And who is this new reliable witness?" Haye asked, finally.

"Erm..." Graham fidgeted in his seat for a moment and just before taking another sip of coffee he murmured, "Vatican."

Just when Graham thought that Hayes' eyes could not get any wider, they seemed to widen again, like two saucers peering back at him across the desk.

"Sorry, my old ears must be playing up." Hayes scoped, "Who did you say the witness was?"

"Vatican, Sir." Graham said again, louder and clearer. Hayes leaned back in his chair, lacing his hands in

131

his lap, "So you would like me to reopen a case on the say so of some psychopath vigilante who likes to dress up and play super hero?"

Graham looked at him hopefully, but realising that this was going to be a more difficult task than he had first thought.

"I also have reason to believe that Webb is responsible for the increase in Stardust distribution in the city."

"Oh you do huh?" Hayes nodded, "Vatican tell you that too?"

Graham nodded and looked down bashfully at his coffee, taking yet another sip.

"You've come to me before with some really out there requests, Graham, but this one takes the biscuit!"

"Have I ever let you down before, Sir?"

"That's beside the point, Graham!" Hayes scoffed, "We put that costumed freak in the box and we'll be a laughing stock!"

"Even if it means putting away the guilty party?"

"The man's insane, Graham!" Hayes growls, "Just look at him? If anything I should be reprimanding you for not arresting him when you had the chance!"

"On what grounds?" Graham snapped, finding himself sounding like Vatican himself.

Hayes leaned forward on the desk and sneered at Graham.

"The case is closed, detective!"

"That's the final word on the matter?"

"It is!" Hayes announced standing back up, "And I tell
you one thing if Valentine didn't do it, it was Stone."
Anger bubbled inside Graham and he launched himself out
of his seat, splashing himself with coffee.

"How dare you!"
Hayes stepped back for a moment and then smirked.

"Be very careful, detective. That badge and gun can
easily be confiscated you know."
Graham said nothing else and turned to leave.

"You were right about one thing though, Graham."
Hayes said as he headed for the door.

"Oh yeah?" He snapped back, "What's that?"

"You were right to turn your back on Stone."
Graham felt his fist clench tightly and his face becoming
overcome with heat. But did nothing just stood shaking.

"Don't you ever talk about Eric." Graham growled, "I
let him down and I don't need you to remind me of that."
Hayes smiled.

"Oh you haven't heard then?"

"Heard what?"
Hayes strutted passed him and opened the door revealing the
erratic scene being played out before their eyes.

"Did you not notice any of this?" Hayes scoffed, "You
need to get your head out of your ass, detective. There are
much more important matters going on than your sad
personal life."

Graham had the urge to unleash the remaining contents of his cup into Hayes' smug, old face but thought better of it.

"For your information, detective, you're very good friend Eric Stone escaped from Oakland Institute last night."

"What?" Graham looked on in shock.

"Somehow managed to get his hands on some cleaning products and lighted match and well, Kaboom! The rest as they say is history."

"But..."

"Who knew he had a degree in chemistry, huh?" Hayes grinned sadistically, "To make matters worse another patient escaped too, a really nasty piece of work apparently, goes by the name of Nicholas Smith. Suffers from a severe case of schizophrenia."

Graham stared at him open mouthed.

"Murdered his family a couple of years ago, cut them all up pretty bad. A Christmas gathering it was, wiped out the whole family in one evening. Said that the other guy did it."

"The other guy?" Graham asked.

Hayes pointed to his head, "The voice in his head. 'The voices made me do it', you know, that old chestnut."

"So he's dangerous."

"Extremely. And without his medication to keep him calm there is no telling what he is capable of."

Graham stared at him, trying to take it all in.

Damn you, Eric! You fool!

"So!" Hayes clapped his hands together, "If you don't mind getting out there and catching them, detective. That would be a real help."

Hayes grinned at him sadistically as he slammed the door in Graham's face.

Chapter 18

Thomas yawned, his tired reflection gaping back at him didn't little to wake him up. He stuck out his tongue, it felt to him that it had a thick layer of fur across it. He turned on the sink's hot tap and steam immediate filled the small bathroom and began fogging up the mirror, Thomas' tired face disappearing behind a layer condensation.

"These late night patrols are killing me." He grumbled dousing his face with the warm water.

He took his index finger and began to write on the mirrored door of the cabinet, removing the residue left by the hot steam as he wrote, Black Crane Cometh...

"No!" He growled angrily at himself and immediately wiped away all the letters revealing his reflection again, a worried face that he didn't like one bit.

"Maybe I need to return to China. I need to talk to Master Sato. This Black Car... these thoughts, dreams or premonitions are getting too much."

He eyeballed the smaller bottle on top of the cabinet.

"Maybe if I upped the dose..."

He reached for them and stared at the bottle of Alprazolam.

"Maybe that will help."

He removed the lid and sprinkled a couple into the palm of his hand, then added a couple more. He stood naked in the bathroom, his taut physique plastered with the wounds from past battles. The hot steam filled their air and he stared at the white tablets in his hands, it was if they had some kind of hypnotic hold over him.

"Thomas?" Came the call from downstairs.

"Burt." Thomas whispered.

"Thomas! Are you coming down?" Burt called again.

"Be right down!" Thomas replied breezily.

He tipped the tablets back into the bottle and placed them back on top of the cabinet.

Burt placed a brown paper bag and a lidded polystyrene on the coffee table that had a chess set assembled on it. He settled back into his favourite armchair with a coffee in hand accompanied by groans.

Thomas staggered into the parlour sliding the clerical collar in place around the collar of his shirt.

"Oh dear!" Burt chuckled, "You look as though you could have done with another three days in bed, son."

"You're telling me." Thomas smiled.

He loved to hear Burt call him son, it was in all honesty what he was searching for, that father figure. It warmed his heart to see him sitting in his armchair, sipping coffee and surveying the chess board.

"I thought you weren't ever coming down." Burt teased, "I've been to Perfect Java and back already." He pointed to the bag and the coffee on the table, "Breakfast!"

"Thanks, Burt." Thomas smiled removing the lid of the cup and allowing the hot steam from the coffee to escape, the smell soothed him. "You're too good to me."

"I know." Burt agreed.

Thomas tucked into his breakfast croissant like he hadn't eaten in weeks, and helped it down with swigs of hot black coffee. Burt was unusually quiet, normally he would be taunted Thomas on the thrashing he's about to receive, Thomas never has been abled to beat him.

"Something the matter?" Thomas asked through a mouthful of food.

"Was just thinking about Henry." Burt sighed solemnly.

"Oh." Thomas replied.

"I still expect to hear his trumpet bellowing out of his apartment on my morning stroll."

"It was dreadful what happened to him. I wish I could have done more to find his killer, but there was just no trace."

"Oh you can't blame yourself." Burt smiled, "They informed me that his body had been down in that cellar for two weeks along with the others. The police didn't have any leads either. You can't beat yourself up over it, you can't catch them all, son."

"I know." Thomas sighed.

138

"Anyway, let's not dwell on the past, we can't change that. How does your search go for the girl?"

"Still haven't been able to track her down. Elliot says that she came to his aid when he was attacked, but he passed out and when he came round she was gone."

"If Elliot knows her then, surely he will see her again and he can tell her that you want t o talk to her."

"Yes, But she moves around a lot from what I understand. Elliot tells me that she is very untrustworthy of people that's why she stays alone."

They both sip their coffees and then make eye contact, Burt's old eyes narrow as if he were a gunslinger looking to draw.

"Right!" Burt grins mischievously and moves the pawn infant of his king to squares forward. An opening he always seemed to favour.

"You always start the same way, Burt!" Thomas whined.

"And I always win." Burt chuckled.

Thomas dove haphazardly into the game and matched Burt's move.

"You have to think about your pawns Thomas." Burt tutted, believing that he wasn't going to get anywhere by just mirroring his moves.

"What do you mean?" Thomas asked.

"You have to respect the pawn, they're not just cannon fodder to be cast aside to bring out your more important pieces."

"They're not?"

"No," Burt shook his head, "A good chess player treats all the pieces with the same respect. You can manipulate your opponent to place their pieces exactly where you need them, not necessarily where the opponent wants them to be. It's all about manipulation of the opponents moves. If you can do that, then you got'em!"

Thomas looked at him and smiled.

"Now!" Burt clapped his hands together, "Are you ready for an ass whoppin'?"

Chapter 19

"Wake up!"

Nicholas stirred restlessly in the winged back leather armchair, he murmured incoherent sentences through saliva that was forming in his mouth and dripping from his lips onto his Oakland uniform.

"Wake up, Nicholas!"

His eyelids flickered rapidly, tired bloodshot eyes peaked out of a mass of straggled greasy hair that hung over his face.

"Wake up, Nicholas..." He grumbled to himself, his voice hoarse.

His eyes opened fully and swatted away the blurred vision of his environment as he focused on a large room, a study.

"Where am I?" He asked himself.

He sat up in his seat to examine his surroundings, a blanket fell from his person onto a tiger fur rug, it's fierce looking head staring up at him. Nicholas' eyes darted around the room and was met by the gaze of several other eyes, those of mounted animal heads hung on the walls.

"What is this? Where am I?" He said anxiously, scared and frightened not to be in the cold, uncomfortable,

141

but all too familiar room at the institute. Rifles and sabres clung to the walls, relics of a lost age. He turned around and noticed four large mannequins clad in various clothes of warriors past. Underneath a large mantle a fire was dying, he stared at the amber flames dwindling between lumps of coal and remembered.

"The explosion! I escaped... I s-should get back..."

"*No!*" That familiar voice crawled at him.

"You!"

"*Of course it's me!*" The voice snapped back at him "*Who else was it going to be ?*"

"Okay, okay, don't shout at me." Nicholas snivelled retrieving the fallen blanket and wrapping himself in it cowering.

"*Look, we need to get out of here.*"

"We do?"

"*Yes! Remember your mission! you are The Vatican, remember?*"

"Of course!" Nicholas gasped in a moment of clarity, everything coming back to him, but his head remained fuzzy. "But what of the power? Where is it? I-I need it!"

"*The old man has it.*"

"The old man? Yes of course!"

"*you must take it back.*"

"Yes."

"Kill him!"

"Yes, kill... No!" He snivelled, "I can't do that, not again!"

The door creaked open and the old man stood in the door way with a pewter tray, on it was a china teapot, milk jug, sugar bowl and a toast rack.

"Ah, you're finally awake." Came the boisterous bark of the old man, "But, I'm sure you deserve a lie in after your night of adventures." He chortled.

He waddled in, still dressed in his dressing gown and sat on an armchair adjacent to Nicholas who was pulling up the blanket to his nose, cowering behind it. The old man creaked profusely as he lowered the tray onto a table and then settled himself into the chair.

"Would you like a cup of tea?" He asked. Nicholas nodded from behind his blanket.

"It's okay you know." The old man smiled, his moustache wriggling across his upper lip like a thick white caterpillar. "I'm not going to hurt you."

He poured the tea and added three lumps of sugar, not even asking Nicholas his preference, assuming that he could probably do with the excess sugar.

"Now, my name is d'Urberville. Sebastian d'Urberville." He said handing him the cup and saucer.

Nicholas appeared slowly from behind the blanket and took the saucer, in his quivering hands.

"And your name?" d'Urberville asks while staring his own tea.

"Nicholas." He replied before slurping at the tea.

The pug dog that Nicholas vaguely remembered from last nights ordeal came bounding in, barking shrilly that sliced through Nicholas' delicate brain.

"**Shut that fucking mutt up!**" The voice shrieked.

The pug stopped and looked at him, its eyes were glazed over.

"I am sorry!" Nicholas apologised.

"No need." Laughed d'Urberville. "Pay no attention to Worthington II."

Worthington II started rolling around the tiger rug before doing a lap of the room and darting out of the room as though it was possessed.

"What's wrong with him?" Nicholas asked.

"I think he got a nose full from the contents of your parcel." Chuckled d'Urberville as he sipped his tea, his bushy moustache dipping into it like a paintbrush.

"Worthington II?" Nicholas pondered, reaching for a slice of toast and gobbling away at it like some ravenous pig.

"Yes, sadly Worthington the first has been gone quite a while now."

"**He carries on like that and you'll need a Worthington the third!**"

d'Urberville laughed loudly, sapping a meaty hand across his exposed thigh.

"That's a good one!" He hacked, "I see your friend has joined us again."

144

"He's not my friend." Nicholas whispered.

"Indeed." d'Urberville smiled.

"Where is my power?" Nicholas asked through a mouthful of toast.

"The power?" d'Urberville looked confused for a second, "Oh! You mean your little parcel that you had with you on your arrival?"

Nicholas nodded.

"I'm afraid it's all gone. It exploded everywhere when you fainted. It made one hell of a mess I can tell you."

"**He's _lying!_**" The voice growled, Nicholas' face contorted into a hideous creature that no longer resembled the true Nicholas Smith.

"Oh poppycock!" He chuckled, "What does an old codger like me need with a load of cocaine, I ask you?"

Nicholas returns again apologising for the interruption, d'Urberville waves it away.

"So you escaped from the institute did you." Asked d'Urberville helping himself to some toast.

"How did you know?" Nicholas asked, looking terrified again.

"Well, the uniform for one." d'Urberville nodded at him, "Plus we had a visit from the boys in blue not long after you passed out in that chair."

"The police!" Nicholas shrieked and nearly spilt his tea.

"Calm down. I didn't let them in, they know me of old and I can give as good as I get." He laughed loudly,

"People seem to listen to you when you're pointing a Blunderbuss at them."

"So they didn't search the house." Nicholas' eyes flitted around nervously, expecting that any minute now one of those mannequins would come alive unveiling themselves as undercover police.

"Of course not! I'd never let those sods in here!" He boomed. "I told them quite sternly that I hadn't seen or heard anything and then tell them to get off my bloody property before I filled their backsides with gunpowder!"
d'Urbervile then began to laugh so uncontrollably and loudly that Nichols thought that d'Urberville could very easy be mistaken for a patient in Oakland himself.

"Tell this old fool about your mission and then we can leave."

"Your mission?" d'Urberville leant foreword in his chair and grabbed the poker, and drove it into the coal to stir it up again. "That sounds very exciting."
He leant back in his chair and seemed to reminisce.

"Missions, I remember those... Trudging through the jungles of India sitting atop a giant bull elephant. Those were the days I can tell you."

"He's Vatican."

"Shut up!"
d'Urberville was snapped from his woolgathering and looked at Nicholas intriguingly.

146

"So you're the myserteous Vatican I have been hearing about?" He asked, bushy eyebrows rising high to join his receding hairline, his monocle falling from his eye.

"Y-Yes!"

"Now I see why you were the cape and the mask." Nicholas rummaged around for the mask that had fallen around his neck and pulled it into place.

"That's better! Now I recognise you. You're just like the image I've seen in the newspapers." d'Urberville smirked as he put his monocle back in to his drinking socket.

Nicholas looked around the room for a moment not knowing how to take d'Urberville's cool reaction that he was a masked vigilante.

"I see you are admiring my collection." Nicholas nodded.

"I am a bit of a collector you see. I just adore old artefacts of bygone eras, especially weapons and armour."

d'Urberville stands up and walks around the room surveying his collection. Nicholas rose to his feet, still holding the cup and saucer in his hands, and followed him closely as he pointed out African spears, Persian swords and medieval axes.

He heard the voice in his head tell him to seize one of those axes and drive it into the back of his head, but Nicholas managed to fight the urge.

"These are some fine pieces." d'Urbverville announced proudly gesturing towards the mannequins.

"This is a Tatami Gusoku from the 17th century in Japan." He beamed proudly as he ran his fingers over the curved armoured plates of the samurai armour.

Hit him! Hit him with something, kill the old bastard!

Nichola smiled uncomfortably and nodded along with d'Urberville's history lesson.

"This one is an exquisite piece!" He bellowed, "An Afghan royal soldier's garbs from the 18th century Durrani Empire." He felt the quality of the garbs and gestured for Nicholas to do the same, which he did.

Kill him, kill KILL HIM!

Nicholas grinned as he brow became laden with sweat, trying with all his might to fight the cruel instructions being fed into his head.

"And you must see the weaponry too." d'Urberville said excitedly pointing to the long slender spear that stop around six and a half feet in length, and encrusted in gold and jewels. "And the matching Kirpan." He gestured to a bizarre shaped knife that was hanging from the belt of the outfit. He unsheathed the dagger and swished around in front of Nicholas, "Isn't it beautiful! The jewelled handle..."

Take the knife! Stab him! Listen to me, KILL HIM!

Nicholas stood staring at the dagger, the cup and saucer shaking in his hands, sweat pouring down his face.

"I said are you okay, Nicholas?" Nicholas nodded.

"This next piece is a real heavy-duty suit of armour, late 15th century, from Germany."

KILL HIM NICHOLAS! IT'S WHAT VATICAN WOULD DO!

"No!" Nicholas yelled out loud. d'Urberville looked at him in shock.

"I mean no way it can be that old!" Nicholas smiled trying to cover up his outburst.

"Oh but it is." Laughed d'Urberville.

As the reached the last mannequin, d'Urberville chuckled to himself, his arms outstretched like the wings of a bird, as he grandly drew Nicholas' attention to a black Knight's Hospitaller outfit.

"Notice the lighter chainmail underneath the surcoat. Complete with hooded cloak."

KILL KILL KILL KILL KILL KILL KILL KILL KILL KILL

Nicholas felt dizzy, any second now he would surely vomit. You're going cold turkey now, Nicholas. You haven't had your meds, soon your mild will be all mine!

"Unfortunately this particular piece is missing a white crucifix that should be sewn on the chest, I'm hoping to change that very soon."

As d'Urberville turned around beaming, Nicholas' face contorted and he screamed "**KILL HIM!**" as he lashed out with the cup in hand and struck him on his temple. d'Urberville fell to the floor unconscious.

"**Now! Finish him off! Kill him Vatican!**"

Nicholas stood over him and stared at the blood that trickled from the old man's head, snaking down the curvatures on his wrinkled skin and ripping onto the carpet. Worthington II burst in again, ran around the room and then stopped to

149

sniff the blood seeping from his master's head. He looked up at Smith and growled loudly.

"No, I won't." Nicholas wheezed breathing very heavy, he turned his attentions to the Knight's Hospitaller outfit and caressed it with a shaky hand.

"But I will take this!" He sneered, his face seemingly trembling between two faces.

Chapter 20

The Webheads had been ushered into Robert Devine's luxury penthouse office, where they waited impatiently. Spider stared longingly out of the wall of glass surveying the city beneath, while his colleagues wandered around examining the pieces of contemporary art that Devine had positioned throughout his office space.

Spider squinted as the sun emerged from behind a billowing cloud. He looked deep in thought paying no attention to what Boris and Dallas were doing. He had always wanted to be powerful, looking out at Studd City from this height made him realise that there were a number of levels of power. He had once thought that becoming leader of The Doomsday Gang would see him sitting pretty at the top of the mountain, he chuckled to himself and shook his head.

Look how that turned out? Can't go anywhere incase anyone sees me! I'm like a fucking recluse, stuck on that old boot with these two buffoons. That isn't what I had envisioned. But this, this is power.

Unrelenting sniggers broke out behind him and ended his reverie, he turned around to see them both doubled over laughing and pointing like school children at a particular piece of art.

"What're you too assholes up to?" Spider asked.

They were unable to answer him, due to an uncontrollable laughing fit. They pointed at a piece of sculpted art that topped a plinth. Spider's eyebrows rose and then he smiled mischievously, golden teeth glistening in the sunlight.

"Did they use me as a model for this?" He scoffed.

"You wish!" Dallas laughed.

The sculpture was of a large, erect male sex organ. Spider positioned his hands around the shaft of the object and vigorously mimicked masturbation, which was too much for Dallas and Boris to take and almost collapsed.

"I see you are admiring my Jack Heron piece." Came the voice of Robert Devine, who was now standing in the doorway with a stern look on his face, Famu stood behind him smirking.

"Sorry man, we were just messin'." Spider said quickly removing his hands from around the smooth specimen.

"No harm done." Devine smiled as he entered the room, Famu closing the door behind him and remaining there, "Boys will be boys and all that." Devine chuckled.

He passed them by and too a seat as his desk.

"But I would like you to know that that particular piece of art cost me $1.5 million."

The Webheads looked at him dumbfounded. "Damn!" Spider announced.

"Indeed Mr Webb." Devine replied.

"So you know who we are?" Spider asked approaching the desk and slouching on it.

"I do." Devine looked a little uneasy with Spider lolling
around on his desk, but fought the urge to say anything. "I hear you are just the men I'm looking for."

Boris and Dallas approached the desk to and Devine met there eyes, "Please help yourself to a drink." Devine added and gestured over to the bar that was ladened with several bottles, "You'll find your poison there I'm sure."

Dallas and Boris didn't need to be asked twice and they hurried off to fix themselves drinks.

Spider remained on the desk looking at Devine with intrigue.

"So what do you want from us?" Asked Spider. "I need someone taking care of."

"Really!" Spider nodded, "Dead?"

Devine smiled, his eyes seemed like they were on fire, it sent a shiver down SPider's spine, but he didn't let him know that and remained pokerfaced.

"Yes!" Devine shrugged, "Why not."

"That's gonna cost."

"Yes, well I was thinking..."

"Let me tell you what I was thinking." Spider interrupted him, "We have to be talking at least half a mill. At least!"

"Really!" Devine smiled sitting back in this chair.

Boris and Dallas looked over from the bar, and Spider winked at them.

"Shall I tell you what I has thinking?" Spider stared at him but said nothing.

"I was thinking $1 million."

Spider nearly fell off the desk and in the background Boris dropped his glass of Volkoff vodka which drew Devine's attention.

"Don't worry about that," Devine said clicking his fingers at Famu, "Famu can you clean that up." Famu nodded and made his way over to the bar, Boris and Dallas joined Spider at the desk realising that this had just gotten serious.

"One mill?" Dallas asked. Devine nodded.

"Shit." Boris whistled.

"Most be one hell of a scalp you want mister." Dallas chuckled before taking a swig of his Whiskey.

"Oh it is." Said Devine.

"Who is it then?" Spider asked.

"So we have a deal?" Devine asked his exquisitely manicured fingers stretching out in front of him, calling for a handshake.

"Deal." Spider said grabbing his hand and shaking it forcefully.

"Good!" Devine said retrieving his hand and making sure he had all his digits, "Thats quite a grip." He laughed. Spider smiled, "So who, when and where?"

"The when and the where will be let up to Famu, he'll be dealing with the logistics of it all but the who, well I can tell you that." He paused a moment, he wanted to build the moment of suspense for his own amusement to capture a mental picture of their faces when they hear who is numero uno on Robert Devine's hit-list.

"Vatican."

Boris spat his vodka out, Dallas almost choked on his whiskey, but again Spider knew how to play it cool and remained neutral.

"Okay." Spider nodded, His companions looking at him as if he were crazy.

"Spider!" Dallas whispered, "How are we supposed to kill that guy?"

"Should have asked for 2 mill." Boris sighed emptying his glass.

Devine laughed out loud.

"How the hell we gonna track down..." Dallas said but was cut off by Devine.

"Like I said, Famu will put all the pawns in place, all you have to do is, well do the deed as it were." He grinned sadistically.

"We can do it!" Spider announced.

"Good!" Devine clapped his hands and then clicked his fingers at Famu again, "Famu, the money."

Famu approached with a briefcase, he lay it down on the desk and open it to reveal five hundred thousand dollars in

$100 bills.

Boris whistled loudly.

"Wait a minute, that's not one mill!" Dallas snapped.

"Shut the fuck up, Dal!" Spider snapped at him, "Thats a retainer."

Devine nodded.

"Indeed Mister Webb! How shrewd of you." Devine smiled, "Half now, half when the deed is done."

Spider nodded.

"That's no problem." Spider said, staring at the money almost lovingly. Devine suddenly shut the case quickly.

"Good, I'm glad we are agreed gentlemen. But I want to inform you of some ground rules."

"Oh here we go!" Scoffed Boris, "The fine print."

"Cute!" Devine scoffed, "Rule number one don't go splashing lots of cash around straight away, people will ask questions."

"Of course!" Spider nodded.

"Number two. Don't go leaving the country now that you have my money, because I will find you."

He stared at them, almost through them, they all felt the same frosty chill cut through their bodies as he did so.

"Number three. Do not unmask him."

"Why not?" Dallas asked.

"I would like to have that pleasure, Mister Orton."

Dallas shrugged.

"Number four. If you are caught, then you do not

156

receive the rest of the money, and if you mention my name to anyone you will all wind up dead."

They all laughed and looked at each other, then back at Devine and realised he was serious, stopped laughing.

"No problem." Spider announced taking the briefcase. "Can I ask you something?"

"By all means." Devine leans back in his chair again smiling.

"Why do you want this guy dead? Why don't you just get Free Willy here to kill the fuck?" Famu sneered at Spider.

"Well, Famu has tried before and failed miserably, this time I thought it may be beneficial to get him some help, safety in numbers I guess." He laughed. "And as for why, well that's my business." He scowled.

"Hey man whatever!" Spider smiled and flung the briefcase under his arm and they turned to leave.

"Not that it hasn't been a genuine pleasure to meet you all," Devine called after them, "But, I don't wish to see any of you again." He smiled sadistically as they left the office.

"Famu!"

"Yes Sir?"

"Make sure you sanitise everything they touched."

Chapter 21

Sebastian d'Urberville finally started to stir, he came to on the floor of his study, his face being brushed vigorously by the moist, soft tongue of Worthington II.

"Alright, man, alright!" d'Urberville groaned, "Stop fussing over me! You know I can't abide you fussing!"
His head had become stuck to the carpet, and it took him a few attempts to pry himself out of the puddle of dried blood. Worthington II immediately began sniffing at the bloodstain.

"Bloody hell, would you look at that!" d'Urberille sighed, rubbing at the wound on his head, "That's one stain that's never going to come out."
He fixed his monocle into place and used a nearby piece of furniture to pull himself up, his weary joints creaking like the rotor blades of an old windmill. He staggered for a moment becoming overcome with dizziness. He leant on the armchair for support, and tried to shake the effects of what was probably a severe concussion.

"My head is splitting!" He groaned, "That bloody little shit!"

Worthington II started yapping at him, the shrieking pitch of his cry caused d'Urberville to wince.

"Alright old man, knock it off."

Worthington II stopped immediately and sat down, figuring that he wasn't going to receive any attention from his master he set about cleaning his private parts.

"Oh, how lovely!" d'Urberville cringed and tottered over to a row of alcoholic beverages that were gathered together in a cluster on an antique credenza.

"I just need to kick start the old ticker, that's all and I'll be right as rain." He winced with each attentive step.

"Now where's that firewater?" He licked at this his bristled moustache and searched through the bottles until he found an old half empty bottle of Hackenschmidt whiskey and with a very shaky hand poured some into a glass and with one swift swig he empty it.

"That's better!" He exhaled, wiped the excess from his moustache with a roaming tongue.

Again he filled the glass, hand still shaking.

"Curse that little sod!" He growled "Out of the goodness of my heart I had taken him in and hid him from the law. Fed and watered him and this is how repays me!"

He looked ver at Worthington II, who had stopped his ablutions and was looking at his master with bulging eyes.

"But we know who got they last laugh don't we?" He chuckled to himself sipping the whiskey now. "Now I am possession of a heap of Stardust." He laughed loudly.

159

He started to walk around the room again, a look of smugness consuming him as he calms sipped at his whiskey.

"Yes, that does put me in a very good position in deed. I am supposed to be at Geko's grand casino opening!" He sighed "How I loathe those pretentious social gatherings, but I guess I could easily load the Stardust to some socialite with more money than sense, yes I could do that." He thought for a moment, "But I guess I really should return it to its owner. Ms Martel should be returning in a few months time and I guess I could keep it safe for her."

Worthington II looked up at him and barked.

"Oh no." d'Urberville shook his head, "I never touch the stuff, not really my thing you know?"

He raised his glass to nobody in particular and made a toast.

"Here's to doing the right thing!"

But as his monocled eye glanced over at his collection of warrior outfitted mannequins and his monocle suddenly fell from a saucer like eye and he spat out the whiskey, showering poor Worthington II.

"M-My collection!" He whimpered and he scampered over to the mannequins, "He's taken the Hospitaller!" He roared and launched the glass across the room, it exploded on impact, causing a firework display of glass and whiskey.

The mannequin had been completely stripped of the black Knight's Hospitaller outfit, as well as the red garments of the royal soldier and the gauntlets from the samurai outfit.

"How dare he!" d'Urberville shouted, "How bloody dare him! That looney!"

He ran his hands over the items and shook his head in disbelief.

"He's single handedly lowered the value of three bloody items, the bastard!"

As he seethed his fiery eyes noticed something else, and those same eyes began to water.

"No!" He snivelled "He's only gone and taken my Kirpan and spear too!"

He stood in silence and then a shaking hand came up and smothered his mouth as he staggered backwards knocking over the suit of medieval armour, that caused such a ruckus that Worthington II fled out of the room. d'Urberville fell into the armchair and whispered, "I've only gone and armed the lunatic!"

Chapter 22

Nicholas Smith had found his way to Studd City, hitchhiking most of the way. He had left mutilated bodies of the drivers slumped over their steering wheels. He now sort refuge in an abandoned apartment block on the corner of Finkle and Murray. He stood for the longest time taking in his new look in a broken shard of mirror that still clung to the decaying wall somehow. A strange, sadistic grin was etched on his gaunt face and his greasy hair hung in front of his face in matted worms.

"*Are you there Nicholas ?*" The croaking voice asked.

There was no answer from the timid and confused Nicholas that once was. His smile widened, slicing upward towards his protruding cheekbones, it would appear that that Nicholas had been silenced, the helping hand could have been the lack of medication and just that the entity within had finally taken full control. He stood admiring himself, a makeshift ensemble of different eras and cultures, that had no place together or should really ever work together, but in a way it actually did. The long black surcoat and hooded cape of the

Knight's Hospitaller, over the vibrant red under garments of the Afghan royal soldiers made his limbs stand out like four sharp bloodied knives. He clenched his fists tightly inside the armoured samurai gloves.

"*you're not The Vatican*." He said with a shake of his head, "*you'll need a new name of course.*"
His black leather boots swept away the dust and debris that had built up on the floorboards beneath. Each tie he moved to inspect his outfit at another angle, the boards creaked in agony. He walked over to the corner of the room where the body of a homeless man lay. The golden spear was wedged into his fleshy gut and stood erect and the jewel incrusted dagger lay discarded in a puddle of blood that oozed from his open throat, which still gurgled, although his eyes were glazed over and quite dead.

"*you have a nice belt, if I remember rightly.*"
He removed the thick leather black belt that was worn and tired, the leather cracked in several places, but Nicholas didn't mind. He took it from the corpse and slung it around his waist, tightly fastening it into place with the large golden buckle. He posed dramatically with his hands on his hips and laughed loudly, the sound was almost maniacal.

"*you are ready!*" He exhaled and with that strode across the room, picking up the dagger and sliding it into the rear of his belt, which was hidden discreetly by the cape. Then retrieving the spear that had skewered the homeless man he climbed out through the window onto the fire escape. He looked out at the city, he had never seen such bustle and heard such noise. The sun was still shining in the sky and Nicholas leapt from the fire escape five stories up and hurtled towards the alley below. There was a moment of self doubt in Nicholas' face and his face quivered, returning to that terrified face that he used to wear. He came to an abrupt end when he collided with a dumpster that was brimming with bags of garbage, which luckily for him broke his fall. He pulled himself out of the garbage and shook off the effects of such a hefty landing and then started to shriek with uncontrollable laughter, 'Well, at least we know you can't fly!"

Suddenly the sound of a woman screaming resounded down the narrow alleyway and Nicholas bounded from the dumpster and stuck another chivalrous pose and listened intently as the words 'Help!' wailed painfully in his eardrums.

"Someone is in trouble!" He whispered and was about to set off into direction of the screams when he stopped. realising...

We need to protect our identity. We need a mask!" He tugged at his surcoat that hung down covering his thighs and tore of a Long piece of it. With the help of his dagger he had soon shredded out two holes in the material and satisfied by his handy work, he tied it around his head, positioning the holes over his eyes as best as he could.

Another sinister smile caressed his lips and he was away, running down the alleyway, the sunlight glistening off the golden spear he carried in his hand.

He skidded to a halt as he was faced with a scene that not only shocked him but aroused him slightly and he gnawed at his bottom lip as he watched one man savagely driving his manhood into a defenceless woman who was being held down by another man. She screamed, gargling on her own tears as the man relentlessly had his way with her.

This awful scenario seemed to be even more despicable in the light of day, surely this kind of thing only happens when the sunsets and evil oozes out from the dark crevices of the city. Unfortunately the latter is not true, this type of thing happens far to often, perhaps these degenerates know that Vatican is not there to help the people of Studd City in daylight, maybe they feel that they can get away with their sickening activities. Maybe Nicholas can be the saviour in the light?

"Don't wear her out, Tony!" The man holding her laughed, "Save some for me."

"Shut up, Buzz!" Tony grunted, "You're breaking my concentration."

Nicholas stood rooted to the spot, saliva dribbling down his chin with an enchanted look on his face, an erection was developing quickly between his legs and then his gaze met the woman's.

"Please!" She snivelled, "Please help me!"

The men followed her gaze and saw Nicholas standing watching them.

"Hey, this ain't now peep show!" Tony growled through gritted teeth and harsh pelvic thrusts. "Buzz, take care of this pervert!"

"With pleasure!" Buzz grinned and released the woman's wrists, she immediately started thumping against Tony's face and chest but it did nothing but spur him on.

"You got a problem sicko?" Buzz barked at Nicholas, grabbing a nearby piece of wood and thumping it into his had as if it were a truncheon. Nicholas saw this and panicked for a moment, remembering the truncheons that the orderlies would use on him when he played up and the red mist descended.

"Leave that woman alone!" Cried Nicholas, the old Nicholas had somehow managed to return.

"Oh I don't think so!" Buzz growled and swung the bulky piece of wood at Nicholas, it connected with his temple and he fell to the ground in a heap, losing his grip on the spear and allowing it to fall to the hard concrete creating an ear splitting din.

"Is this how you get your kicks?" Buzz shouted and began striking the downed Nicholas with the wood.

"Hey, Buzz?" Tony called, stuffing his rapidly shrinking penis back into his jeans, "Your turn bro."

"Alright!" Buzz cried and quickly made his way over to the woman who was snivelling and trying to crawl away. Buzz got down on his knees and pawed at her exposed backside, "It's okay, I prefer doggy-style!" And began to enter her vigorously, she yelped out and still the tears flowed.

"So what's this fags problem?" Tony said kicking at Nicholas who was curled up in a ball, whimpering. "Is that it? You just gonna lie there? Fucking faggot!" And gave him another soft kick to the head, before turning around and watching Buzz have his turn on the poor defenceless woman. Nicholas's head span, around and around before this eyes opened again and that crazy face had returned, that gaunt evil looking face. He rose up and retrieving his dagger seized Tony by his hair and dragged the blade across his throat, tendons and arteries split and blood erupted from the wound. Tony collapsed to the ground clutching at his neck as blood sprayed everywhere like a garden sprinkler.

Nicholas stood behind the unknowing Buzz, blood flicking up at him, specks dotting his expressionless gaze. The woman's teary eyes locked on to Nicholas' glazed stare and willed him to do something to help her, and as if they had a telepathic link, Nicholas stooped down and retrieved the spear. The afternoon sunshine slicing through the surrounding buildings and glistening on the blade, the coloured jewels fixed into its neck winked at him, dazzling him with their seductive colourful dance. Nicholas smiled at the blade and then turned his attentions to Buzz who was evidently coming to the end of his gruesome act, his breathing pattern now

167

rapid and his exposed rear end eagerly driving back and forth. Buzz pushed forward one more time and released everything he'd had built up, arching his body, but before he could straighten up he felt severe excruciating pain as Nicholas forcefully skewered him through his rectum, the tip of the blade piercing through his throat and showering the poor woman in her attacker's blood. Nicholas retrieved the spear swiftly and Buzz's carcass toppled over leaving the woman staring up at Nicholas, covering in blood and frozen in shock.

Nicholas approached her, his face was friendly and calm as he wiped the blood from his spearhead on his cape.

"You are most welcome ma'am!" He beamed.

She stared at him, a rollercoaster of emotions twisting through her.

"I said... *you're welcome!*" Nicholas murmured, his face starting to twitch as if that voice was about to take over the steering wheel of this runaway wrecking machine.

"T-Thank you." She stuttered. Nicholas, turned to leave.

"Who are you?" The confused woman murmured.

He span around on the spot and said in a gravelly voice, "I'm... *I'm...*" He stopped and looked down at his outfit and then his spear confused, "Who are we?"

"We?" The woman blurted out as she tried to stand on trembling legs, "Are you nuts or something?"

Nicholas screamed and his face contorted with sheer anger,

he dived at her, kicking her to the ground and climbing on top of her.

"I am not nuts!" He erupted, saliva spraying all over her terrified face. He held her down, his hollow dark sockets homing two piercing bloodshot dots, that seemed to burn a hole in her soul. She was paralysed with fear, the whole ordeal had been too much, she had no fight left in her.

"you think that I was some angel sent her to save you? Maybe an angel of death! yeah, I like the sound of that!" He shrieked with laughter, a sound that was so delirious that the woman lost control of her bodily functions and urine started trickling down her legs and onto the floor of the alley.

"The Vatican isn't going to save you, he's not going to save anyone now, I'm here to make sure of it! God's precious angel..." He growled and retrieved the dagger from his belt and drove it into her throat, carving down her sternum aggressively, her flesh peeling with ease as Nicholas was met by her exploding torso, before swiping wildly across her stomach, allowing her intestines to escape into the alley.

"What have you done?" Nicholas whimpered as he stood up and staggered backwards, dropping the dagger onto the floor and staring at the blood on his gloved hands.

The voice laughed and it was sickening.

"you mean what have 'we' done, Nicholas! Look at it, such a thing of beauty!"

169

The woman was quite dead, her torso opened up in a crooked looking crucifix. He looked at this lavish engraving, his eyes squinting, an upside-down crucifix glared back at him.

"*Yes!*" He nodded feverishly and licked blood from his lips, tasting her, it sent a shiver down his spine, and caused another stirring in his loins. "*So beautiful, like a work of art. Not even God could create something so exquisite it could only be the work of a being more powerful than any God...*"

He bent down next t the body, caressed her fleshy breast that was now dangling at her side, his fingers tiptoed up and down her exposed ribs and the he delved into her stomach, and then retrieved a fist full of organs.

"*I know who we are, Nicholas!*" He wailed holding up the visceral entrails as if they were a trophy, "*I know who we are!*"

"Who?" Came the response, which was almost as whisper now.

Nicholas laughed again as he used his findings to draw a large upside down cross on the floor next to the body of the woman.

"Who?" He asked again.

Nichola stood up and took the bloodied hand and wiped it down and across on his surcoat making a dirty looking used down crucifix.

"WHO!" Nicholas shouted at the top of his voice.

"We are..." He cackled ferociously before falling into a sinister whisper, "...THE ANTI CHRIST!"

Chapter 23

Burt shuffled slowly back up the path towards St. Vincent's church, the usual Perfect Java breakfast gathered in one hand, his walking stick clutched in the other. Whistling some Motown classic by *Gladys Knight and The Pips*, his aura emitted an aura of happiness. He reached the door, stopping to retrieve a letter that was protruding from the wall mounted mailbox. His old eyes flitted across the golden overly elaborate handwriting and noticed it was addressed to Thomas and stepped through the door into hall of the church, his joyous tone carrying high up into the rafters accompanied by the tapping of his walking stick on the solid floor. As he approached the altar he noticed Thomas sitting on the front pew.

"Oh, good morning!" Burt announced as he approached, "I didn't think you would be up and about yet." Thomas turned to look at Burt, eyes bloodshot with fatigue, concealed behind his glasses.

"I'm awake, Burt." He said horsily, "I don't think I've slept in all honesty."

Burt sat down next to him and handed him a coffee.

"Here get some caffeine inside you, that will perk you up."

"Thanks." Thomas smiled taking the polystyrene cup.

They sat in silence for a few moments, the only sound was the gentle sipping of coffee through the plastic lids.

"So what's kept you up?" Burt asked, breaking the silence.

"Sometimes we come across scenes that will haunt us for the rest of our lives." Thomas sighed.

Burt nodded in agreement, "I know what you mean, Son. Some of the things I witnessed in Vietnam..." Burt shook his head, lost in a reminiscent daze. "...Horrible, horrible sights they were."

"Sorry Burt, I forget that you have lived through your own war."

"No need to apologise. It all seems so long ago now that sometimes it feels like a dream. But no matter what I witnessed over there, I don't think any of it filled with more dread than watching my poor Doris die."

Thomas looked at Burt, who's eyes were glazing with moisture, but he had no words of comfort.

"To watch her suffer like that and not be able to do anything to save her..." He choked and Thomas draped a caring arm around his crooked slouched shoulders, "...War is different. You always have a chance of helping, a chance to make a difference with the skills that the good lord provided

173

you with. When a cancer takes over there is nothing left to do but pray."

Burt wiped at his leaking eyes with the back of his hand and Thomas rubbed his back sympathetically.

"I wish there was something I could say to make you feel better Burt, I truly do."

"There are no words, Son." He turned to him smiling,

"At least I have the memories of her, the cancer couldn't take that away."

Thomas smiled.

"So." Burt sniffed and blew his nose on his handkerchief before stuffing it back into the deep pocket of his favourite cardigan. "Tell me about what has been keep you up." Thomas thought about telling Burt there and then about the Alprazolam and how he took three of them last night, but even that couldn't block out the horror that he had witnessed.

"I arrived at the scene early into my patrol, just before SCPD, so I was able survey the situation for a few minutes. A part of me wished I hadn't been given that luxury. But, from the safety of a nearby rooftop the scene resembled a painting more than a massacre, the main colour on the pallet, red."

"What happened?" Burt asked shaking his head.

"Three victims, two men, one woman, I overheard Detective's Graham and Freeman discussing that the woman had been raped and then murdered."

Thomas saw Burt's fist clench into a tight ball, it was one thing that Burt could not abide, to him in it was the worst of all crimes.

"The bodies of the two men lay in puddles of their own blood. One of them had had his throat cut the other had been impaled through his anus by something." He looked at Burt who's eyes had widened.

"Whatever was used had been removed and taken with the killer."

"And the woman?"

"That's the worst of all!" Thomas announced, stopping to take in a considerable amount of coffee as though he needed it to get through the next sentence. "Her torso had been opened up. Her contents had been left to spill out beside her."

Burt had no words, just a slow shake of the head.

"Graham believes that she had been raped by the two men, but had been interrupted by and unknown assailant who had murdered the two men."

"So you think the killer tried to save the woman and was too late?" Burt asked.

"No!" Thomas shook his head, "I would say that the two men were responsible for raping the woman, but not murdering her. I think this mysterious assailant murdered all of them."

"What? You mean, try and save the woman and then kill her?" Burt scoffed, "But that doesn't make any sense?"

"I know." Thomas agreed, "But when you have a bird's eye view of things appear differently. The one body was a few feet away from the woman's final resting place. As if he was watching his ally... doing the deed as it were. The other man was lying next to the woman and how he was brutally penetrated must have meant he was killed in the act."

"But why kill the woman?"

"I have no idea, the work of a deranged mind perhaps."

"Is it possible that it could have been Stone or the other patient that escaped the Oakland?"

"It's possible. But who knows!" Thomas shrugged. "But there is one thing that frightens me a little, one more thing that I haven't told you that changes everything."

"And that is?"

"Next to the body of the woman, smeared across the floor in blood was a gigantic crucifix."

Burt said nothing.

"If the tabloids get wind of that particular part then, surely they will jump to conclusions and..."

"Drop it on you!" Burt seethed.

"Exactly!"

"So what we're dealing with here is a murderous vigilante that saves the victims of crime only to then sacrifice them." Burt speculated.

"It leaves a lot for us to ponder." Thomas added.

"This must take priority over your search for Spider." Thomas nodded in agreement and the two sat in silence for a while in contemplation.

"Oh, I almost forgot." Burt said suddenly and handed him over his mail.

Thomas surveyed the flamboyant penmanship before opening it.

"What is it?"

"It's an invitation to Greta Geko's grand opening of her casino in Regal."

"You're moving in influential circles now I see." Burt teased.

"It would appear so." Thomas laughed, "But, I have no right spending my evening's attending just pretentious gatherings when there is a psychopath on the loose."

"Shame." Burt sighed, "It says you get to take a plus one. I'm a wiz on the old roulette table." Burt smiled.

Thomas laughed, but inside his head images of crimson crucifixes throbbed alarmingly.

Chapter 24

Under the shadow of the Griffin to Alexandrea line elevated train track, blue and red lights flashed on an off in rapid succession, causing the blood stains on the asphalt to appear magenta in tone.

"Another fucking corpse." Sighed Detective Graham as he and his partner Detective Freeman stand over the flayed body of a middle aged man, "In the middle of the day as well. You believe that Rich?"
Freeman shakes his head in false disbelief, of course he believed his eyes, this was Studd City and all bets were off.

"Nothing surprises me now, Sid." He sighed as he almost nonchalantly opened up a stick of gum and jammed it into his mouth and began to chew rapidly.

"Same M.O as the others." Graham added crouching down to take a closer look at the gutted carcass, next to the body lay a grand crucifix, smeared across the floor with the victims entrails.

"Sick puppy this one." Freeman replied, not bothering to join Graham that close to the action, he had had enough of the view from ringside, he much preferred watching the show from the cheap seats these days.

"And what's with the cross of blood?" Freeman asked.

"I don't know." Graham muttered as he surveyed the dead man's groceries that had poured out onto the street, there was something nauseating about the pieces of fruit splattered with human gore.

Freeman was busy surveying the obscene seemingly biblical calling card of this new killer.

"Hey, you don't think Vatican has anything to do with this do you?" Freeman asked through chomping jaws.

"No!" Snapped Graham immediately, "Of course not!"

"Whoa!" Freeman took a step back in surprise, "Take it easy."

"Sorry!" Graham grunted.

"You never know what these guys arc capable of. Vatican could have been lulling us into false sense of security and then flipped the tables."

"No!" Graham snapped again and rose to meet Freeman, who was now wearing a bewildered expression.

"Vatican had nothing to do with this, Rich."

"But how do you know?"

"I-I just know, okay!"

"Sheesh! I didn't know you two were such good friends." Mocked Freeman.

"We're not... I'm not..." Graham scrambled over his own words.

"Hey Sid, settled down." Freeman now looked a little concerned by Graham's bizarre behaviour, "I'm on your side." "Yeah, I know."

An officer wound yellow police tape around the scene, penning the two detectives in. Freeman leant in closely and whispered to his partner, "Is there something you're not telling me, Sid? Do you know something about this Vatican character?"

Graham stared at him for a few moments, part of him wanting to spill the beans. He hated keeping secrets from his partner, but he wasn't about to tell anyone that he had been having midnight conversations with a vigilante dressed as a Knight's Templar.

"No, Rich." Graham smiled and quickly changed the subject, "Let's get out of here. We've got all we're going to get out of this mess."

Graham led the way out the crime scene, ducking under the tape they headed towards Graham's old Ford County Squire, a red cherry perched on top bathing them in its vibrant glow. Graham attempted to get in the car when Freeman halted him with a hand on the shoulder.

"Sid."

Graham turned to face him.

"Are you sure everything is okay?" Freeman looked very concerned.

"Yeah, sure!" Graham scoffed, "I've just had a lot on my plate at the moment."

"Yeah I know you have." Freeman chuckled, watching Graham squirm uncomfortably and reach inside his jacket for a cigarette.

"What is that supposed to mean?" He stuttered grumpily.

"Nothing." Freeman shook his head, "By the way, where is Officer Nash tonight?"

"She's working undercover on the Mandrillus case. Nearly got enough on him to put him away for a long time."

"Are you seeing her tonight?"

There was a pause as Graham took a drag on his cigarette, he knew that Freeman was about to make him feel real bad about himself.

"No."

"Oh, so you're actually spending the night at your own house for a change?" Freeman asked with a side order of sarcasm.

"Yeah." Graham grunted.

"In your own bed?" Freeman continued to probe.

Graham nodded, scowling at his partner.

"With your own wifc!"

"Stop it!" Graham snapped.

Freeman slapped him on the back, "I'm only yanking your chain, Sid."Freeman laughed.

"Look I know you don't approve..."

181

"Hey, it's none of my business." Freeman held his hands up, "If you wanted my advice, you'd ask for it, right?"

"Go on then."

"What?"

"What advice do you have for me? I'm all ears."

"Oh now you want my advice!" Freeman laughed.

"Well if you're gonna be a smart ass…"

"Quit being such a grumpy bastard, Sid. How can you be so miserable when your tapping Nash's peachy ass every night!"

"Because of Mae!" Graham snapped. Freeman smiled and nodded.

"Exactly! Even with everything you've got going on your first thought is Mae. Doesn't that tell you something?" Graham took another hefty drag and said nothing.

"You hardly ever go home anymore do you? Guilty aren't you?"

Graham nodded solemnly.

"Damn well should be too!"

Graham attempted to snap back and dropped his head again and sat on the hood of the car.

"You know you're in the wrong too, I can see it in your eyes. Nash is a lovely girl, and hotter than beelzebub's pitchfork. But you gotta think of Mae, and the kids, Sid! Think of the kids."

"I know you're right, Rich." Graham sighed and then flicked the cigarette bud out into the road just as the el train came roaring over their heads.

They looked at each other for a moment as the trained passed over them, the screeching of the metal wheels on the rusty track was dreadful and both of them wore faces of discomfort.

"Those poor kids." Freeman shook his head, "When was the last time you did anything with them?"

"I'm taking them to see the wrestling this week! I've had the tickets for months!" He announced defensively.

"Good!" Freeman nodded, "Thats a step in the right direction, you just need to make up your mind what it is you want, Sid. Mae doesn't deserved being treated like this."

"What are you going to tell her if I don't?" Graham scoffed.

"No." Freeman sighed taking a seat next to him, "You know I would never do that to you. I am your best friend."

"Glad to hear it."

"And best friends don't do that."

"Double glad to hear that." Graham laughed.

"But that also means that best friends should listen to each other's advice. You hear me?"

"Yeah. I know you're right, you're always fucking right." He laughed, "I've just pinned myself into a corner."

"There's a crowbar in the trunk if that will help prise you out of this dilemma."

"Funny man."

They both laughed, both of them knew that particular conversation was over, Freeman had said his piece and that was that.

"So what do you think of this crucifix killer?" Freeman asked.

"I have an inkling that this might have something to do with the Oakland breakout."

"Eric? You think Eric is responsible for..."

"No, not Eric!" Graham interrupted Freeman before he ran away on his high horse. "I know that what has happened to him as left him a little unstable, but he couldn't do something like this."

"Then you mean the other guy, Smith?"

"Yeah, we'll have to take a look at his file, see if what he did in a prior life looked anything like this."

"I still think it's got something to do with Vatican." Graham shot him a look again.

"It's not him."

"You keep going to bat for this guy, why?" Freeman's eyes saucer and then he excitedly squealed, "Do you know who is?"

"Settle down, Rich!" Graham replied looking around to see if any of the other police on scene heard him, but they were all to busy.

"No, I don't know who he is, but I did have a conversation with him a few nights ago."

"Holy shit!" He squealed and then whispered, "For real?"

"Yeah, he's a real nice guy." Graham chuckled and left the hood and made for the driver's side.

"Wait a minute! Don't walk away from me!" Freeman called after him and ran around to the passenger's side, "You can't drop a bombshell like that and then leave me hanging!" Graham winked and open the door.

"Sid, come on!" Freeman pleaded.
Graham retreaded the cherry and flung it inside the car.

"How about I tell you all about it over a coffee and donut?"

"You're on!" Freeman chuckled.

"Damn right we're on, because you're paying."
Graham slid into the car leaving Freeman to ponder, "I always have to pay for the damn donuts! I'm gonna see whether I can claim on expenses for those damn things!"

Chapter 25

Boris and Dallas sit in an old run down Volkswagen Beetle, its bright canary yellow coat in need of an urgent pick me up. Boris surveys the street, but he cannot fight the urge to glance at the large donut that pulsates pink neon in the window of Perfect Java on the corner of Royale and Quebec. Dallas shuffles through his deck of playing cards, his cowboy boots up on the dashboard.

"What are we doing here again, Dal?" Boris groans. "You know why we're hear, Shamu said..."

"You mean Famu." Boris interrupted.

"Yeah, whatever!" Dallas rolled his eyes, "Guy looks like something I saw at Sea World once anyhow!"
Boris had now stopped probing the streets for what they were looking for altogether and had he sights set soul on donuts that he could see on display inside the diner.

"Can we just go and grab some donuts?"

"No!"
Boris sighs and taps away at the steering wheel while humming some forgotten tune from the old country.

"Were you even paying attention?" Dallas asked, snapping Boris from his salivating.

"Yeah!" There is silence.

"Remind me one more time who we are looking for?" Boris smiles a maw of broken teeth grinning at an annoyed Dallas.

"Jesus Christ, Boris!" He mocked, "How were the Russian's ever consider a threat."

"I keep fucking tell you I'm from the Ukraine." Boris growled.

"I know, I know." Dallas laughed, "Keep your hammer and sickle on!"

"You son of a..." Boris roared balling up a fist and lunging towards Dallas, the playing cards erupting into the air and showering them in reds and blacks.

"Easy big fella, I'm only messin with ya!" Dallas howled.

"Just watch it!" Boris barked.

"Okay, okay." Dallas sniggered.

"Well, it's incredibly racist!" Boris sulked.
Dallas laughed quietly as he sat up and looked up and down the street.

"As I was saying, Famu said we need some bait to lure Vatican in."

"Maybe we could lure him in with a hot coffee and a cinnamon twist." Boris said dreamy almost salivating.

"Will you quit it with the donuts!" Dallas snapped, "Fuck your cinnamon twist!"

Boris turned to him with an almost hurt look on his rough exterior, "Blasphemy!"

"Look man, we can't fuck around here!" Dallas said sounding serious which was a characteristic that wasn't usually familiar to him, "This is a huge deal! Working with Devine could lead to more work and the pay off for this is gonna be immense!"

"How much we getting?"

"Enough to send you back to Mother Fucking Russia and visit your comrades!"

"Fuck you! I'm Ukrainian!" He snapped and then his face calmed, "That much though?"

Dallas nodded.

"So what are we fucking wasting time sitting in this bumble bee..."

"It's a beetle."

"Whatever!" Boris shrugged, "Why don't we get out there and nab... anybody? Surely this hero guy will come and save any normal peon."

"Cus that ain't what we've been asked to do. Apparently this guy has bee seen with Vatican on numerous occasions."

"What' he look like? Do we have a name?"

"We're on the look out for a bum called Vermin."

"Vermin?" Boris scoffs, "You American's have such silly names."

"Yeah, I blame the Kardashians." Dallas laughed, "No, Vermin is a nickname that his fellow bums have christened him."

"Bums!" Boris moaned, "Why'd they call him that?"

"Looks like a rat apparently." Dallas shrugs nonchalantly.

"Poor guy." Boris sighed checking his own rugged reflection in the rearview mirror.

Dallas smirked at Boris.

"You're no oil painting yourself Boris!" Laughed Dallas.

"Fuck you!" Boris groaned, "I'm the most handsome of all the Volkov brothers!"

Dallas stared at him and then burst out into a fit of laughter. Boris ignored him and continued to scour the busy streets.

"So why are will sitting here and not searching for him? Surely that would be quicker?" Boris stated.

"There's really no need."

"Why?"

"I've been told that he passes through here daily with his shopping cart. Always checks the dumpsters at the rear of Perfect Java."

Boris' face contorts, disgusted by such information.

"Hey, guy's gotta eat." Dallas shrugged.

"Yeah, but c'mon, not out of the trash!"

"Maybe they're filled with day old cinnamon twists." Dallas smirked and chuckled as Boris' eyes lit up.

"Yeah, the guy has to eat." Boris nodded, "Maybe we should go around back and check if he's there. You know, just in case?"

Dallas burst out laughing and Boris playfully thumped him in the arm until Dallas saw their target shuffled passed them.

"Thats him!" Dallas cried and Boris immediately stopped fooling around to focus at the strange hooded figure that appeared crooked as he waddled down the sidewalk, the squeaky wheeled shopping cart leading the way.

"Let's get him!" Boris announced excitedly as he attempted to open the door.

"No." Dallas yelled, grabbing by his jacket sleeve and jostling him back behind the wheel. "We can't do it here, in the middle of the day you idiot!"

"So what do we do then?"

"Follow him, just keep your distance."

Elliot Hays turned off Quebec Street and head towards the rear of the place responsible for the best donuts in Studd City.

"He's going round the back." Dallas smiled slapping Boris on the shoulder, "See! What did I tell ya?"

Boris started the car up and slowly pulled out and headed in the direction that their target had gone.

"He'd better not have eaten all the cinnamon twists." He muttered under his breath.

Chapter 26

SCTV News vans surround the gruesome scene of Nicholas Smith's latest sacrifice. Popular reporter Donna Winkle, fixes her hair as her cameraman starts a countdown before going live. A wide overemphasised smile bursts into to life, glistening pearls of white framed with two ruby lips, that shines for a moment as she introduces herself to the viewers.

"This is Donna Winkle of SCTV News with this breaking news report." Her face changes and that pleasant smile disappears immediately.

"Another dark shroud has fallen over our poor city." The camera pans across to try to get a decent view of the body. A shallow quagmire of blood seeps out from the hollowed out torso of an elderly, black homeless woman, her internal organs floating on the surface like misshapen buoys.

"A killer has struck again, claiming yet another victim. This time, Ms Saphron Whistler, a defenceless homeless woman, known in the community as 'Sweet Sapphire', has been brutally gutted and left to bleed out right here at the rear of Sika's Samoan Snack Shack in Alexandrea."

The camera zooms in on the round face of the victim, her eyes bulging from their sockets in terror, her mouth gaping like a dead fish. A police officer guarding the scene walks in front of the camera blocking the view.

"There has been no statement released from SCPD on this, the second murder committed today. Just hours ago the body of Mr Matthew Brown of Montreal Square was found just a stones throw away from here. Both murders appear to be linked."

The police officers try to shoo away the reporters and cameras gathering round. Winkle is shoved out of the way with the masses, her prim, professional expression almost faltering.

"But our sources have informed us that the authorities believe that these killings could all be biblical sacrifices."

The picture of Donna Winkle reporting from the scene becomes distorted for a moment as a flickering electrical haze consumes the image. Burt and Thomas sit teetering on the edges of worn armchairs as they watch this breaking news unfold on their ancient television set.

"Here we go." Murmurs Thomas.

A blurry photograph appears on screen of a visceral crucifix haphazardly pasted on the floor.

"Eye witnesses have even been quoted as saying they saw a strange hooded figure running across a nearby rooftop carrying what they believed was a spear. Could it be that our very own Angel of Justice has turned his back on us?"

193

"I knew it!" Annoyed about what he was seeing unfold before his very eyes, "They're going to try and pin the whole thing on me."

Burt looked at him sympathetically, but he had no words, there was nothing he could say to make things any better and his glance returned to the screen, where Donna Winkle had reappeared.

"The authorities have not released any images of this crucifix that has appeared at three murder scenes now. Why? Why are they protecting this maniac?"

The bloodied crucifixes flash up on screen from each murder scene.

Thomas stood with his hands on hips, shaking his head in disbelief.

"Vatican if you're out there, how could you..."

Burt turns off the television and rises to join a perplexed looking Thomas.

"What am I going to do Burt? They'll all be gunning for me now. It will be a watch hunt!"

"There's only one thing you can do now. You must catch this lunatic and end it before it really picks up momentum."

Thomas nods, and suddenly they are interrupted by a high pitched beep echoing from Thomas pocket.

"Phone call?" Burt asks.

"No!" Thomas looks at him confused, hand rummaging in the inside pocket of his blazer. "Pager!"

"Pager? But who...?"

"Elliot, he must be in trouble."

Thomas Looks at the small pager screen, the name Elliot Hays flashes across in pixelated digits.

"I've got to find him." Said Thomas, flustered and pacing around the church's small living area, "That maniac might have gotten to him and..."

"I'm sure it's nothing so extreme." Burt intervened trying to extinguish Thomas' increasing build up of anxiety.

"I've got to go... now!" Thomas announced striding towards the main hall of the church, "I won't let that beast take him, I won't!" His raised tone echoing around the hall.

He picked up his pace and sailed over to the organ and pulled out tall the stops activating the hidden entrance. Burt struggles to keep up with him.

"Thomas!" Burt calls, "But, it's the middle of the day! You'll be exposed."

Thomas came to an abrupt halt at the top of the stairs that lead to the secret cellar. The cool spring breeze took hold and swept up the staircase, dosing him with its refreshing kiss.

Burt had taken this break in Thomas' quick departure to catch him up.

"Settle down, Thomas, you must stop to think." He said wheezing slightly, as he tried to catch his breath.

Thomas looked at Burt with sad eyes, "I won't let him die, Burt."

"But how do you know?"

"The pager was only to ever be used in life or death situations. Elliot is very proud, you notice he didn't even use it when he was attacked. No, something is different this time. I must get to him."

"Then you must go." Burt agreed.

The two disappeared down the stairwell and the stone knight gripping the shield that guarded the secret slip back into place.

Chapter 27

Vatican bounded over the rooftops, his surroundings familiar but with one exception, today the backdrop was not his ally. A fleet of doughy cloud drifted across a sea of cornflower blue, was luscious and awe-inspiring, but it didn't help Vatican. Determination etched on his face and the bright ball of light in the sky blinded him on several occasions, causing him the take extra consideration when vaulting from ledge to ledge. *Someone has got to have seen me. Burt was right this isn't a smart move.*

He dropped down onto a fire escape and used several spiralling, aerial manoeuvres to move down to the lower levels of the city, vaulting over freshly hung washing strung between buildings, like colourful bunting at a bazaar.

But sometimes we have to push the envelope and do things that we don't normally do.

His quick, nimble feet crisscrossed across narrow window ledges before coming to rest on a protruding quoin of a building that overlooked the elevated train line. He waited, using the time to catch his breath and surveying his surroundings that looked almost alien to his eyes. Each

197

building looking awake to him, not dozing, shrouded by a blanket of night, the way his eyes usually saw them.

The sun reflected in the building's mirrored windows, blinking at him and for a moment he really took the time to take in how picturesque Studd City was.

It has it's flaws, boy, did it ever! But on days like this, when God manoeuvres that great ball of fire in the sky at points it this way, wow!

He found himself descending into old memories that had been stored in the back of his mind for a while. The beautiful landscape had brought forward images of the places he honed his parkour craft. Places such as Rome and Paris, no matter how brightly the sun shone on Studd City it could never hold a candle to the beautiful scenery that Thomas saw in Italy and France. Nor could the shining sun cleanse this city of the quagmire of corruption, deception and death that it had found itself consumed by. Vatican quickly return to present day, he couldn't allow such fond memories to become smeared by such ugliness.

Get it together Thomas. Put it into perspective will you! You can't compare Studd City with the Piazza San Pietro of Vatican City or the Place du Trocadéro of Paris. Just because the sun is shining doesn't mean that sinners see the light.

The sound of the train approaching stirred Vatican from his musing and he turned to see the train, and readied himself to mount it as it slowed down at the corner beneath him.

You have a friend out there that needs your help. Whether

*it's under the cover of darkness or by the light of the day,
you owe it to give him your all.*

Vatican rose, teetering on the edge of the sturdy corner stone
of the wall, preparing himself for another leap of faith, this
time to catch the train to Alexandrea in search of his friend
Elliot. He readied himself and was about to jump when a
blinding light shone in his eyes dazzling him enough that he
took a few steps back and nearly lost his footing. He
managed to grip the side of the building and growled with
annoyance as the train moved away and out of sight.

The dazzling shining light was still shimmering with an
almost hypnotic pulse.

"What is that?" He said to himself staring over at a
neighbouring rooftop. He retrieved his binoculars from a
rear pouch and directed them to the vicinity that the flashing
was coming from.

Through the binocular's lens' he could see the girl he'd been
looking for twisting something reflective in her hands, it was
catching the light.

"It's her!" Cried Vatican, "But, now is not the time!"
The girl lowered the object and began smiling and waving
her hands at him. Vatican watched on as she gestured for
him to venture over.

"What could she want?"

He thought for a few moments, Elliot was in trouble he knew
that much, should he cease his current crusade to see what
she wanted?

"I should ignore her and move on, but Elliot did say that she came to his rescue..." He pondered and finally it was curiously that won out and he made his way majestically around the buildings towards her. He could see the awe in her eyes as he neared.

"Vatican!" She called, at first Vatican took her look as excitement, but as he arrived on the ledge of the rooftop it was panic that he saw on her face.

"What's wrong?" Vatican asked stepping down and approaching her quickly.

The girl couldn't catch her breath and she collapsed to her knees.

"Are you okay?" Vatican shouted, demanding an answer.

She held her finger u as she caught her tried to catch her breath. Vatican could see she was suffering from malnutrition and whatever exerting exercise she had been doing had obviously taken it out of her.

Vatican knelt down and rest a hand on her shoulder, "Is everything okay? Can I help you in some way?"

"Do... you... know..." She panted, "how difficult... you are to keep... up with?"

"You've been following me?" She nodded.

"But why?"

"Ver...min..."

"Vermin?" Vatican thought about it for a moment and then realised that was the horrendous nickname that the homeless community had instilled upon Elliot. "Elliot! You mean Elliot?"

She nodded.

Vatican reached around into a rear pouch and removed a small bottle of water which he handed the girl.

"Here, drink this."

She took it and smile, it was innocence personified and it warmed Vatican's heart.

"Thank...you." She stutter and then empty the bottle, then whipped at her mouth and chin with sleeve.

"What has happened to Elliot?"

"How'd you know?"

"I received a distress beacon from him."

"You mean this old thing?" She said retrieving Elliot's pager from her pocket.

"But how?" Vatican asked in shock and then his face contorted into a stern scowl, "I hope you haven't stolen that and are playing some kind of prank!"

"No, no, it's nothing like that!"

"So, has something happened to him?" She nodded with a look of angst.

"Do you know what happened?" Vatican pressed.

"Yeah." She nodded and tried to get to her feet, Vatican steadied her and ushered her over to the ledge to sit on.

"What happened?"

"They took him."

"Who? Who took him?" Vatican felt a sickening feeling like a yoyo bobbing up and down in his throat.

"Two of the Webheads."

"Webheads! Spider's gang?" She nodded again.

"What exactly happened?"

"Elliot was on his rounds, you probably know that he likes to do a lap of the neighbourhood each day to see what he can find."

Vatican nodded.

"Well, he had stopped off to check the dumpster's at Perfect Java, sometimes there are some good finds to be had there, you know?" Vatican smiled and she carried on, "Well, they came out of nowhere in a banged up old beetle, a pissy yellow colour it was."

Vatican chuckled at her sharp vulgarness.

"They hit him a few times and then threw him in the back of the car."

"How do you know all this?"

"We were in the dumpster..."

"Wait a minute? I'd have thought that Elliot's dumpster diving days were long gone!"

"No, not Elliot!" Sighed Penny rolling her eyes, "He's way too old to go searching in dumpsters. I meant we as in me and Kasper." There was shuffling sound from inside her oversized hooded sweater and then a moving bulge appeared and Kasper's friendly face appear out of the neck hole.

"Kasper!" Vatican was taken-aback and then smiled greeting the rat with a tickle to the chin, he appeared to like this, before disappearing back down into the comfy, warm nook he had discovered.

"So we were rummaging around to see what we could find. Was a good haul, two jam, a custard, whole bag of cinnamon twists..." She stopped herself from disclosing the whole of Perfect Java's stale menu and smiled at him, returning to the matter in hand, "Yeah, well, they didn't even notice us!"

"I tried to give chase and follow the car but it was too fast. They threw this out the window. I'm surprised it still works." She handed over the pager and Vatican took it in his hand.

"You did your best." Vatican said with a smile, and then looked out at the city, wondering where they had taken him and how he was going to find this particular needle in a city of haystacks.

"Oh yeah I did!" She announced with sass, "You don't think I gave up that easy do ya?"
Vatican turned to face her, his brow rising high over his crimson face mask.

"So you know where they took him?"

"Damn straight! I know exactly where they have taken him." She said proudly.

"Care to share that information?" Vatican chuckled.

"Chinatown. Old Chinatown."

Vatican stared at her in awe, his face mirroring the face he saw when he grandly made his entrance.

"Do you know whereabouts in Chinatown?"

"Well," She groaned looking a little coy, "Okay, I may have exaggerated about knowing 'exactly' where they went. I lost them as they moved into the old meat market."

"I'll find him." Vatican smiled, "You may have saved Elliot's life..." Vatican paused, "By the way, what is your name?"

"Penny. Penny Ling."

He held out his hand and she shook it.

"Pleased to meet you, Penny ling. You're one clever girl."

"Thanks, I know." She shrugged, "What's your name?"

Vatican laughed.

"Maybe one day." He winked and climbed up on the ledge of the rooftop.

"Save him Vatican... please." She said solemnly, "He's the only real friend I've got."

Vatican nodded and before he leapt from the building he looked at the pager in his hand and tossed it to Penny, she caught it and looked up at him.

"Keep this, incase you ever need me."

"Wow, thanks!"

Vatican steadied himself to leave when Penny spoke again.

"Be careful out there, Vatican."

He turned again, her face looked pale and serious.

"There's someone out there parenting to be you. He'll kill you."

"How do you know?"

"The eyes and the ears my friend." And winked at him. He had one last smile for her before her raced one towards Old Chinatown.

Chapter 28

The smell of freshly slaughtered animal meat hung in the air, hovering over the Hu Meat's slaughterhouse like a leaking rain cloud. Boris and Dallas dragged a dazed and confused Elliot across the gravel cover roof of the building and unceremoniously dumped him next to the large skylight that rose from the roof like an ugly, transparent pyramid.

"Sit down old man!" Boris growled menacingly.

Elliot slumped up against the skylight, cowering under the shroud of his hood he looked exhausted. His hands bound by rope, a piece of material gagging his peculiar shaped maw.

"You won't need this." Dallas snapped as he removed Elliot's hood.

Boris and Dallas' faces squirmed, contorting in disgust from the sight that met their eyes.

"Ugly bastard aren't ya?" Dallas scoffed.

They casually held their handguns limply as if holding any ordinary household object.

Eliot thought about trying to take one of the guns, until Boris whipped him across his uneven skull with the nose of his gun. Something sang in Elliot's ears and his eyes rolled back into his head as he fought to stay conscious.

"Go easy on him, Boris." Dallas said, "He already looks like he's gone twelve rounds with 'Left Hook' Lewis Johnson."

"Only twelve rounds?" Boris laughed, "He was eyeing up your gun, I saw him."

"He was?" Dallas asked, "Motherfucker!" He growled as he too struck him across the face with his gun too.

They laughed as Elliot's face bled, old scars being reopened and staining his cratered flesh with fresh blood.

Elliot stared at the two giggling idiots that stood over him and he felt a sudden surge of self loathing consume him. He wished he wasn't this old and decrepit, a part of him wished he was dead instead of quivering on the roof of some slaughterhouse in Old Chinatown, being used as bait to catch a god friend of his. He felt like utter shit for allowing himself to be put in this predicament.

I'd have shown you! You pair of punks!

Elliot became overcome by reverie and foggy visions manifested in his mind's eye, visions of the past, he was younger, stronger and would not be bullied, by anyone.

You two would have been trounced and pissed your pants by now if I were...

Visions of his clenched fists drove into faceless degenerates and then something shimmered before his eyes, his eyelids quivered rapidly, almost blinded by the reflected light for a second.

...younger.

He shook of the effects of yesteryear and noticed the setting sunshine, catch Dallas' gun and shine in his eyes. "I think this guy has lost it?" Boris mocked staring at him inquisitively.

"Must have hit him too hard." Dallas shrugged, "C'mon we best get out of sight." He added as he forced his gun in the waistband of his jeans as he strode away to take cover behind some broken meat tubs and bloodstained tarpaulin.

"Now, don't go trying anything stupid." Boris whispered as he leant over the defenceless Elliot, "Or I'll but a bullet in that ugly head of yours."

He pressed the barrel of the gun to his head with smooch force that both men gritted their teeth.

Dallas called to Boris and he left Elliot alone to join his comrade.

"Do you think this is going to work?" Boris asked with a whisper.

"Of course it is." Dallas snapped back, "He'll come for him, I'm sure of it."

"But how will he know where we are?"

"The girl?"

"What girl?" Boris looked at him perplexed.

"Don't tell me you didn't notice the girl hiding in the dumpster at the rear of Perfect Java?"

Boris looked at him the way a confused dog would look at its owner.

"Maybe your senses had become overwhelmed by the smell of stale cinnamon twists." Dallas mocked, "Shit, Boris! She was trailing us for fuck's sake!"

"I didn't see any girl!" Boris snapped back, "What girl?"

"It's the girl we sometimes use to move the stardust?"

"Oh, the chink?" Boris bellowed, Dallas immediately covered his mouth and shushed him.

"Quiet, you idiot! Fuck me!" He said shaking his head, "You're such a hypocrite."

"What are you talking about?"

"You talk about racism all the time, about how you're not Russian..."

"But, I'm not Russian."

"I know that idiot!" Dallas rolled his eyes, "Then you come out here calling people chinks!"

Boris just looked at him and shrugged.

"Just forget I said anything. Vatican will come, she'll have made sure of that."

"Oh you paid her off." Boris smiled.

"No."

"But you said she has worked for us moving Stardust?"

"Yeah, those kids are homeless and starving, they'd do anything for a few bucks. But no, I meant he'll come because they're both righteous, do-gooders who want to 'do the right thing'!"

They both laughed.

"Quiet!" Dallas whispered, listening intently.

A figure bounded up the fire escape that hugged the side of the building, each heavy step that fell on the rusted metal steps echoed around the rooftop. It was in such a fashion that it was though the ascending strange did not mind that he could be heard. A hooded figure leap onto the roof with such vigour and excitement that he laughed loudly when he witnessed Elliot slouched in an unattractive heap, looking so vulnerable.

"**A SACRIFICE!**" Anti Christ cackled, as he removed his hood, unveiling his sharp features that protruded from his gaunt face.

"**WE HAVE FINALLY BEEN ACCEPTED BY THE PEOPLE OF STUDD CITY!**"

He smiled and twirled his spear around in his has hands as he approached Elliot, who looked at him with frightened eyes because Elliot was the eyes and the ears of the city and he knew exactly who stood before him, the one they had christened 'The Crucifix Killer'.

"**I THINK I SPEAK FOR THE BOTH OF US WHEN I SAY HOW HONOURED WE ARE FOR SUCH RECOGNITION!**"

The Anti Christ turned around on the spot with his arms stretched out wide, his golden spear shimmering in the dying sunlight.

"THE HILLS ARE ALIVE!" He sang as he span in a circle faster and faster, until he almost toppled over, only leaning on the spear saved him the embarrassment of falling face first into the gravelled roof.

"FORGIVE ME MY FRIEND, I KNOW THAT THIS MAY BE A TRYING TIME FOR YOU, BUT I PROMISE IT WILL ALL BE OVER SOON." He smiled sadistically, his bloodshot eyes pulsing from behind the confines of his black mask. He approached Elliot and crouched before him.

"What a shame." Nicholas said with a grieved gaze, sighing deeply, his gloved fingers gently running over the horrendous scars on Elliot's face like a blindman would explore braille.

Elliot was taken aback by the change in his expression and voice, it was almost as though two different people were addressing him. Then a shudder was sent hurtling down his spine when he saw that face change. With his beak like noise, sharp scowling forehead and saliva dripping from his barbed teeth he resembled some kind of ravenous bird of prey.

"YOU WILL HAVE THE HONOUR OF BEING MY NEXT OFFERING!" He stood up and gestured blood that had dried on his surcoat in a grungy looking Petrine cross, "YOUR BLOOD WILL HAVE THE PRESTIGE OF JOINING THE MANY THAT HAVE BEEN SACRIFICED BEFORE YOU TO HELP CLEANSE THIS CITY."

Anti Christ held the spear aloft and then pointed it at Elliot's chin, its tip drawing blood effortlessly.

Boris and Dallas watch on bemused.

"Who the hell is this asshole?" Whispered Boris.

"Well, it's not Vatican, that's for sure." Dallas shrugged.

"Maybe we'd better do something about it?" Boris asked, "I mean a dead hostage isn't worth much is it?"

The two attempt to rise when they notice someone else standing on the rooftop, the sunset painting him in warming yellows and oranges.

"You harm one hair on his head and as God is my witness..." Growled Vatican.

Anti Christ's grin widened, the thin layer of skin stretching like elastic over his sharp protruding cheekbones.

"WE KNEW YOU WOULD COME!" Anti Christ whispered, still staring at Elliot.

"Step away from him." Vatican snapped.

Anti Christ turned around slowly to face Vatican, pointing the bloodstained spear head towards Vatican.

"YOU ARE INTERFERING IN THE RITUAL VATICAN!" Anti Christ snarled through the sinister smile, "NOW IF YOU WOUD BE SO KIND AS TOO WAIT KINDLY, WE WILL SOON GET TO YOU AND YOUR BLOOD WILL JOIN THE MANY. YOU TOO WILL CLEANSE THIS CITY OF ITS FILTHY WAYS!"

"You know it's funny." Vatican laughed, causing Anti Christ's brow to quivered with suspicion. "I too have something similar planned."

Anti Christ stared at him, his Redding eyeballs pulsating, a strange muscular twitch had now started to take hold, attacking his nostrils and eyelids.

"But it never involved gutting people as though they were animals." Vatican sneered.

Anti Christ's face spasmed relentlessly.

"Going cold turkey I see." Vatican said moving slowly towards him, "You need your medication."

"No!" Whimpered the voice of Nicholas Smith from somewhere deep within this menacing shell.

Vatican continued to edge ever so closer, his hand now outstretched towards Anti Christ.

"I want to help you." Vatican said, "I want to get you help, get you medicine. But first you must trust me."

Anti Christ's whole frame went limp, his head and shoulders slouched forward and he hung there, spear only just balancing in the bent tips of his fingers. He looked like lifeless, a strange grovelling whimper came from his rapidly moving lips.

"That's it, you just have to trust me." Vatican said again, moving closer and closer all the time, "Do you trust me?" The mop of dirty blonde hair that hung over his face nodded slowly.

"Good! Good!" Vatican smiled, "I need you to step away from Elliot for me."

213

Anti Christ shuffled sluggishly a few steps away from Elliot and stopped. Vatican smiled and reached out towards the spear, "I'm just going to take this off your hands okay?"

Anti Christ again, Vatican gripped the spear and began to pull it away from him.

"That's it! That's it!" Vatican urged.

When it seemed that Vatican had control of the spear there was resistance. Vatican looked on as Anti Christ's depraved eyes blazed through a veil of dirty hair.

"*YOU ARE TOO TRUSTING VATICAN!*" Anti Christ sneered and pulled the spear out of Vatican's hand and swung it at him viciously. Vatican stepped back quickly, leaning out of harms way as the spear's tip faced in front of his face. Vatican immediately retrieves his three piece staff from his thigh holster, rotates it in his hands fixing it into place creating his bo staff. The two of them stood staring at each other, their metallic weapons gleaming in the fading sun. Two warriors stood, both of them waiting for the other to make the first move. Anti Christ did not leave Vatican waiting for too long and with a psychotic war cry he charged at him, the spear he'd leading the assault. Vatican side stepped the oncoming Anti Christ and the momentum took him passed him, he skidded to a halt and turn to face Vatican again, the scene reminiscent of a quick footed matador taking on an uncontrollable bull.

"*HOLD STILL! IT WILL BE EASIER FOR US ALL IF YOU DO!*" Anti Christ grumbles as he thrusts the spear unsuccessfully at Vatican, each time the

214

well trained and well prepared Angel of Justice too nimble and quick.

"There will be no blood spilt today, not by you." Vatican glares, the spear singing as it connects with a well placed block from Vatican's bo staff.

"This little game of yours is over." Vatican booms and with a well placed strike to the wrist of Anti Christ sees his grip loosen and Vatican moves in to disarm him and then sweeps him with such fluid action that it was almost as though he were made out of water.

"I will not have you ruin all my hard work! I will not have your actions besmirch my name."

Vatican kicks the spear away, with bounces and rolls on the roof with irritating clamour, and with it now out of arms reach for the fallen Anti Christ, Vatican moves in hesitantly, bo staff gripped tightly in a protective position.

"PLEASE DON'T HURT ME! FORGIVE ME!" Anti Christ grovels.

"Get up!" Vatican snarls.

Anti Christ rises to his feet, his upper body now smothered by his ragged cape. Vatican's eyes flit to the restrained Elliot which was a rookie mistake, in his angst state he took his eye off Anti Christ who leapt at him like an uncoiling spring and grabbed Vatican by the throat. Vatican dropped the bo staff, it too serenading them with an almost identical rendition of the song sang by the spear.

Anti Christ mounted Vatican, his fingers clawing at Vatican's throat, cutting off his airways and causing Vatican's complexion to turn an unhealthy shade, the colour of red wine.

"REST NOW LITTLE ONE, SHHHHH!" Spluttered Anti Christ, saliva bursting from his mouth and dribbling down his chin and dripping onto the helpless Vatican, **"ROCKABYE BABY, ON THE TREE TOP!"** He sang, swaying back and forth with Vatican's limp head in his unrelenting grip.

"MY MOTHER USED TO SING THAT SONG TO US, DIDN'T SHE ?" The swaying motion stopped as Anti Christ seemed to be somewhere else for a moment and he relinquished his grip on Vatican's throat allowing him much needed oxygen, Vatican gasped and collapsed, his face slowly returning to its usual colour.

"SHE WOULD SING IT TO US EVERY NIGHT!" He added solemnly, looking at his gloved hands, that were frigid in blood stained claws, **"WE HATED HER!"** He growled, turning his attentions bad to Vatican who was trying to find his feet, he stalked him, hands still fixed like talons, **"THAT'S WHY WE SLIT HER THROAT!"**

He screamed and dove at Vatican, but this time he didn't underestimate his opponent and grabbed his wrists, preventing those threatening claws from seizing his windpipe once more. Vatican pulled Anti Christ in swiftly and brought up his knee to meet Anti Christ's jaw, the sound was sickening and Anti Christ staggered backwards dazed, his eyes rolling like two red billiard balls. Vatican rose quickly and when Anti Christ shook off the effects and charge again, Vatican struck first with a brutal tiger claw strike, the palm of his hand connecting with the bridge of his nose, breaking it instantly. Blood trickled from his nostrils and fell to the ground holding his face, screaming out in agony.

"Please, stop! Please don't hurt me anymore." Nicholas snivelled, looking up at Vatican with tears in his eyes, a face they didn't resemble the monster he'd bee fighting with just seconds ago.

"Who are you?" Vatican asked, a bemused look on his face now.

"Nicholas. Nicholas Smith!" He coughed and spluttered, blood seeped out through the gaps in his crooked teeth.

"I think you need some help." Nicholas nodded and rose gingery to his feet.

"Elliot, are you okay?" Vatican called, Elliot replied with a nod of his head, his eyes suddenly doubled as if to warn Vatican. Anti Christ was on him again and with a demonic shriek he drove his dagger into Vatican's side, the blade cracking two ribs as it forced its way through. Unluckily for Vatican, the blade found the only gap in his kevlar under armour. Vatican winced and managed to thrust an elbow into Anti Christ's already shattered nose and watched as he collapsed on the roof in a heap.

Vatican removed the dagger and let it drop to gravel, he gurned with discomfort and made his way over to Elliot.

Excruciating pain writhed around in his insides, like a floundering electric eel. He grimaced as he knelt inform of Elliot and removed his gag.

"Are you okay?" Vatican asked, through gritted teeth.

"I was going to ask you the same thing." Chuckled Elliot.

Vatican smiled and then winced as he clutched his side.

"It's just a flesh wound." Vatican replied, staring at the mass of blood that was now dripping from his fingertips.

"Yeah, I know." Elliot replied, "Seen enough of those in my time to know. Just missed your vital organs, you'll be okay."

"I wish I had your wisdom, Elliot." Vatican laughed as he untied, his wrists. The rope had begun to slice into Elliot's flesh and had left deep, sore indentations.

"You realise that this is a trap don't you?" Elliot groaned as Vatican helped him to his feet.

"Don't move bible boy!" Came the growl of Dallas' Texan drawl.

Vatican looked up at Dallas and Boris who had surrounded him, guns pointed at his head. He glanced around, taking in his bearings, the bo staff, spear and dagger were all too far away to retrieve. The carcass of the Anti Christ lay motionless several feet away. He held Elliot up, tightly to protect him but he made sure that he did not show any signs of discomfort from his wound. He could not let them know how much he was hurting. His main priority now was getting Elliot out of here to safety.

218

"What do you want?" Vatican asked, his eyes flitting back and forth between the two gunmen.

"Certain people want to talk with you." Boris grinned an ugly smile.

"Oh yeah?" Vatican scoffed, "What people?"

"We can't tell you." Dallas said quickly, he didn't want to allow Boris to blurt out any information, "Let's just say it's a surprise."

"Spider?" Vatican said and watched as Boris' face gave him all the answers he needed.

"Just come on, get moving!" Dallas growled shuffling closer, he had been on the receiving end of a Vatican ass kicking a long time ago and did not wish for another.

"No!" Vatican answered defiantly, gripping at weary Elliot.

"No?" Boris barked, "What do you mean, No?" And with that strode forward and pressed the nose of his gun against Vatican's temple. The metal was cold against his warm, clammy skin and in a way it was soothing. Vatican remained defiant and did not move, just stared into Boris' eyes.

"You won't shoot me!" Vatican said calmly.

"Vatican what are you doing?" Elliot stuttered, "They'll kill us both."

"Yeah," Dallas chimed in joining them, "You'd best listen to the old man."

"They won't kill me, Elliot. It's fine."

"Fine?" Elliot cried, "There is nothing 'fine' about

this situation!"

"Don't push us!" Boris growled and pressed the gun into his temple harder, Vatican remained unfazed. "Please stop doing that."

Boris pressed even harder, the barrel cutting into his skin now. "Shoot me then." Vatican said cooly, calling their bluff. Their stunned faces informed Vatican that his judgement of the situation was correct.

"You see, Elliot." Vatican smiled, "They already played their hand. They informed me that there was a high power at work here, these two are nothing but winged monkeys!"

"Hey!" Boris yelled, "Who are you calling a winged monkey!" Boris prodded him again and too quick for Boris to react, Vatican had grabbed the gun, twisted it out of Boris' hand and threw it across the rooftop. Boris stood looking at him in awed bemusement.

"I did ask you to stop doing that." Vatican sighed, "As I was saying, they are eating on someone's instructions and if they kill me then I presume their employer will not be too happy about that. I can only presume that he or she wants that pleasure for themselves."

He made eye contact with Dallas, he looked speechless, this let Vatican know that everything he said was true.

"So if there's nothing else you want to discuss, we will be on our way." Vatican said and started to lead Elliot towards the fire escape.

"Not so fast!" Dallas cried as he grabbed at Elliot's ragged over coat and pulled him towards him, placing his gun to Elliot's head.

"You're right about everything. You're one clever son of a bitch, you know that?"

Vatican grinned, masking the grimace of pain that longed to ripple across his face.

"You should be on *Who wants to be a millionaire* or something!"

"But, I don't wish to be a millionaire." Vatican chuckled, "The only wish I have is to have the streets free of cockroaches like you. I don't think there is a gameshow for that yet though."

"Cute!" Dallas grinned "Boris, get your gun."

Boris scurried across the rooftop to retrieve his gun as Dallas laid down a new ultimatum for the Angel of Justice.

"Well, you see the thing is, you are right that we aren't going to kill you. Not yet anyway!" He smiled at this, possibly envisioning the future act, "But, we don't need this old bastard. So if I put a bullet in his head..."

"Okay." Vatican intervened, "What do you want?"

"I told you, the boss just wants to talk."

Boris returned, out of breath and lifting his gun, also aiming it at Elliot.

"If you let him go free, then I will come with you freely."

"Vatican, No!" Elliot struggling in Dallas' grip.

"It's okay, Elliot." Vatican smiled at him.

221

"He's gonna try something tricky as soon as we let the old guy go." Said Boris anxiously.

"You have my word." Vatican said holding his hands in the air.

Dallas nodded and let go of Elliot.

"Are you sure about this, Dal?" Boris stuttered, his gun wavering back and forth between Elliot and Vatican.

"It's cool." Dallas said, "Go on old man. Your ugly ass gets to see another day."

Elliot stumbles forwarded Vatican catches him.

"Vatican..." Elliot whispers.

§"It's okay, Elliot." Vatican winks, "Just get out of here."

"But..." Elliot tried to find words to make him change his mind, but he knew it wouldn't help and he shuffled towards the fire escape.

They waited until Elliot had disappeared out of sight and then Dallas and Boris sandwiched Vatican, guns aimed at his legs now and Vatican knew that he was safe from being killed (for the time being) but there was nothing stopping them putting a bullet or two in his kneecaps if he got smart again.

"Well, then gentlemen." Vatican said holding his hands aloft, "Shall we?"

Vatican knew that he could easily disarm both of them and leave them unconscious in about three moves, even with a gapping hole in his side. But in all honesty he was intrigued as to who wanted to 'talk' to him, not to mention being a man of his word. And if it was indeed Spider (who he expected) then he would have the chance he has been waiting for months for and that was to take in the man responsible for the Doomsday murders.

Boris and Dallas gestured over to a door that would lead to the inside of the building and were about to move when there was a subtle sound of metal being scrapped across the gravelled rooftop and the golden spear of Anti Christ cut through the air and impaled Vatican through his back, the spearhead slicing smoothly through his right shoulder, it's glimmered tip protruding out through his deltoid. Vatican staggered forwards from the shear force and the unexpected pain and growled through tightly gritted teeth.

Boris and Dallas turned in shock to see Anti Christ shuffling towards them, sliding his dagger back into the sheath on his belt. His gaunt ace horrific as each orifice dripped blood.

"THE SACRIFICE HAS BEEN CLAIMED!"

He announced as he approached, not focusing on Boris and Dallas at all, his eyes of fire burning solely on Vatican who refused to yield, he would not fall, but he's knees buckled as he tried unsuccessfully to reach the spear and remove it.

"THE CITY WILL BE CLEANSED, THE ANGEL OF JUSTICE WILL FALL!"

Anti Christ grabbed the spear and reclaimed it swiftly and for Vatican, painfully. His knees buckle and he almost collapsed to his knees. But still he remained defiant and he managed to slowly turn around and face his attacker.

Anti Christ's face was crimson from hairline to chin, Vatican watched as each droplet of blood fell from the point of his chin and hit the gravel, each drop sound like a muffled gunshot. Vatican was on the verge of passing out.

"YES," Anti Christ hissed, "THE ANGEL OF JUSTICE SHALL FALL!" And with a shriek he kicked a defenceless Vatican in the chest sending him hurtling backwards towards the skylight. The glass shattered on impact and Vatican fell from the roof accompanied by a barraged of broken glass before he struck the concrete floor below. He lay immobile, blood seeping from a fresh wound in the back of his head.

"CITIZENS OF STUDD CITY!" Anti Christ cried, holding the spear in the air, as Boris and Dallas watch don in amazement and fear. "YOU HAVE WITNESSED THE CLEANSING! I TOLD YOU ALL THAT THE ANGEL OF JUSTICE WOULD FALL..."

He looked around like a victorious gladiator would survey the crowd in a coliseum.

"AND THE ANGEL OF DEATH WOULD RISE!"

Anti Christ pulled his hood into place, shrouding his bloody mask in shadow and departed the roof swiftly down the fire escape.

Boris and Dallas looked down through the broken skylight at the motionless Vatican below.

"Well, that worked out nicely." Boris said.

"As long as he isn't dead it did." Dallas replied.

Chapter 29

The night air was filled with pretension and arrogance as Studd City's privileged and wealthy, retreated from their luxury stretched limousines that were filling the street in Regal. Elaborate gold and green bulbs burst into life, drawing everyone's attention to the ostentatious signage that hung above the entrance of the building, that the Studd City's elite were being drawn to in droves, like spellbound bluebottles being attracted to a pulsating bug zapper.

Geko's Casino, were the words that lit up the night, the grandiose event reminiscent of a film premier from an almost forgotten era. As the gaggle of socialites sauntered through the doors into the majestic lobby, a succulent female voice purred through the building's tannoy speakers, welcoming them in what sounded like a subtle German accent.

Gold and gild was the theme for the venue's vulgar decor, spiralling staircases circled the lobby leading to other large open plan rooms of entertainment, as gigantic golden chandeliers hung from the ceiling on thick chains. Decorated with small green lizards throughout.

Waiters handed out free complimentary glasses of the finest champagne, the guests sipped at it graciously as they began to mingle with their fellow upperclass acquaintances.

Detective Sidney Graham shuffled in reluctantly, arm in arm with his wife Mae, who was beaming and looked very pretty with her auburn hair twist and tied up tightly for the occasion.

"Oh, Sid, it's so splendid!" She gasped as she glided into the bustling lobby, her silver even gown hugging her curves flatteringly.

Sid grunted as he dug a finger down the collar of as tiff new shirt that he had (uncharacteristically for him) buttoned up tightly accompanied day a flamboyant purple tie, which was also knotted tightly and causing him much frustration.

"Stop messing with it!" She hissed out the corner of her mouth.

"But..."

"Just leave it alone!"

"Fine!" Sid grumbled as Mae dragged him towards the waiter with a tray of champagne flutes.

They each took a glass and then strode over to the corner of the room where several tables of canapés had been laid on for the guests.

"Oh, Sid, look!" Mae gasped, her gaze being drawn from the canopies and focusing on the large lizard sculpture that had been painstakingly chiselled from ice. "Isn't it beautiful!"

"I guess." Sid shrugged, cramming several minuscule, smoked salmon mousse Canapés into his mouth. Much to the horror of Mae, who subtly nudged him in the ribcage with the point of her elbow.

"What is the matter with you?" She whispered, flashing false smiles at any nearby onlookers who were looking on in disgust.

"What?" Sid gurgled, canapés debris falling our of his gorged maw.

Mae grabs his by his arms and pulls him into the corner of the room, away from prying and pompous eyes.

"You actually bring me out for a change and you act like an actual pig!"

Sid stared at her, wiping crumbs from his best suit, and inspecting a suspicious looking stain on his tie.

"I mean look at you!" She sighed, retreating a handkerchief from her evening purse and dabbing away at the stain with it,   "Sometimes it's like having three kids."

"Sorry mom!" Sid scoffed, rolling his eyes until he was met by Mae's intense stare.

Mae then looked away and sighed, her head dropping, "Maybe you should have brought somebody else to this thing."

"Mae, I didn't even want to come but I was told I had to attend. I thought you would have liked it"

"Well, I do, but it's been so long since we did anything together... and look at you! You just can't stop being

228

a cop can you?"

Sid shrugged, "But I am a cop."

"I know." She sighed "but you're not on a stakeout now with Richard, chomping donuts and slurping coffee. This is a big deal with important people."

"Important people!" Sid laughed mockingly.

"Well, they're more important than Clive the mail man or Corey the paperboy!"

Sid looked at her a little confused.

"These are the only people I see day in and out, Sid." She sighed, "You just don't understand."

Sid dropped and arms round her shoulders, something he hadn't done for months. In fact it was a very strange feeling to have such intimacy with her, he almost removed his hand from her warm flesh as it felt forbidden.

"Look I'm sorry, Mae. I understand how bored you must be stuck at home on your own all day."

She turned to him and embraced him, he was taken aback at first and then smile, tightening his arms around her. Mae pressed her head against his chest, she could here the fluttering of his heart, it soothed her, it was like old times.

"I just get the impression that these days you don't want to spend time with me. Maybe you should have brought someone else to this function. Somebody like Sergeant Nash." Sid's eyes widened, but he said nothing, he couldn't.

She knows! Does she know? Why would she say Valerie? She must...

He swallowed hard and pulled her to him even tighter.

"If I've got to be at this thing then there's nobody I'd rather be her with than you, Mae."

They looked at each other and they smile, she kissed him, it was nice, familiar.

"Thank you for bringing me, Sid." She said and then laughed as they sipped their champagne and walked away from the seclusion of the corner, "Besides I bet she's sick of the sight of you anyway."

Sid swallowed hard and almost choked on his champagne.

"Seeing your old miserable face at work everyday would be enough to put anybody off." She laughed again.

Sid grinned and then quickly downed his champagne, before swiftly seized another full flute from a passing waiter.

"So, where are all these important people you were talking about?" Sid teased.

She sneered at him playfully and then surveyed the room.

"Oh look there's SCTV news anchor, Rex Redford." Mae gasped pointing excitedly.

"Don't point, Mae." Sid looked around anxiously, "It's embarrassing."

"Oh Sid, Look!" She swooned, "It's Bret Lennox!"

Sid glanced over to the centre of the lobby, where sure enough Hollywood's own Bret Lennox stood surrounded by young females all of them pushing and showing to get close to him. He wore a bright cerise suit, and sunglasses and every few seconds would check his reflection in gigantic golden lizard that clung to a pillar that rose up to the ceiling, making sure that his slicked black hair had not fallen out of place.

"He'd be at the opening to an envelope that one."

"Oh but he's cute."

"You and Rich need together, he's the chairman of the Bret Lennox fan club."

"Stop teasing." Mae chuckled.

"I mean look at him!" Sid griped, "Wearing sunglasses inside, what a dick!"

"Emmanuelle M'Caw!" Mae shrieked, startling a few unsuspecting guests next to them.

"Who?" Sid asked confused, looking around.

"There! Look!" She pointed to a small, wiry looking man, lipstick glossing his pert lips, a shock of blue hair sporting from the top of his head as he stood looking bored and lackadaisical as several people commenting on his beautiful macaw feathered coat.

"Who the hell is that freak?" Sid whined.

"He's a world famous fashion designer, Sid!" Mae shook her head in disgust.

A group of men from the far corner of the room caught Sid's eye and one of them nodded at him and Sid smiled back.

"Who's that?" Mae asked.

"That's Dr Flint, the head of Oakland Institute and was the man in charge of Eric."

"Oh!" Said Mae and there was a silence between them that seemed to last a while. Neither of them had discussed Eric since he had escaped.

"Who are the other stiffs he's talking too?" Mae asked.

"All boffins!" Sid said, trying to remember their names, "Calloway, Copeland and Cumberbatch, I believe."

"Not very exciting are they?" Mae groaned.

"Well, it gets better." Sid nudged her to a bunch of elderly men guffawing. "A meeting of the minds, Mayor Luger, Tobias Thorn..."

"Who's Tobias thorn?"

"He was Mayor of Crimson for what seemed like eternity."

"Well, he looks like he's ready to keel over." Mae scoffed.

"The old fellow in the wheelchair though, I have no idea who that is."

They stared over at the pale pile of shrivelled up flesh that sat in a wheelchair, cackling away at what Mayor Luger had just said. A tall, gaunt man stood behind the wheelchair, hand gripping the handles tightly, his piercing eyes fluttering around the room uneasily.

"That would Mr Grey, I believe." Said a voice from behind them, they swivelled on the spot and were faced by the smiling monocled face of Sebastian d'Urberville.

"Good evening Detective!"

His thick, white moustache, contorting into a friendly smile.

"Lord d'Urberville." Sid shook his hand, "Nice to see you again."

"And is this your beautiful wife?"

232

"Yes, Mae, this is Lord Sebastian d'Urberville."

She offers her hand and he kissed it, his moustache lapping at her hand like a paintbrush made her titter.

"You look very smart indeed, Lord... erm, Mister Lord. What do I call you?"

"You can call me anything you like as long as you call me, my dear."

They both laughed, Sid rolled his eyes and took another sip of champagne.

"It's a beautiful suit you are wearing." Mae smiled, her eyes dazzled by a row of medals hung on his chest.

"Oh this old thing." d'Urberville chuckled, "This is old mess uniform. I brush it off for special occasions."

"Wouldn't have thought that the opening of a casino was a special occasion." Sid scoffed.

"Well, it beats being stuck in watching reruns of the Wheel of Fortune doesn't it."

Mae laughed again, Sid could tell that she found the old man very charming.

"So who is this Mr Grey?" Sid asked.

"I'm not entirely sure what he does, I know he's got his fingers in lots of pies back in the land of Blighty. But couldn't tell you what pies, I only know him by name."

"And what's the name of that miserable looking vulture pushing him?" Sid asked as his eyes watched as the sinister looking man pushed him along to another group of people.

"Mr Raptor." Whispered d'Uberville.

"Strange name." Sid scoffed.

"Strange man."

"Why are you whispering?" Mae asked.

"Well, my dear, I have heard that he has very attuned ears. I wouldn't want him to hear me gossiping about him would you?"

Mae looked over at his protruding beaklike nose, and two dark menacing flitting from side to side under a hideous scowl.

"No, I guess I wouldn't." She said with a shudder.

"They say he has the ears of a hawk!" d'Urberville whispered into Mae's ear.

"Okay, okay." Sid scoffed, "He's just trying to scare you, Mae."

d'Urberville took out his monocle and breathed on it before wiping it on a handkerchief before stuff it Ito his pocket.

"I just repeat the things I hear, Detective."

"A dangerous game."

"Indeed!" d'Urberville said while positioning his monocle back in place.

They gazed around the room again in silence, people watching.

"Oh there's Sophia Valentine." d'Urberville sighed sending sorrow for her.

"I'm surprised she's got the nerve to show her face."

"Oh come now, Detective. You can't blame her for the sins of her husband now can you?"

"If you believe she didn't know what her husband was up too then you're..."

"I concede, Detective!" d'Urberville interrupted, "I can sense the scars are still fresh so I won't reopen them." There was an uncomfortable pause for a few seconds when d'Urberville spoke again.

"There's William Fairfax." d'Urberville nodded over at an attractive man in a light suit, with long blonde air standing very close to a man in a dark suit with olive skin and an ugly scar running down his left cheek.

"And who would that be?" Sid asked.

"Another ponce from my homeland. Bloody pillow biter that one. Seems he is getting very cosy with Frankie Fazzini."

"And who is Frankie Fazzini?" Mae asked.

"A crook from Sanctuary City, owns a string of his own casino's over there. Probably here to check out the competition." Explained Sid.

"Oh isn't this fun!" Mae squealed, smiling from ear to ear, "You seem to know everyone, Lord d'Urberville."

"I do like to keep a breast of things, my dear. But there is one person here that I don't know."

"That does surprise me." Sid said with a roll of his eyes and a swig of his drink.

"Who would that be?" Mae asked.

"That fella over there! The one by the foot of the stairs, all on his lonesome."

They glared at the suave looking man, with love skin and slick dark hair with flashes of grey on either side, dressed exquisitely in a tuxedo, that was topped off with a voluptuous red rose. He too appeared to be people watching, a cigar clenched between his fingers while he sipped on what appeared to be water.

"Seen him around mind." d'Urberville added, "But no idea who he is. Doesn't appear to be a fan of champagne either."

There was a deal of excitement as several new guests arrived and on seeing Elizabeth Martel sashay, provocatively into the room, immediately gaining everyone's attention, in a figure hugging maroon dress, that was cut down to her navel allow the ripeness of her pale flesh to be displayed. She whipped her ginger hair out of her face and let go of her fox fur that shrouded her exposed shoulders. It fell behind her and was snatched up immediately before it hit the floor by her valet, Reginald. A little person with a face wrinkled like an old prune, but dressed very smartly in matching maroon tailcoat.

"Must dash." d'Urberville announced before approached the newcomer, "Lovely to meet you Mrs Graham." He called over his shoulder.

"Who the hell is that!" Mae announced wide-eyed, automatically drawn to her impressive cleavage.

"That's Elizabeth Martel." Sid answered, he too was having some trouble tearing his eyes away from that dress.

"Who?"

"She owns The Martel Circus."

"Well, she seems to have brought two big tops with her."

Sid nearly choked on his champagne and they laughed out loud. They watched for a little while as d'Urberville greeted her, obviously old friends he escorted off to another corner of the room, Mae giggled at Reginald as he scuttled after them. More guests piled in and Sid scoffed shaking his head, "It would seem they're letting anybody in to this shindig!"

Mae averted her gaze to the door and witnessed a black man in a snakeskin suit and fur coat, a wide smile spread across his face.

"He looks happy." Mae chuckled.

Two tall ladies joined him and took an arm each. Each one of them wearing very little in the way of even gown, their large silicone breasts unmoving as the giggled falsely.

"Oh, no wonder he looks happy." Said Mae, "Who is this guy?"

"That's Charles Samuels, they call him 'Cheshire' Charles on account of that ridiculous grin that's always painted on his face. He's the owner of the Cat's Whiskers club, and the neighbourhood pimp."

Mae's eyes widened, "So they are his... girls."

Sid nodded.

"What are there names?"

"No idea!" Shrugged Sid, even though he did. That was a conversation he didn't wish to have with his wife how he knew the names of two strippers/hookers. He wasn't

237

going to tell her that these two under dresses ladies were Honey and Loretta.

"How could they let these type of people into an event like this? Disgusting!" Mae hissed, her face contorting with outrage.

Sid smiled at her, she looked at him and asked him what he thought was so amusing.

"You're now seeing the 'real' celebrities of Studd City, Mae. The lowlives that I have to deal with on a daily basis." Before Mae could reply she heard Sid groan and a small sinister looking man scuttled in clad in a tweed suit and a trilby, slanted forward to through his pock covered face. He grabbed a champagne flute and disappeared into the mass of people. Mae looked at Sid for confirmation of this latest guest.

"Cockney Stan." Mae looked on taken aback.

"Stanley Cox, he's a legitimate London cockney. Thief and all-round nasty little worm."

More strode in, Robert Devine walked in like he owned the place (technically he used to), Famu dressed smartly for a change, bringing up the rear. An East Asian party followed slowly, the leader a middle aged man with long black hair and moustache, dressed in traditional gold and red garbs that were decorated with dragons, His hands concealed in wide sleeves. Mae swooned over his beautiful ensemble.

"That's Motou Chun-Po, A businessman from China. He's new to the city, I believe he is currently here to do business with Devine."

Motou was shadowed by two younger individuals, one male one female, with matching stern looks and traditional garbs in black velvet.

"I believe they are his children." Sid added as they congregated around Devine and helped themselves to champagne.

Beatrix Roux of Masquerade's burlesque club entered last, fashionably late, a beautiful long sleeved, black dress that consumed the ground around her giving the illusion that she had now feet and was almost gliding across the polish floor. Her jet black hair was curled and styled meticulous giving her the look of a gothic gorgon. Holding her by the arm tightly was a very tall, almost Amazonian looking, she looked intimidating. A perfect figure was hugged by a magenta leather dress, and matching stiletto heels. A mass of bright red hair clashed against the magenta of her garment, cascaded down the one side of her face as if concealing a secret.

Sid was about to tell her who the lasted guests were when he was surprised to see her gazed had been averted to the staircase and her face was and explosion of awe as a beautiful women appeared on the stair, where she seemed to wait for everyone to notice her.

The constant babble of voices and singing of glasses soon died down and the massive room was eerily filled with silence, all eyes fixed on this beauty that had appeared before them. She smiled almost bashfully, a natural beauty in a long silk evening gown of emerald, trimmed with various

239

elaborate gold fringes. Her black hair plaited loosely and allows to fall casually on her right shoulder.

Mae's eyes were drawn to the golden colour that she wore around her neck, a long golden chain hanging from it appeared to move in the light. There was something peculiar about the collar and chain that seemed to disappear over her bare shoulder. From her manage point she could not make out what it was.

"Ladies and Gentlemen!" She spoke, her accent almost German sounded, Sid leaned over to whisper in Mae's ear and inform her that this was indeed their hostess and that she was from Switzerland.

"I would like to start by saying how ecstatic I am. And if I'm completely a little relieved!" There was a whirl of laughter that drifted through the crowd and she lifted her hand, but not for silence but to fidget with her collar. The crowd became silent again and watched on intently as she seemed to scratch the back of her neck, then tug gently on the chain.

"We were both unsure whether you would all come to this the grand opening of my new venture, Geko's Casino!" There was a flurry of applause, which died again after a few seconds.

"I say we." She chuckles still tugging on the thing golden chain, "My business partner seems to be a little reluctant in making an appearance tonight." She smiled at the people below, all of them looking back her with contorted brows of confusion.

"I am Greta Geko and this is Bobo!" A large tokay gecko clambered over her shoulder and scurried over the plunging neckline of her dress before settling on her collarbone as if it were a living brooch. The crowd gasped and then applauded again, as the wide eyed lizard stared at them inquisitively, a small emerald encrusted collar around his own neck, joined to his master by the chain.

"Say hello Bobo." Greta said and a handful of the guests said it back in unison, which made everyone laugh including Greta who stroked her fingers across Bobo's lumpy sea foam coloured flesh.

"I welcome you all, eat, drink and be merry and above all! Spend lots of money!"

Music erupted and Greta disappeared into the lobby and was swarmed by a line of guests clambering to talk to her.

Robert Devine stood alone sipping his champagne and watching on intently as the rabble gathered around this new foreign beauty that had arrived in Studd City. He smiled to himself, realising how much of the Greta family fortune had been transferred into his bank account and wondered how much she had left. Famu stood several feet behind him engrossed in a cell phone conversation.

Devine scanned the room saw all the familiar faces and some unfamiliar ones too. He noticed Detective Graham and his wife filling their faces with more canapés, and scoffed. He did love surveying a crowded room and realising that he was the most powerful man in it, which was usually every room he was ever in. His thin lips slid into a smug smile and he looked very content.

Famu appeared at his shoulder and leant down to his level, "Mr Devine." He murmured.

"I hope you're not going to be whispering sweet nothings in my ear all evening." He sighed.

"No, Sir, it's just, there has been development."

"Go on."

"They've got him."

"Really!" Devine smiled again, the mischievous grin of a boy with a magnifying glass on a sunny day. "Apparently there was..."

"I don't wish to know anymore details, Famu. Especially not here, you should know that!"

"Yes Sir, of course."

"I think you should go and oversee the situation personally."

"Of course." Famu nodded and then hovered around behind Devine for a few seconds unsure of what to do.

"Go Famu." Devine sighed with a roll of his dark eyes that resembling beetle's shells.

"Are you sure, Sir?"

"Yes, I am capable of taking care of myself."

"Yes, of course."

"I will be along tomorrow morning, and Famu?"

Famu moved in closer realising that Devine wished to whisper something to him that was not for other's ears.

"Don't kill him. I would like that honour."

"Sir." Famu nodded.

"Oh, and the mask."

"The mask?"

"Leave it on. I would also like to have that honour too."

"Of course."

Famu disappeared out of the door as Devine smiled again, wider than even 'Cheshire' Charles, everything was going in his favour. That was until he saw a familiar face through the crowd of people, it was Spider and he grinned a mouthful of sparkling golden teeth at Devine. The smile dissolved from Devine's face and was replaced with a scowl as Spider made his way toward him, clad in a garish leopard print suit.

"Yo, Mister Dee-vine!" He bellowed, "How's it hanging?" He grabbed at Devine's hand and shook it.

Devine retrieved his hand quickly and glared at him.

"What do you think you are doing here?" He growled.

"Celebrating of course!" He cackled, downing a champagne.

"You're not supposed to bringing attention to yourself. You're supposed to be laying low!"

"Hey, a guy has too get out once in a while, let it all hang out you know?"

Devine looked him up and down, and his nose writhed in distaste from the red suede shoes he was wearing to the garish leopard print suit he was wearing with no shirt.

"Oh you're worried about this get up?" Spider laughed, "Thank I'm drawing attention to myself? Man, take a look around, I'm undressed for this gig."

"You need to leave!" Devine hissed through gritted teeth, "There are people here that could make life very difficult for us."

"Okay, okay." Spider rolled his eyes, "I'm going. I'm going to work over bible boy with a pair of pliers and a blowtorch anyway." He said as he attempted to leave, Devine grabbed his arm.

"No!" He whispered, it hissed into Spider's ear like leaking gas. "Tomorrow, we will both pay him a visit."

"But why?"

"Because I want him to suffer through the night..."

"Oh I'll make him suffer alright."

"I don't trust you." Devine bit and the two of them stared at each other, Devine became aware that prying eyes may be peering at them so he let go of his arm and Spider brushed off and adjusted his suit.

"Yo, watch the threads man!"

"You are too reckless. I can't trust that you wouldn't go too far. I want this to take time, to make the bastard feel that he won't see the morning, to install that fear in him. Only then after we have taken hope will he be ripe for the picking."

"Yeah, whatever you say. So tomorrow then yeah?"

"Tomorrow!" Devine whispers and Spider disappears out of the front door surfing an eating champagne flute into an unexacting waiter's hands.

Devine looked around the room, his eyes flitting back and forth suspiciously, surely some of those prying eyes had seen them, that could spell trouble for Devine, who was hoping this would run smoothly without having talk his way out of anything. Devine breathed a sigh of relief as all the familiar faces were engrossed in their conversations and he sipped at his champagne again. Then he looked over at Detective Graham and noticed that he was looking over in his vicinity with a curious look on his face, their eyes locking for a moment before Greta Geko waltzed across their line of vision as she greeted Elizabeth Martel, the gaggle that followed her blocking the inquisitive detective's view.

"Are you okay, Sid?" Mae asked, "You look like you've just seen a ghost."

"I think I have." He murmured.

Chapter 30

The distant sound of dripping water roused Vatican from a long unintentional slumber. His eyelids felt heavy, it was an effort to even try and open them, when he finally did he was met by a dark haze. His other senses had now also seemed to be have woken up and his nostrils convulsed with the dreadful aroma of dead animal flesh that seem to linger in the air. He lifted his throbbing head, the rear of it felt strange as though it was filled with broken shards, that swept around his skull with the slightest of movements.

"C-con...concussion...neh!" He mumbled, slurring with a mouthful of cotton.

His eyelids flickered rapidly and slowly the haze that hung in front of his eyes lifted to reveal a dark depressing looking slaughterhouse. In the distance he could make out the hollowed out carcasses of pigs dangling from hooks through a curtain of transparent strips of plastic that where covered in stains. Stains that appeared to be brown, Vatican soon realised that it was not dirt but the dried blood of animals. He held the vomit in somehow and then looked around at the large damp space. The floor covered with once white tiles,

246

some of them cracked, he stared at them wondering if his skull resembled them. Drain holes dripped water as though the area had been hosed down earlier on in the evening, some of the tiles still remained stained pink by the animal blood.

He tried to move and realised that he couldn't, not because he was in pain but it seemed that some confines were preventing him from doing so. He tried to move his arms and realised that they were being held out either side of him, being restrained around his wrists by some kind of metal shackle and as he fidgeted and tugged at them, he heard the singing of chains, a sound that carried around the old slaughterhouse's high ceiling, before escaping out of the huge Vatican shaped hole in the skylight above. He clenched his fists and realised he was gloveless, he tugged away at the shackles again and excoriating pain stabbed at his wounds in his shoulder and side. His teeth gnawed down on each other uncomfortably as he grimaced with unrelenting pain. Luckily for him the blood from Anti Christ's attack had congealed, clotting the seepage of any more of his precious bodily fluid. His head lolled forward, he realised now that his chest was bare, his surcoat and under armour had been removed. Earpiece removed, most likely destroyed. He moved his whole body, his legs ached after being made to kneel on the hard surface as he was suspended by the two lengths of chain that he could only resumed were fashion to each wall. The utility belt and thigh holster was also gone.

"They've taken everything." He murmured, realising that they must have taken his mask too, and it was only a matter of time before the world knew his true identity, he sighed and looked down at his knees that scraped the tiles each time he moved, but being thankful that at least they allowed him to keep his dignity by not removing his leggings or boots. He hung in the gloom waiting, for what he did not know, would they kill him?

Probably. They wouldn't go to all this trouble to just threaten me. No sir, this is the real deal, one of those situations that you thought could one day happen, took your eye of the ball Thomas. And paid for it.

There was the sound of voices from behind the plastic curtain. He heard a loud chattering in Mandarin and a gargantuan Asian man shuffled past the dirty veil, wearing nothing but a blood-soaked apron and a large meat cleave gripped in his hand. He was yelling angrily in his mother tongue, seemingly to himself, as he unhooked a hanging pig carcass and dropped it over his shoulder. He stopped and turned and peered into the vast room where Vatican was knelt, he one eye seemed wide open staring at him, while the other seemed closed as though the beast of a man was winking at him. He turned to his left and shouted something. It had been many years since Vatican had needed to use Mandarin, he was rusty at best after all this time but to him it sounded like the man had annoyed that Vatican was conscious. The man scoffed and waddled away, numbing under his breath.

Boris, Dallas and Famu steeped through the curtains and into the room, Dallas was shuffling his playing cards back into some order then stuffing them into the back pocket of his jeans. They all looked pretty pleased with themselves, Vatican scowled at them and even if they didn't realise, it would have been a very different situation if he hadn't have been ambushed by Anti Christ.

Famu spoke, his booming voice echoing throughout the warehouse, Vatican had met Famu before and was now confused as to why he had joined forces with two Web-heads. Maybe he was the mastermind behind all of this, to gain revenge for Vatican making a fool out of him.

"Can you hear me Vatican?" Famu spoke again. Vatican nodded.

"Good!" Famu smiled.

They stood in front of him and grinned sadistically at him, with smiles so sharp, they looked ready to take their pound of flesh from him.

"Why weren't we allowed to remove his mask?" Dallas asked.

"That's what the boss said." He shrugged, "Said he wanted to have the pleasure."

"Fair enough!" Nodded Dallas.

So Famu isn't in charge then. So who?

"Pity, I bet he has a pretty face, this one." Boris chuckled.

Then it brings it back to Spider. It has to be.

249

"So, Vatican!" Famu smirked, "You've been a thorn in the ass of our boss for too long..."

"Isn't it a thorn in his side?" Dallas interrupted. Famu glared at him.

"Isn't it pain in the ass?" Boris added.

"Does it fucking matter!" Famu barked.

The other two shook their heads nonchalantly.

"So..." Famu began but was cut off again by Boris. "When do we get to hit him?" He asked with a twinkle in his eye.

"Fuck it!" Famu cried, "I had a whole fucking speech laid out for this and you guys have made me lose my train of thought."

"Sorry comrade!" Boris apologised.

"Please, be our guest." Dallas said gesturing to him that the floor was his.

"No! You've ruined it now." He snapped, almost petulantly.

"So, we are free to hit him now?" Boris asked. Famu sighed and nodded.

Boris smiled and approached Vatican unleashing a meaty right hand that connected with Vatican's face. His head whipped back and forth as thousands of tiny stars erupted like fireworks before his eyes.

The look of sheer elation on Boris' face was evident as he drilled Vatican's face with unrelenting force, the sound of his flesh splitting under the impact of his rigid knuckles. After a few minutes of tenderising Vatican's face, Boris was forced to stop to catch his breath.

"Lightweight!" Laughed Famu.

"Fuck...You!" Boris gasped, "I'm just out of practice." Vatican amazingly still conscious, shook of the effects of Boris' blows. His face was already beginning to puff up in places and a trickle of blood ran from his nostrils. He spat violently, sending a wad of bloodied saliva hurtling towards the tiles below. He scoffed and grinned at Boris, showing off a gleaming pink teeth. "Shit, Boris." Dallas mocked, "Don't think you got

through to him."

Famu and Dallas laughed at a now scowling Boris.

"Oh yeah!" He growled and again balled up his fist, "I guess I'm going to have to hit him harder then."

He ploughed into Vatican's face again, his head rocking back and forth once more, blackness appearing before his eyes every so often before being immediately bought back to the moment by another blow. Boris staggered back and hacked, he tried to get his wind again, dry heaving and almost tumbling over.

The slaughterhouse was filled with laughter again as Dallas patted Boris on the back, "Let me show you how it's done, Comrade!"

Dallas stepped forward and smiled at Vatican who was now looking at him a little woozy, his face now hand deep lacerations a blood was seeping out of his nose and chin.

"He hits like a child." Vatican murmured.

Famu and Dallas laughed out load and Boris was about to go for Vatican again, but the sudden movement had caused him to dry heave again.

Dallas flexed both sets of fingers and practiced a few jabs at the air like some sparing boxer.

"Lets see how you handle someone that's ambidextrous." Dallas grinned and began jabbing at Vatican's face with both fists. His blows were more precise than Boris' wild hammers and Vatican felt every blow meet its designated target. Dallas bobbed and weaved around the helpless vigilante strike him in various place on the face and ribcage. There was the sound of bone cracking as pain exploded in Vatican's torso and he grimaced with discomfort.

"Oh we have a winner." Panted Dallas as he lay another body shot to the same place, over and over again. Dallas finally backed off out of breath too, but the damaged had already been done. Vatican's head lolled forward, and blood dripped onto his chest. His side was already bruising and Vatican was struggling with his breathing.

Broken rib or ribs, difficult to tell. Must be pressing on my lung.

Vatican again refused to show any sign of weakness and after again shaking of the cobwebs that seemed to be constantly spun in his head he gazed at his captors and tried to smile. It hurt to smile.

"You gotta hand it to him though." Famu said as he removed his jacket, "He's one tough son of a bitch."

252

Famu unbuttoned his cuffs and slowly rolled up his shirt sleeves, revealing two massive forearms that resembled two thick slabs of meat.

"Aren't you, Vatican?" Famu smiled showing off the biggest fists Vatican had ever laid eyes on, "But even the toughest nut will crack eventually."

Famu drove his gigantic fist into Vatican's face, his broke on impact, he swallowed a mass of blood and finally he blacked out.

Chapter 31

It was the early hours and with a belly full of warming coffee and his blanket wrapped tightly around him Burt had reluctantly nodded off in front of the computer. A gust of cold night air had drifted in through a crevice in the old church's cellar. It bit at his wrinkled cheeks and he stirred, then bolted upright in angst.

"What time is it?" He asked himself scrambling to remove his arm from the confines of the blanket to access his watch.

"Must have dropped off, but for how long?" He asked himself, wiping his eyes and slotting his glasses back into place and staring at the computer screen that had automatically switched to a screensaver and he watched for a moment as colourful pixelated balls bounced around the screen. He activated the mouse and the screen burst into life again, a red dot pulsated indicating the whereabouts of Vatican.

"That's odd!" Burt said with a curious scowl, "He appears to be in the same place as where I left him?" He tapped at the screen vigorously as if that would make any difference to the situation. "Maybe it's a glitch with the system or the tracker." He told himself before taking a swig of his coffee and recoiling at its coldness, placed the mug back down on the table.

"Maybe he has circled round and ended back in the same place." Burt shrugged, "Its possible."

He checked his phone and there were no missed calls, no messages on the pager either.

Burt didn't have to search his gut long to know that something was wrong. Quickly he found Vatican's number (under 'V' in the cell phone) that would connect him with his handsfree earpiece. Nothing, the line was dead.

Burt felt something in the pit of his stomach stir, a sick feeling of anxiety seemed to emerge from his bowels like some kind of acid indigestion.

"Something's wrong!" Burt murmured franticly trying the number over and over again.

He rose from the chair the blanket dropped on the floor when the pager started to beep. He looked down at it and it informed him that Vatican was indeed trying to contact him. He breathed a sigh of relief and sat back down on the chair and tried the phone again but nothing, there was still no answer, the line was still dead. But yet the pager continued to beep, he pressed the button to deactivate it but it started straight up again.

"What is going on here?" Burt puzzled, "Why doesn't he answer?"

The pager continued to beep and Burt grabbed it and switched it off before hurtling across the cellar. He was annoyed at himself for not knowing what was going on.

"If you'd have stopped awake you'd know what was happening you stupid old bastard." He growled.

He rose again from his seat and thumped the table, everything situated on it rattled and swayed.

"Call the police." He announced, "Yes, call the police." He reached for his cell and hesitated, "What are you talking about you old fool! What are you going to tell them?"

He sighed heavily, not knowing what to do. He had never gone this long without hearing from Vatican, he was starting to worry and the worst kind of thoughts had managed to creep into his head.

He's dead. That's why his tracker is lying dormant. He's dead! Good God!

Burt felt dizzy and sick, he lent on the table to stop himself passing out.

"What do I do?"

There was a subtle sound of rapping coming from the door that led to the sewers. Burt's eyes saucer and slowly he turned to face the metal door. The rapping continued on the other side. Burt stepped away from the desk and stared at the door, the knocking on the other side became more and more vigorous. Burt's first thought was that something had indeed happened to Vatican and now they were looking to infiltrate his base.

"Not on my watch!" He growled and made his way over to the weapons rack that homed several types of martial arts weaponry, from sais, bo staffs, tons and various swords. "I'm not going down without a fight." And with that he retrieved a katana from its stand and relieved it of its sheath and waddled slowly towards the door that was now seemingly being kicked.

He adjusted his grip around the handle of the katana and crept forward towards the door. The banging stopped abruptly, Burt too stopped in his tracks and waited.

Maybe it's Thomas? Maybe he is injured!

This spurred him on to reach for the locks and think about sliding it out of its slot, but something caused his hand to tremble and hang in the air of the bolt.

"What if it's not Thomas?" He murmured and his bulbous bottom lip quivered.

Then a voice spoke, a gentle cooing of a voice, a child's voice. "Hello? Is anyone there?" The voice asked.

"A child?" Burt said aloud and was obviously heard on the other side of the door because the child called louder and banged on the door again.

"There's someone there isn't there? I can hear you!" The voice called. "Vatican needs help!"

That was all Burt need to hear and he cared not for who or what was standing on the other side waiting for him, all he knew was that his fears had become reality and his friend need to help. Burt flung back the bolts and still keeping a firm grip of the katana he swept open the door as quickly as he could. Penny was standing in front of him, Vatican's pager in her outstretched hand.

"Who are you?" Burt asked, his hand naturally loosening up on the handle of the sword.

"I'm Penny... It's Vatican they've got him." She said through teary eyes and trembling lips, "They're killing him!" Burt's stomach lurched again, the words that he feared the most had just spilt from this child's lips and it terrified him. But he couldn't let her know how scared he was, she needed comfort too, he could see that and autopilot took over and he became that loving father figure of Burt again.

"You'd better come in and tell me all about it."

Chapter 32

"What is..." Whispered Vatican.

All there seemed to be left was darkness. Vatican felt like his mind had become disconnected from his body, as though he had become detached from reality, floating in a void of nothingness. If truth be told the fists of his captors continued to rain down on him like jagged chunks of ice in a hailstorm. Vatican could not feel any of the blows that fore his flesh and chipped away at his bones for he had become numb to the torture and continued to sit in box of blackness.

Visions exploded in front of mind's eyes, imagery of noises that meant nothing to him. A red rose grasped in his hand, his fingers wrapped around the long stem ever so tightly, reluctant to release it even though its severed thorns punctured his flesh. No matter how tightly he squeezed the silky red petals continued to fall as blood seeped through his fingers. A wheelchair flashed before his eyes, rusted and forgotten in a cobwebbed nook. The image of his mother lying on the floor, heavily pregnant and dead from an overdose caused by years of abuse. An X-ray of a as shattered spine. A bottle opener flicks of the top of an ice cold beer and spins in the air, it catches the lights and shines in his eyes, causing him to squint, there is gold shining in his eyes, gleaming like bars of bullion. A bat's wing spreads out before him, its leather look consumes him flapping at his face, the texture cold and sickening as it touches his face. A diamond sits in the palm of his hand, it is reluctantly released and it spirals as it falls into the abyss, it sounds like the hissing of a snake as it disappears.

What is this?

He spoke to himself, his voice echoing in the nothingness, reverberating around walls that he could not see, the invisible walls of his mind.

What are these visions that sting my eyes?

A masked face growls at him, saliva dripping from its wearers cracked teeth.

WHAT...

The kiss of a beautiful woman, her lips look familiar to him. He fights an urge to stop but does not, a guilty feeling as though he has been seduced by a forbidden fruit.

IS...

The crimson crucifix of his surcoat, swivels and settles upside down, blood drips onto it and is smeared by an unknown hand, the surcoat is torn and ripped to shreds a scream of paining thunders through the corridors of his mind.

THIS?

The screaming face of Burt in pain tears at his heart, the pain of that vision worse than any pain his physical body is

260

receiving. *NO!*

His screams were bloodcurdling and there was nothingness again.

What is this? What is going on... Is it the future I see, the past?

"It is both." Says a voice, muffled and weak.

Sato! Master Sato is that you?

"My time is short here, Thomas. Ask what you need to ask, before long I will be gone."

But why? Why must you be gone? What are these visions? They hurt, the pain... How come you have left me.

"The connection between us is now weak, I no longer have the power to hold it."

I don't understand.

"You will, one day you will understand why, but that is not important now. Ask the important question before I go." *The... visions! What are the visions?*

"I have answered this question, Thomas. You need to concentrate and not waste this time we are given. The visions are the past and the future that you see. You may never see these things again or maybe you will. The past cannot be changed, this we know. But the future lies within your hands, these visions are mere sketches of what could be."

But, Burt... He... he was in pain...

"This is not the question you should be asking. You are wasting our time here, Thomas. Concentrate."

I don't understand, I don't know what the question is!

"Concentrate."

The same visions play through his head again in high speed, flashing passed before his eyes rapidly like the carriages of speeding train. They blur and merge and Vatican feels as though his brain will explode, he screams to hold on to the visions, to find the question that needs to be answered. "It's too late." Sato sighs and the link is severed.

Sato? Master Sato? No... I don't know the question you were asking for, I...

A red ruby glows in the darkness, it seems too far away to grasp, Vatican feels as though he is reaching for it, his fingertips skimming over its smooth surface. A sound sends a shudder down his back, the sounds of feathers ruffling and then beating the stale earthy air.

The question!

The wings flap hard and slow sending a gust of that foul stench of death towards him, caressing his face. The glowing ruby becomes an eye and the eyes grows nearer in the darkness, accompanied by that hypnotic thrashing of wings.

The Black Crane! What is... The Black Crane!

The question was asked but it was too late and the menace known only in the dark corners of his mind comes for him, shrieking with terror his sees the beak, it's long curved talon, the red eye and then... Another fist is drove into Vatican's swollen face, his eyes open as much as his bloated eyelids will allow and he is in the slaughterhouse, still shackled and still face to face with his tormentors.

"I think we're finally getting to him." Famu pants almost out of breath, his knuckles raw and peppered with fresh blood.

"Did you hear him cry out?" Dallas laughed, "Been a few hours since he made any noise."

"At least he's not dead." Boris scoffed driving a well placed boot into Vatican's ribs.

Vatican grimaced and suddenly the pain was all to real.

"Tell me something, Boris is it?" Vatican stuttered. Boris nodded with a bemused furrow of the brow.

"Which soccer tots team do you play for?" Vatican smiled defiantly as blood dribbled down his chin.

Boris looked confused as Famu and Dallas laughed and pointed at him like some court jester that doesn't realise he is the punchline.

"I don't get it." Shrugged Boris, "But you've made me feel stupid so I'll have to hit you harder!" Boris ploughed him in the face and again the blackness of unconsciousness was with Vatican.

At least there is no pain in the dark.

The light shimmers through the gigantic stained glass window of St. Vincent's church, the light brings with it all the colours of the spectrum bathing him in peace and serenity.

What will my congregation say when they see my broken carcass up in the pulpit on Sunday? What will Father Lamont say?

He could feel no pain in his mediative state and unconsciousness was his friend, it allowed his mind to

263

wonder away from the dastardly scenes that were taking place at the slaughterhouse. But a part of his mind tells him that if he thinks he is turning up anywhere else but the bottom of the Hennig River come Sunday, then he's deluded.

What will happen to the good people of Studd City? The followers of St. Vincent's that have raised there is hope and have all banded together since I arrived? I can't worry about that, I must change my train of thought, negativity is not an option. Losing my grip now hat is happening to me is not an option. Dying... is not an option.

Ice cold water is thrust into Vatican's face and he is jolted awake once more. He exhales deeply in shock as water mixes with his blood and sends a pale pink mixture swirling down the drained of the slaughterhouse floor.

Dallas stands over him with an empty bucket in his hands, "Stay with us big guy, we're not even close to being finished."

His hand delves into the bucket, dipping his fingers in the dregs of water that remain before flicking it playfully at Vatican's face and laughing again. Another Flying fist from Boris collides with his cheekbone. Dallas drops the bucket and the singing of the metal on the tiles makes his eardrums ring, Dallas smashes him on the chin, rocking his head back and forth again as if it were no longer attached to a neck. Famu's left hand then right hand collide with his face and then stars dance around the inside of his eyelids again. The strikes keep coming relentlessly but oddly the individual behind the punch changes which each strike. His father, Ricky the bully from the orphanage, A young Xing, Spider,

Vinnie Valentine, Elvis Valentine, Father Lamont, Father Harrison, Sniff, former boxing champion 'Left Hook' Lewis Johnson, Robert Devine. He shakes his head to try and rid himself of these images but still they keep coming, but these are strange faces now, people or things he has never seen before, could these be people from his future? False faces, masked faces, looking at them, he hopes not.

More punches come faster and faster, a man in metal gas mask, a man in a torn Luchador mask, a masqueraded mask on a beautiful woman, a man with one eye, something green and glowing like radioactive sludge whips at his face, then Anti christ smiling over him striking him.

The screams inside his head rattle his skull as the faces change again, Detective Graham, Elliot, Penny... Burt! The people he trusts the most now unleashes their anger, tenderising the flesh of his face.

"No!" He screams and it all stops and there is only darkness again.

He hears the falling of footsteps as some approaches through the darkness, it is a version of himself attired as Vatican, a scowl on his face.

No...

The Vatican unleashes strike after strike, pummelling his face, bloody erupting from his face in vulgar spirts until his face is churned to nothing. Vaticans gasps for air again as he is revive by another ice cold blast from Dallas' rusty bucket.

"I think that's enough for one night, don't you?" Famu says.

265

Vatican looks at them and the only positive he can take from this scene is that they look completely exhausted.

They turn and walk away from Vatican, who's limp body hangs from the chains that shackle him, his body broken and bloodied, but he smiles and manages to call after them, "See you in the morning."

The trio stop as they reached those transparent strips that act as curtains and they all raise their eyebrows in shock and in someways respect. Then they smile and it is oh so very sadistic.

"You think that's it?" Asked Dallas, "We're just going to catch some Z's."

"Don't worry though Angel, the night shift is here." Famu grins as he holds open the curtain and the huge Chinese man appeared. The same giant of a man that crept passed the curtain hours ago, or was it days? Time has been lost to Vatican now and all that awaits him is death.

The trio left and the gigantic mass of Y'ao Hu approaches. He seemed to be wearing only loose fitting trousers that cut off just below the knee and his feet were bare, as was his chest that was only covered by a bloodstained apron. He carried with him a brown parcel that looked as though it was made of leather. Vatican swallowed hard as this behemoth grabbed a table and pulled it along the tiles which caused an horrendous sound. Hu did not take his eyes of Vatican and came to a halt in front of him, one eye looks wide and bloodshot the other almost closed in suspicion. He smiled at Vatican and spoke in Mandarin, each word whistling due to

266

the meagre amount of teeth his mouth was homing. A long great beard hung from his chin and soaked up fresh blood like an artist's paintbrush soaks up paint. Vatican could not understand what Hu was saying to him, his head was spinning and interpreting Mandarin was the last thing on his mind. Hu lay the parcel on the table and unravelled it to unveil an impressive collection of knives and cleavers, he smiled at Vatican and again his bald head crinkling with how ecstatic he was.

"You don't have to do this..." Vatican murmured on the verge of blacking out again.

Hu turned to the table, a bear of a man hunched over surveying his tools and then finally he retrieved a large cleaver and held it in the air, light gleamed of the blade and Vatican had settled in the darkness again.

Chapter 33

Detective Graham rolled over in bed, his own bed for a change. He stared at the ceiling, watching the shadows of crooked branches creep across it like witches fingers. He heard Mae stir, burrow down under the covers and sighed with contentment. Graham remained motionless until he noticed a change in her breathing and realised she had meandered into dreamland. He turned his attentions to her and watched as she breathed in and out calmly, her mass of red hair still curled from the evening's event. Graham turned his attentions back to the ceiling where those branches danced in the moonlight that surged it through the open curtains. He sighed a heavy sigh that seemed weighed down by guilt, he wanted so much to reach fro his pants and retrieve the crumpled packet of Freebirds in his pocket, but he'd promised Mae he had given up, that was yet more deception in an ever-increasing pile of lies. The truth is he had had an exceptional evening. He had enjoyed his wife's company immensely and it was as if they were dating again, it was like the early days of their relationship. In fairness there was nothing wrong with Mae whatsoever and Sid knew this, the sex was amazing when they had it, granted in recent years it was few and far between but amazing, but he never held that against her, there were times when he had come of several long shifts and he was in no fit state to perform either, they just both had busy lives and it took its toll on them. Sid knew he was to blame for the way he felt, that chain of guilt seemed to increase in length as he hauled it around everywhere he went. He was just a weak man that had his head turned by a beautiful young woman and wasn't man enough to say no, granted it was when his emotions were at their most vulnerable that he finally submitted to her feminine wilds, but still that was no excuse. Sid could still smell her scent on him, the evening did end with them making love, the curtains remaining open as Sid liked it so he could gaze upon the contours of her body that were gently kissed by the moonlight. Just the thought caused his manhood to stir again in his briefs, but it was a passing fancy, he was content, maybe he thought that he should realise that he was content and stop fucking around. He turned over and tried to close his eyes, he still saw Valerie when he closed them as if he should now feel guilt for sleeping with his wife instead of her, he growled with annoyance and writhed under the sheets facing away from the mass of red hair on the pillow next to him. His cellphone suddenly burst into life, illuminating the room and vibrating coarsely on the bedside table, the noise like the buzzing of an insect caused Mae to stir. Sid glanced at the screen and saw

269

the name Valerie Nash glaring back at him, he swiped it up and switched it off immediately, dropping it on the floor.

"No more," He whispered to himself, "this has to stop." Sidney Graham closed his eyes and slept.

Chapter 34

Burt Simmons hung up the phone and shook his head, "They still can't get in touch with Detective Graham." He said. Penny looked back at him, her dirty hands wrapped around a mug of hot cocoa.

"Don't know how you can trust those pigs." She scoffed.

"Tho..." Burt began to say and then thought better of it, pausing to clear his throat, "Vatican trusts him, he's a good cop and a good man."

"If you say so!" She shrugged, "Speak as I find myself. No pig ever helped me when I was need and believe me I've been indeed for years."

"Have you ever though that you're too proud to accept the help?" Burt smiled.

"No!" Penny bit and then felt a little embarrassed knowing that there might be some truth in what Burt was saying. She decided to stay sum and contours to enjoy the cocoa.

"I thought that he may have been able to help him." Burt sighed.

"So what do we do?" Penny asked anxiously, "It may be too late now."

Burt refused to think like that and he waddled over to the computer again.

"The last place you saw them was on the roof of a slaughterhouse in Old Chinatown, yes?"

"Yeah" She nodded, "But they have moved him somewhere. I helped Elliot back home, he was very weary and then made my way over here."

"How did you find us by the way?"

"Elliot told me."

"Elliot knows?"

Penny nodded and then shrugged, "There's not much he doesn't know."

"The eyes and the ears?" Burt smirked.

"Exactly!" Penny winked at him, "But in that time they could literally be anywhere now."

"I don't think they would risk moving him." Burt said turning his attentions to the computer and tapped away vigorously at the keyboard.

"Pretty good on that for an old dude aren't ya."

Burt laughed, "I've been taking evening classes for the last year or so."

Penny stood up and joined him at the desk, watching over his shoulder as he brought up a map again and a red dot contoured to glow in the same spot.

"What's that red dot?" Penny asked.

"That's Vatican, there is a tracker concealed in the heel of his boot."

"Shit!" She gasped and then her face glowed apologetically as Burt cut her a look.

"Thing is he hasn't moved, he's in exactly the same place, which could mean three things. He's lost his boot, he's imprisoned there or..." Burt couldn't bring himself to think it, let alone say it. Penny being the braver of the two finished his sentence.

"Dead!"

They looked at each other, Penny could see the pain in Burt's eyes and realised how much he cared for Vatican and she so wanted to help him, she also wish that someone would have that love burn in their eyes for her.

"We need to save him. It's down to us!" Penny announced, downing her cocoa and wiping away a brown moustache of foam away with the back of her hand.

"Where is he?"

"Well, according to the map," Burt typed away, "If I cross-reference it to a map of Study City he is at an established called, Hu Meats."

"I know where that is." Penny cried heading for the door and positioning her hood into place.

"But wait!" Burt called after her stopping her in her tracks, "what can we do?"

"Don't underestimate me dude." She snapped at him.

273

"I meant no disrespect, Penny, it's just I'm an old man and you're a kid."

"I may be just a kid, but I have seen things..." She snapped.

"I daresay you have." He interrupted in that sweet tone of his, making it impossible for Penny to annoyed at him, "We have all seen things, Penny. Terrible sights." Burt was lost in thought for a moment, a flashback to Vietnam perhaps or the suffering his wife, Doris went through in her last days.

"Are you okay?" Penny asked and it brought him back from whatever memory clouded his mind's eye.

"Yes, Penny." He smiled at her, "Right! What can we do?"

"I'll go and find out exactly where he is and try and help." Penny said carrying on towards the door with great purpose and grabbing the discarded katana that Burt had place on a table, "I'll take this, just incase." She smiled mischievously.

"Wait a minute!" Burt cried, "I can't let you take that!"

"Too late, Gramps!" She winked as she pulled open the door to the sewers, "I'll be okay I promise."

"What should I do?" Burt called rising from his chair.

"Keep trying that Detective friend of yours." She exited into the large sewer passage and called as she closed the door, "Don't worry about me, I'll be fine." The door was slammed shut and Burt shook his head as he sat down and began to laugh.

"Unfortunately that's what I do my dear, worry. It's my lot in life."

Chapter 35

Vatican drifted in and out of consciousness throughout the remainder of the early hours. He could hear the scrapping of metal on metal as Y'ao Hu sharpened his various tools, the constant clamour of those implements being discarded on the table echoed through the slaughterhouse. He heard the sickening squelching of the blades slicing through flesh, but he felt no pain. He had had learnt to shut out the pain through the mediation that he had learnt all those years ago at the top of Mount Lao by his master Sato. His body wanted to shut down from the pain but his mind was able to shut out any pain and remain in an unconscious state. But still Vatican heard that Hu cutting and could only imagine what horrors awaited for him when he once again became conscious, if he was lucky enough to do so that is.

Vatican had drifted into nothingness again the occasional sound of Hu's cackling and his rapid spitting of Mandarin as he enjoyed whatever torment he was causing the powerless Vatican. In the darkness the stained glass window of St. Vincent's Church stands before him, dazzling with shards of all colours of the spectrum, it seems to move as if it were a gigantic kaleidoscope. Each transparent shard is illuminated by a light on the other side, he imagined his face bathed in a comforting shroud of colours, suddenly the light was extinguished and with it disappeared the comforting dancing colours. There was darkness again and he watched as an elevator dropped in the darkness and stood there for a few moments before the doors opened up to reveal a gaping maw of raging flames. In the flames he saw buildings fall and glass exploding from skyscrapers, before the door closed again. The floor counter appeared above it in glowing red digits showing zero, the counter burst into life and cycled through numbers rapidly as the elevator tore up into the darkness and out of sight. Mandarin again chattered in his ears, but he still could not fathom what was being said.

The nothingness was again interrupted by a familiar sound, the haunting sound of digging. He could hear the sound of the spade striking the earth and scooping it up, then falling like heavy rainfall. He could smell the soil and damp grass, he shivered as if he was outside, stood next to a freshly dug grave. Suddenly the heavens opened up as lashed down above the scene with reckless abandon. The grave looked deep, a manmade crater that seemed bottomless. The cascading rain ran down its walls creating a watery tomb. The headstone was cheap sandstone and Vatican read the large words that were expertly chiseled into it... HERE LIES... "Vatican!" Came the call that echoed around his head. He ignored it and there was darkness again, the gravesite filled up, covered with circles where a spade had been used to flatten it. The headstone was covered by a splattering of mud and made it impossible for the name of who's grave it was to be read, he reached out with his hand (somewhere he heard the rattling of chains) He attempted to wipe away the mud and reveal the name.

"Vatican!" Came the call again, it echoed around his head and then there stood the stained glass window again.

"VATICAN!" Came the bellowing cry and the stained glass window exploded in a shower of shards, colourful sharp raindrops drenched him and then he was awake again. The pain was the first thing he noticed, everywhere hurt, his face felt like the face of his skull was broken and rattling underneath his skin. The wounds in his back and side throbbed irritatingly and he heard his tormentors calling his name. It was Boris mocking him.

"He's awake." Boris said.

"Good morning bright eyes." Dallas said.

Vatican opened his eyes, it was a struggle as his lids had become glued together by dried blood. The first thing he noticed was daylight, it hurt his eyes and he had to close them again and ready himself before he opened them again. Early morning sunlight cascaded through the broken hole in the skylight and shone down on him like a beacon as if he had been chosen by the lord himself. The table sat in front of him with pieces of freshly cut pig, Hu's tools were sat next the to various cuts of meat. Vatican breathed a sigh of relief, he realise that Hu had not picked away at his flesh with his instruments, nor sliced away limbs just for fun. No wonder Hu had been laughing Vatican thought, he knew now that he was just there to keep an eye on him through the night and maybe inflict a little psychological suffering while he was at it. He managed to do just that.

Famu stood back by the curtain on his cell phone, as Boris and Dallas stood gawping at him.

I must really be a mess if their faces are anything to go by.

The proprietor of the establishment was nowhere to be seen, Vatican deduced that he was merely a pawn in Spider's game, just someone paid off for the use of the location.

"So you survived the night then?" Asked Dallas.

"Do I have to call for room service or is Boris going to serve me breakfast in bed?" Answered Vatican defiantly as he groaned, a groan that mimicked his body's stiffness.

Dallas fount great humour in Vatican's quick wit and laughed loudly, Boris however did not.

"Well, here's your early morning wake up call!" Growled Boris as he struck him across the face with the back of his hand. Vatican's ears rang but there was no pain, his face was too numb, but he blamed out for a moment again, longe enough to see the grave again, and read the words 'HERE LIES VATICAN' staring back at him. A hand burst out from the soil, fingers grasping for him like the tentacles of some man-eating sea creature. He gasped as if tasting fresh air and he was back in the slaughter house, with those three sadistic faces staring back at him.

Famu had hung up the cellphone and joined them, "He's still alive then?"

"Bright as a daisy!" Dallas smiled.

"Good!" Famu nodded, "They will be here within the next few hours."

They?

"Can we use these?" Boris asked as he picked up a banana shaped skinning knife from the table.

"I don't see why not." Shrugged Famu, "But, let's go and get some breakfast before we start." He turned and left, Dallas followed, Boris lingered for a few moments, he smiled at Vatican as he toyed with the knife in his hands.

"See you in a little while Angel!" Boris laughed, placing the knife back on the table and then left.

They? Whose they? Someone is going to a lot of trouble to get rid of me.

He looked around, even the slight movement of his head swivelling was excruciating, he knew that if he didn't find a way out of this soon, he would soon be repackaged as Hu Meat's pork loin.

Chapter 36

Detective Graham yawned as he strolled into his office, shuffled over to the coffee maker and switched it on. Before he had had chance to sit down he was greeted by his partner Detective Freeman, who sauntered in after him a pile of folders grasped to his chest.

"Late night Sid?"

Graham nodded as he continued to yawn.

"Must have been one hell of a night." Freeman laughed as he settled into his usual resting place on the corner of Graham's desk. "I heard that there were quite a few interesting characters at that shindig."

"Too right!" Graham agreed as he collapsed into his chair, "Very interesting!" Graham said with a faraway look in his eye.

"You look like you want to tell me something Sid?"

"You'll think I'm mad if I tell you though."

"I think you're mad anyway," Freeman shrugged, with a playful smile stretched across his face.

"I think I saw Spider there."

"Really?" Said Freeman taken-aback, "Surely he wouldn't be that stupid to show up at that thing."

"Maybe I'm wrong, maybe it was just someone that looked like him. I don't know," He sighed, "maybe it was the excitement of an evening out, free champagne and canopies."

"He'd have an awful lot to lose if someone saw him there. I saw the guest list, there were quite a few there last night that would gladly see his head on a spike."

"Exactly! Thats why it couldn't have been him." Said Graham, but he still didn't sound convinced, "It was only a quick flash anyway, didn't see the guy properly, so, yeah it was probably just my mind playing tricks on me." He shook his head, "Just standing there he was talking to Robert Devine."

"Oh, well there you go then." Freeman declared, "It can't have been him then. Why would a worm like Spider be rubbing shoulders with a big wig like Devine?"

"Yeah," Graham nodded, "You're probably right." Graham left the comfort of his chair, removed his jacket and discarded it on the filing cabinet and moved over to the coffee maker that was bubbling away and poured the thick black substance into two stained mugs that looked as though they had never ben washed up.

"So what's the plan of action today?" Graham asked returning to the desk, handing Freeman his mug and sitting back down.

"Well, the paparazzi continue to bang the same drum, they believe that Vatican is in fact the crucifix killer."

"He's not!" Graham snapped defensively.

"Okay, okay!" Freeman grinned, "I know he's your new bestie and all..."

"Don't be a dick, Rich."

"I'm only playing. I don't think it's him either, but you now what these newspapers are like, anything to sell a story. I mean look how they treated Eric and his wife, made her out to be a junkie and him a serial killer."

Graham said nothing just stared into his thick black coffee.

"If you asked me, it was those tabloid bastards that drove Eric to take out Sniff. I think even he started to believe their hype."

Freeman could see that this particular conversation was going nowhere, he knew how Sid felt about the whole situation and it was better left alone.

"Anyway, it's been quiet on that front. The crucifix killer has not struck since."

"Well, that's one thing I suppose."

"Besides I believe I have some evidence here that changes the perspective on the whole case."

"And what's that?" Graham asked intrigued.

Freeman dropped the file on the desk and Graham opened it up to reveal photographs of the crucifix killer's victims. Graham wasn't even fazed by such a gruesome sight, even if it was early in the morning, this job had made him numb.

"Take a look at those." Declared Freeman rather pleased with himself.

"But I've seen these Rich." Graham fanned them out staring closely at them.

"You have indeed. But what everyone seems to have missed is that the crosses are in fact upside down."

"Upside down?" Said Graham through a furrowed brow of concentration as he inspected the photographs closely.

"Yeah, the cross of St. Peter or also know as the Petrine cross. But we al know that lunatics that are involved in the occult use this as a symbol in their worship."

"Well, I'll nee damned." Graham smiled.

"I'll make sure the SCPD release a statement on this so that the people of Studd City and its cheap rag of a paper that we are dealing with someone who is married to the occult. That should take the heat of our vigilante friend."

"Well done, Rich." Graham smiled handing him back the files.

"Hey, I'm not just a pretty face." He winked scooping up the file.   "Oh, and talking of pretty faces, I hear that Nash is about to bring in Mandrillus Kalu."

"For real? She got enough evidence to make it stick?"

"You sound surprised, Strange that you would doubt her abilities."

"I don't doubt her abilities."

Freeman raised his eyebrows playfully at Graham.

"I mean her abilities as a police officer!" Graham snapped.

"But anyway that's all over no isn't it?" Freeman probed.

"Yeah, actually I think it is."

"Good!" Freeman rose from the desk smiling, "She was too hot for you anyway, you were punching way above your weight there."

"Oh yeah?" Graham chuckled.

"Hell yeah!" Freeman laughed back, "But come on we got to go and help her take him in."

"Oh, okay. Where is it all going down?" Graham took a deep swig of his coffee and then grabbed his jacket.

"Buchanan Suites. She has some officers in uniform shadowing her, but it wouldn't help to give her some back up. This is a huge deal for her."

"Yeah of course! Let's go."

As they attempt to leave the doorway is blocked by Sergeant Richards.

"I've been looking for you Detective." Richards whistled through his large protruding front teeth.

"Well, now you've found me, Bugs." Announced Graham.

Richards sighed and adjusted his glasses, he did so hate his nickname.

"Make it quick, Bu... Richards!" Graham added.

"There has been a man calling here for you every hour since the early hours, it has become exceedingly tiresome."

"Well, who is it?"

"I don't know wouldn't leave a name, sounded urgent though. He was quite frantic and he insisted on speaking to you and only you."

Richards stared at him through his thick lenses.

"And?" Graham shrugged, "What would you like me to do with that information?"

"Well, I thought you may be at least intrigued."

"Very intrigued, but if that's ally have for me then I can't help you." Graham said and marched away, Freeman in tow.

"Well, really!" Richards scoffed, "Getting ruder and ruder that man." Richards returned to his desk, muttering under his breath. "Thinks I'm his personal answer phone service now does he? Really!"

Chapter 37

Vatican glanced around the slaughterhouse, with the sunlight streaming in through the skylights he could no take in his surrounds and look possible ways of escaping.

He was wide awake now and his body was tender, he felt as if he had been used in some kind of voodoo ritual as a poppet filled with pins. Luckily for him any bleeding from Anti Christ's attacks had stopped and his body had naturally fought against the wounds, blood drying up and melding together to seal them. They would still need stitches of course. His face was sore, flesh had been split, he was pretty sure that his nose had been broken and possibly chipped some of his ribs. Strangely his legs felt just as bad yet they had not been attacked like his he'd and torso, hours spent kneeling and had a severe effect on his muscles they felt tight as if even the smallest movement would cause them to rip.

There has to be a way. There is always a way.

He looked at the shackles, cleaning his fists and pulling against them, the chains rattled and then went tort, but all it did was causing screaming pain in his shoulders, the shackles cut into his wrists which each tug of the chain.

Get to your feet, it may give you a different view of the situation.

The chains slackened as he stopped pulling against them as the pain softened. He shuffled his feet on the damp tiles, trying to get a grip to help him to his feet. He slipped and slid, luckily there was no way he would fall as his shackles held him in place. Finally after several attempts he managed to make it to his feet, his knees shook and knocked together under the strain and his thighs ached with paresthesia. He steadied himself and managed to circle around on the spot and survey the situation. The chains had been hooked onto meat hooks that where situated on either wall, Vatican notice that the chains had not been secured or fastened and if he could create enough upwards thrust the chain may well leave the hook.

"There is a chance." Smiled Vatican, even a menial feat such as smiling hurt.

He shuffled across to his right side which automatically caused theft chain to tighten, he did so until there was no more slack. Vatican then started to thrust his right arm up and down, as if he were a large bird trying to flap a damaged wing. The chain whipped up and down as if it were waves on water, the last link of the chain wobbled up and down the hook but would not rise enough to detach itself. There was considerable amount of effort put into this and Vatican collapsed to his knees, sweat drips down his body and glistening in the sunlight. He groaned in pain and anguish.

"It's no use." He groaned to himself on the verge of tears.

Is that it? Had enough? Does the crusade end here?

Vatican knelt in a puddle of his own sweat and blood, beaten. *You think you were chosen for this crusade to just die in a dirty slaughterhouse next to trotters and pig's ears.*

"No." He whispered, he clenched his teeth and pulled himself up again and continued to whip the chain as high as he could. Several times it balanced on the very tip of the hook before falling back into place, but somehow Vatican stayed focussed and with one massive attempt he launched himself off the ground with the chain and it left the hook and fell onto the floor in a massive clatter.

Vatican had freed up the one side, the chain was still shacked to his wrist but at least he was no longer restrained by the wall, he could now move freely and was on his way to the other side of the slaughterhouse, very slowly and tentatively as he dragged the free chain behind him.

"He's free!" Called a voice and as he instinctively turned to those dirt strips of plastic and saw his tormentors returning from their breakfast.

"Get him!" Shouted Famu and Dallas and Boris ran towards Vatican, they slipped and skidded on the wet floor but just as Vatican attempted to release the second chain they both tackled him down to the floor. Vatican felt like he had been hit by a bulldozer, the air leaving his lungs as if trying to escape from the dilapidated shell.

289

"You sneaking fucking bastard!" Dallas scoffed ploughing him with a right hand, Boris followed suit by laying in some swift kicks to the ribs.

"Stop fucking around and get him back into place! They'll be here soon."

They... They? Who are they?

Dallas and Boris took the loose chain and started to drag Vatican back across the tiles, over the drain were the stench of forgotten pig meat and stale blood wafted up through the shafts and attacked his nostrils, he wretched and almost vomited, but luckily they dragged him past the drain before he lost the lining of his stomach.

"The boss is going to be pissed if he finds out he got loose." Famu said, his voice almost quivering at the thought. Whoever his boss was even the big rhino, Famu feared him.

As Vatican's bruised, lacerated face slid unceremoniously across the uncomfortable cold and wet tiles the table came into view and as if he were acting on autopilot he thrust a kick towards the leg of it and sent it hurtling across the tiles into Famu, the cleavers and knives exploded from the table as it made impact with the large Hawaiian and scatted off in all directions. This was the distraction that Vatican was going for as Dallas and Boris had naturally stopped in their tracks to see what the ruckus was all about.

"What the fuck..." Dallas started to yell when Vatican was up on his feet and jerked the chain they were holding, sending them down the floor with sudden violent impact that their heads collided with the tiles.

"Get him you fucking fools!" Famu bellowed as he tried to free himself from the unwanted table and pieces of meat he had been showered in.

Dallas and Boris struggled to get to their feet but when they did, Vatican had almost reached the second chain, the y grabbed the training chain and yanked him away from it again. Vatican bandaged to slides across the tiles and did not fall, his body was on fire and felt as if his limbs could fall of at any moment, but he closed his eyes to ficus al his inner energy and strength on the matter in hand.

They charged at him angrily, blood trickling from the fresh wounds on their heads, Vatican flicked the chain out of their moist hands and then swung it around his head building up the momentum before whipping it at their ankles and sending them both hurtling to the floor once again.

"Have I always got to do everything myself!" Growled Famu who came stomping towards him and through several punches at Vatican who managed to duck and dive out of each of his massive fists, and hitting him with some lacklustre palm strikes that had not really behind them. Famu smiled and nailed a head butt that staggered Vatican and almost caused him to black out again, he fell to his knees and tried to shake it off.

"Even when you were at full strength you had to cheat to beat me." Famu snarled, "No little toys to help you now is there?"

"No you're right." Stuttered Vatican, "I had to fight dirty last time."

Famu grabbed him by his soaked hair and lifted him off the ground.

"Yeah you did!" Famu nodded and attempted to strike him with another head butt, but Vatican manoeuvred himself out of the way and managed to wrapped the free chain around Famu's massive neck, and he pulled with all his might, immediately cutting of his windpipe and Famu started to spit and splutter, his face turning a strange colour of beetroot. Dallas arrived and was met in the gut with a revers kick from Vatican still holding onto Famu's bulk like a cowboy on a bronco, his feet sliding back and firth like some strange dance as he tried to keep the behemoth from escaping. Boris approached with speed and Vatican through a swift kick in his direction but he saw the it coming and grabbed his foot, Vatican twisted around and locked his thighs tightly around Boris' head in a vicelike head-scissors. Vatican was now horizon in the air choking Famu with the chain and Boris with his legs, if he was lucky they would both pass out before Dallas was back on his feet.

Unfortunately he wasn't lucky and a pissed off Dallas drove a meat tenderising mallet onto the back of his head and Vatican collapsed to the floor. Boris and Famu collapsed to their knees gasping for breath but for Vatican there was only darkness again.

Chapter 38

Penny arrived in Chinatown. She had made sure that she had kept to the backstreets, relying on the shroud of the old buildings to conceal her and the katana that she grasped tightly in her hands. If she was seen by the police then she would be in big trouble and she would have to think fast if she were asked where she got such an item and what she intended on doing with it. Way too many questions to answer, as well as not being able to help Vatican if she were to be apprehended on route. Sticking to the shadows suited her fine.

The market was in full swing and as always was ridiculously busy as hundreds of customers packed into the narrow aisles, rubbing shoulder to shoulder as the merchants shrieked in high pitched Mandarin as they attempted to draw people in to buy their goods. Penny reached the wet market and recoiled immediately, the stench of fish and meat that had been left to fester in the sunlight was repulsive. Fighting back the urge to retch she was forced to look away from the gawping fish heads that stared at her as she manoeuvred her way around the rear of the stalls.

Penny looked to cross the market towards the meat section of which integrated into the butcher district, homing market stalls, butcher shops and slaughterhouses, but her route was impeded as she noticed two SCPD officers strolling along the outskirts of the market.

"Shit!" She hissed and crouched down behind a huge tank that was a short-term home for several large lobsters that groped around in the unappealing murky water. There she waited, waiting for the officers to walk on by but they didn't, instead they stopped to chat to with local traders and were handed free beverages from one stall. Penny realised that these scrounging officers were there for the long haul and weren't leaving anytime soon.

"Goddamn pigs!" She scowled, "Always wanting handouts."

She realised that to get to where she was going she would have to use an alternate route, she could not bee seen with this sword or it was game over. She headed into a nearby alleyway and nimbly left up onto a swelling dumpster and tipped across it before leaping into the bottom rung of a fire escape ladder that dropped slightly after it was shocked due to the sudden impact of her weight. Not that she weighed a lot at all, she was if anything malnourished and it was amazing that she had such energy for someone on one meal a day of scraps and leftovers. She climbed the ladder one handed, still clutching the sword in her hand and hiding down by her side, she held it very naturally as if they were old acquaintances. Penny called the zigzagging fire escape steps and settled on the roof where she took time to catch her breath an survey the landscape to see which direction would help her reach her destination quickest.

An abundance of uneven rooftops lay ahead of her, but she could see her destination in the distance, its skylights glimmering in the sunlight like a beacon. She tuck in a deep breath and darted towards the edge of the building, she moved with such speed and her movement was so natural when she leapt over to the other rooftop, tattered sneakers touching down on the unforgiving surface before organically moving into a forward roll where she rose and exhaled with shaky relief. All of this came so naturally to her that it was if it was imbedded in her, as though she were programmed to do it without even thinking. She took in the moment, felt the adrenaline and head towards the ledge towards the next building. There was much more to Penny ling than a feisty, homeless teenager, much more.

Chapter 39

Famu, Dallas and Boris pulled themselves together again and were slightly ruffled at what Vatican was able to do do them, with one arm shackled and after several hours of torture. They looked at each other and back at the unconscious heap on the damp wet tiles. None of them wanted to admit that they just got there rears kicked by that man, the thought that spiralled around each of their heads was, 'What could he have done to us if he had been at full strength?'.

Finally Famu spoke, he made sure that he sounded unperturbed by what had just occurred, "I think we need to show this asshole who's exactly in charge here!"

Dallas and Boris glanced at each other unconvinced by Famu's words, but nodded anyway.

"I think we should unleash a word of pain on this cocksucker!" Famu growled as he eyed up the array of knives and cleavers that were now splayed out on the floor. He grabbed a hefty meat cleaver in his large mitt and caught his reflection in the blade, he grinned with sadism, visions of him taking the cleaver to Vatican's limbs appeared in his minds eye.

"Oh it's time to use the toys?" Boris smiled, almost dribbling with perversion.

Famu nodded, "Choose your weapon of choice boys."

Dallas and Boris knelt down, Dallas quickly scooped up a long bladed boning knife and playfully toyed with it in his hands. Boris however took longer with his decision, wondering which instrument could cause the most damage. His eyes skimmed across the array of misshapen blades, that shimmered invitingly. But Boris bypassed all the knives, cleavers and mallets and scooped up a large serrated fragment of glass.

"You're one sick puppy, Boris." Dallas laughed, "D'you know that?"

"I want this pizda to suffer!" He growled.

They stood in front of the unconscious vigilante and waited.

"Can't we just skewer him now?" Boris asked.

"No, we wait until he's conscious. You want him to enjoy it don't you?" Dallas laughed.

Vatican started to stir.

"Think we should shackle him up again?" Dallas asked. Famu nodded and Dallas strode over to the far side of the slaughterhouse, hoisting up the chain from the floor and dragging Vatican back into position.

Famu's cell phone rang and he immediately answered it, "Yes, Mr Devine, he is still here and yes he's still in one piece." Famu fell silent and nodded occasionally as Robert

Devine talked, "Yes, Sir, certainly." Famu hung up and slotted his cell phone back in to the inside of his once white blazer. "They're on their way."

"Better make this quick then." Boris smiled and gave the rousing Vatican a swift kick, hoping to help proceedings move along. He groaned and slowly started to get to his knees, Just as Dallas hooked the chain back into place.

Vatican's vision returned, blurry and wavering at first, but then he saw the daunting figures standing over him once again and a part of him sobbed, this wasn't just a bad dream, it was real and it was still ongoing.

"Time to clip those wings angel!" Growled Famu and he lifted the cleaver high above his head, when suddenly he was struck in the back of the head by a large nugget of bone, which then collided with the tiled floor and skidded away.

"What the fuck!" Growled Famu clutching at the back of his head, when another came hurtling through the air and hit him on the side of the head, "WHAT IS THIS?" He screamed as another chunk of bone fell to the floor after ricocheting of his head.

"What's going on?" Dallas asked and he and Boris took turns at looking around the room.

The plastic curtains to the entrance trembled as though someone had just passed through them and the trio turned their attentions to it "Who's there?" Called Famu. Another piece of bone came hurtling through the air from a different direction and hit Boris now.

"The fuck!" He growled with annoyance.

"Who's there?" Dallas called and managed to doge an oncoming piece of bone that hurtled passed him and struck the brick wall.

"What the fuck is going on?" Famu sneered, looking very angry indeed.

They heard the pitter patter of feet moving rapidly somewhere in the shadows.

"Show your fucking self, this isn't funny." Famu said glaring into the shadows, his grip tightening around the handle of the cleaver.

"Get away from him." Came the reply from the shadows behind where a groggy Vatican knelt.

"Is that a kid's voice?" Boris asked.

"Show yourself Kid!" Dallas called.

Another piece of bone cut through the air and hit Boris on the nose. Dallas tried not to laugh and shouted again, "And stop fucking throwing shit!"

"Leave him alone then!" Came the voice moving closer, a hooded silted could just be made out.

"Come into the light." Beckoned Famu his eyes narrowed to try and work out the identity of this united guest, "We won't hurt you I promise."

There was a snort of laughter that carried from the shadows at this and Penny appeared slowly behind Vatican.

"Yeah right! I wasn't born yesterday Shamu!" She snarled.

"You!" The trio growled ate same time and then all looked at each other.

"How do you know her?" Famu asked them.

"She used to run the Stardust for us." Dallas answered still in shock.

"Well, I'm not proud of that part of my life." Penny announced, "I'm turning over a new leaf and I have decided that I no longer do business with cockroaches."

"The little bitch!" Boris spat.

"Little girl," Famu said gently, "Unless you would like your old friend Vermin to get the same treatment as your vigilante friend, I suggest that you get your ass out of here."

"His name is not Vermin!" Penny growled and stepped closer.
They laughed at her snarling face.

"I'm so scared." Dallas scoffed, "Are you scared Boris?"

"Very!" He grumbled through a jagged smile, shard of glass gripped in his hands.

"W-who is... it?" Vatican stuttered, slurring over his words as he became conscious again.

"It's me V-Man, Penny." She said calmingly and joined him at his side placing a caring hand on his bare flesh.
"V-Man?" The trio of abusers mocked.

"Yeah!" Penny scowled.

"What's the V stand for, vagina?" Laughed Dallas.

"You carry on and you'll find out what it's like to have one." She growled twisting the katana in her hand so it catches the sunlight and flickers in his eyes.

"N-no..." Vatican slurred, "No Penny, get out of here... they'll kill..."

"Damn right we fucking will!" Famu seethed and waved his cleaver at her.

"I'm not scared." Said Penny drifting slowly in front of Vatican now and unveiling the katana that she had kept hidden down by her side. "I'm not going anywhere."

Vatican watched on through droopy, swollen eyes, his visioned blurred an impaired, he truly could not believe what he saw (or what he thought he saw). Maybe he was still dreaming, lost in that world that was conjured by a state of unconsciousness. The scene he was witnessing was in truth no more inconceivable than anything else he had imagined the last 24 hours. The images again flash rapidly before his eyes of a man in a gas mask, a gigantic man in the torn and tattered mask of a luchador, the billionaire tycoon Robert Devine, The Anti Christ character that he had met just hours ago that's left scars on his flesh that will forever remind him of madness. He had to still be dreaming if these images still appeared, didn't he?

Somewhere in the distance was the wailing of sirens, and Vatican breathed a sigh of relief, it was over and with it probably his crusade for the authorities would surely strip him bare of his mask and identity and shout to from the rooftops for all to hear. A part of him deep down was glad, he felt like a great weight was being lifted from his shoulders and he collapsed to the floor, the shackles had been unhooked and once again he felt the ice cold kiss of the damp tiles. He could hear a voice talking to him softly and reassuring. Wass this the Lord? His limp body was hoisted up into a sitting position, was this indeed the Lord Almighty collecting his soul? Any second now he would continue to ascend towards the heavens, towards that blinding white light.

No, the light is gold. A golden light that will continue to shimmer after I'm gone. It has shone before and it will shine again.

He shook his head, he had no idea what any of that meant.

The light is golden and the crane is black.

The light is golden and the crane is black. The light is golden and the crane is black. The light is golden and the crane is black.

"The light is golden and the crane is black." He chanted.

"Are you okay Vatican?"

He forced his eyes to open and saw Penny's sweet innocent looking face smiling at him, her big brown eyes shining with concern, flecks of blood speckled her plump cheeks.

"What... are you doing?" Vatican asked struggling to hold himself up.

"I thought that was obvious." Penny laughed helping him up, "I'm saving your ass."

Vatican looked around to survey the scene, Dallas clutched his arm that now homed a wound, that was spurting blood that dribbled between his finger tips as he head sat on the floor seething through clenched teeth.

Boris lay unconscious on the floor, nose broken and various small cuts etched on his flesh. Famu stirred groaning, a broken katana blade protruding out of his bare foot, the shaft of the blade piercing through the sole of his flimsy leather sandals.

"What did you do?" Vatican asked her.

"What I had to do!"

"But..."

"I've been doing what I need to survive for the past five years and no-one has given a shit, so don't start reading me the riot act now."

She had spunk and she was feisty, Vatican smiled, it was a thankful smile and he was in awe of this fearless young warrior that risked her life to save his. Maybe his crusade would continue after all.

Cars screeched to a halt outside and the room was illuminated by twitching rays of blue and red.

"I've gotta go." Penny said gently and stood up.

"But, you can't..." Vatican grunted as pain attacked his wounds as he tried to move suddenly.

Penny immediately knelt back down at his side, "You need to take it easy. These guys really did a number on you. I'm surprised you're even still alive!"

"You saved me." He said, "Please stay with me."

"I can't!" She shook her head, "They'll take me away." Vatican shook his head and grabbed hold of her hand and squeezed it as if he would never ever let go of it.

"It's all going to work out fine." He smiled.

"No, I can't!" She cried pulling her hand out of his and standing up. "You don't get it they will lock me up or put me in some orphanage or something! Those kind of places aren't for me, they mess kids up!"

Vatican chuckled and laughed so loud that his horsey tones reverberated around the slaughterhouse.

"Dude, you're so weird." Said Penny with a confused look on her face.

There was a loud ruckus that exploded from the other side of those fluttering plastic curtains. The blaring of aggressive voices filtered through and when Vatican looked again Penny was gone.

"Penny?" He asked, but his the only reply he heard was his own voice. He sighed and tried to move, "I would have vouched for you Penny." He looked at the curtains as the SCPD burst in guns raised, the initial look of shock that consumed their faces and Vatican collapsed on the tiles again whispering, "Thank you."

Chapter 40

"Get these three out of my sight!" Growled Detective Graham as he knelt down to greet the rising vigilante.

"Look like you've seen some action buddy." Vatican smiled as his eyes met Graham's.

"What happened here?" Graham asked, Freeman stood in awe, just gawping at Vatican.

"You know how it is, you step out for some pork loin for the Sunday roast and end up trapped in a slaughterhouse being beaten half to death by three baboons. It happens at least once a week." Vatican oozed sarcasm as he smiled and Graham laughed.

"Well, you're lucky to be alive you know that?"

"Yeah!" He agreed.

"What the hell happened here!" Freeman cried, unable to keep it in any longer as officers led the trio out in cuffs.

"Take it easy, Rich." Graham mocked, "He gets excited when he meets celebrities. You should have seen him when he met Brett Lennox."

"I'm serious!" Freeman groaned, "Look at this place?

It looks like a scene from Maple Falls Massacre in here!"

"How did you get out of this one?" Graham inquired. Vatican looked around meeting the eyes of several inquisitive officers that were coming and going, securing the area and leading his abusers away to hopefully see out the rest of their lives at Skelter Prison.

"I had a little help..." He began and then looked around, realising Penny was long gone, and he did not wish to disrespect her by dropping her name into this particular conversation.

"From who?" Graham asked.

"Oh, from faith!" Vatican smiled. Graham smiled, "Of course."

"Well, at least you've taken yourself out of the running for the title of 'The Crucifix Killer'!" Laughed Graham.

"Yeah, this is one hell of an alibi you've got here." Added Freeman.

"I can tell you who was responsible." Said Vatican.

"You can!" Graham said taken aback.

"It was the work of a guy calling himself 'The Anti Christ'!"

"The Anti Christ?" Freeman repeated.

"He did a number on yours-truly before these boys even got started on me. I believe he may have been that escaped patient from Oakland."

"Smith." Graham nodded, "Nicholas Smith."

Vatican nodded and then finally realised the shackles had

been removed from his wrists and he lifted his hand towards his face, it was strange how light it felt to him, the thick heavy metal had become a part of him. He felt for his mask and he was surprised to see it was still in place.

"My mask..." He began but then he met another understanding smile beaming from beneath Detective Graham's ever growing auburn beard.

"Don't worry, It's still there."

"Thank you!" Vatican spluttered and had to turn away for amount, he felt rather overcome, that someone he hardly knew had taken such measures to help him protect his identity and keep the Angel of Justice alive.

"I ushered them away as soon as I could, they were like kids at Christmas all vying to remove that wrapping."

"But why?" Vatican asked.

"I asked him that too." Piped up Freeman, wanting to know an answer to this particular quandary too.

"I have my reasons." Graham snapped, "That's all I have to say."

"I doubt that will fly with Commissioner Hayes." Freeman sighed.

"Yeah, well that's my cross to bear."

Vatican smiled. "Amen to that!"

"Erm... Detective!" Interrupted Officer James meekly as a gurney being wheeled in by paramedics came to a halt, "The paramedics are here to take, erm..."

"Vatican!" Snapped Graham, "His name is Vatican."

"Er, yes of course. Well, they're here to take Vatican to the St. Vincent's Hospital."

"Yes, of course! You need looking over, you have some nasty wounds there." Graham said in an insistent tone. The paramedics moved forward and Vatican looked to Graham, "Can I at least walk out of here?"

"Think you can manage it?"

"Yeah, but I might need some help getting started."

"Sure." Smiled Graham, He held his hand up to the paramedics to halt the gurney, "Rich give me a hand."
The detectives helped Vatican up to his feet and helped walk him out of the building.

"You sure got your own back on those guys huh?" Graham asked.
There was a delay and Vatican smiled, "Yeah. They didn't know what hit them."
Freeman and Graham glanced at each other, they both had come to the assumption that he was lying.
They neared the ambulance, its rear doors inviting the injured vigilante as he had started to walk unaided but still the detectives remained close at hand.

"Here we are!" Announced Graham as Vatican came to rest on the step that lead to the back of the ambulance.

"Thanks, Detective."

"Please call me Sid." Vatican nodded.

"We'll leave you in the capable hands of these young ladies then."

The two female paramedics smiled at Detective Graham and then looked bashfully at Vatican who was still topless, his ripped physique rippling in all the right places.

"But if I hear of anyone here or at St. Vincent's removing this man's mask, then they will have me to answer too!" Bellowed Graham for all to hear.

The paramedics flinched under Graham's words and nodded vigorously to show that they understood.

Graham winked at Vatican and dragged Freeman away by his arm, or he would have continued to stare at Vatican.

Vatican sat in silence as he surveyed the scene in front of him, police were everywhere, ambulances, cars and SWAT vans surrounded the now cordoned off slaughterhouse as an array of people had shown up to see what was happening. Luckily for him, Vatican was out of view and couldn't be seen by any of the onlookers, most of the attention was on the arrested anyway. A helicopter flew over head that belonged to SCTV News.

"News travels fast in this town." Vatican said aloud more to himself, but the paramedics returned smiles as they continued to check him over. Famu was being hustled into another ambulance on a gurney, accompanied by several police officers, the katana blade still protruding from out of his foot and him crying like a baby. Dallas was holding a compress on his bandaged arm, his other wrist cuffed to Officer Phillips, and being shadowed by Officer Harris as they clambered into another ambulance. Boris was sitting in the back of a squad car looking very grumpy indeed. Vatican could see Sergeant Reeves leading the proprietor Y'ao Hu out in handcuffs, but he knew that there was very little evidence to connect him with anything.

"Severe wound to right trapezius, that's going to need some stitches." On of the paramedics said, "Same with the external oblique. Both wounds are deep but his body has reacted well and the blood has clotted."

As they both worked quickly to examine and bandage him up, each prod and movement was agony, and Vatican's head was swimming again.

"Chipped ribs possibly, broken nose I'd say." Said the other paramedic, "Hell of a lot of bruising, you're going to be tender for a while but I think you have managed to escape without any lasting damage."

Vatican could hear the words but he did not answer.

"Make sure we've got plenty of morphine, Jill."

"Okay, angel let's get you strapped in." Said the other with a caring smile and they helped Vatican onto the gurney, his eyes started to all back and all he wish for was sleep, but the horrendous pain would not allow it and he winced with each strenuous movement. Jim the paramedic climbed in the back with him and the other paramedic slammed the doors behind them.

News reporters from various stations had arrived and were all clambering for the best location to make their report. Graham and Freeman watched on as the ambulance slowly rolled out of Old Chinatown.

"You didn't believe him either?" Freeman asked. Graham shook his head.

"So you think someone else was on hand to take down the three stooges?"

"I do. He was definitely covering for someone."

"So that means we've got another masked vigilante running around Studd!"

"Maybe." Grinned Graham.

"What the hell are you smirking at?"

"Makes my life just that littlest easier if there is, doesn't it." And with a wink and a pat on the arm graham left, Freeman scurrying behind him with a confused look on his face.

Slowly the rear tinted glass of a black limousine lurched halfway down the window. Shrouded in shadow Robert Devine sat watching the scenes that were taking place in front of him, his brow was sculpted into a rigid scowl. His breathing was heavy and his nostrils quivered fiercely like and angry bull.

"Would you like me to drive on, Sir?" Came the voice of the driver.

He said nothing, but his eyes were on fire, the red of the ambulance's lights shone in them giving his slender face a demonic appearance.

"Sir?"

"Idiots!" He murmured under his breath, "FUCKING IMBECILES!" He growled and the window slowly rolled back up into place and the limousine trundled away.

"This town has turned sour." Growled a heavily tattooed black man, who pulled down the sleeves of his sweatshirt concealing sleeves of spiderweb ink. He stood surrounded by an abundance of curious onlookers.

"Time to split this scene." Murmured Spider as he pulled his hood into place and worked his way through the crowd.

Chapter 41

The ambulance's sirens howled through the streets of Studd City, its relentless irritating drone acting as a warning to all that it approached. Inside its rear, Vatican lay restrained, but this time we was no longer shackled by chains and being beaten. Jill had made him as comfortable as she possibly could, but withe each jerking movement or turning of a tight corner Vatican could feel it and he grunted through his gritted teeth.

"Okay, Angel, it's okay." Jill reassured him warmly, as she held his hand. "Not long now."

She smiled at him and then looked to make sure that the morphine was taking effect. The bag of clear liquid painkiller swayed from side to side and she held it still to make sure the drip was taking it. It was and Vatican could feel the effects immediately as it surged into his bloodstream through the cannula inserted into his vein.

Jill was truly a professional and unfazed by the man lying on the gurney and who he was, all she saw was a human being and automatically wanted to care for him. Vatican smiled dreamingly as his pain seemed to evaporate and replaced by a warm euphoric feeling. His drowsy eyes focused on the light above him flickering with each bump in the road, the light became intense, almost blinding in fact, he had to close his eyes and when he tried to open them again he was met by a golden shimmer. It resembled a police shield, he had seen this before, in dreams, in visions and it shimmered and sparkled brightly. He tried to think, but his head was not in the right place and the morphine became completely victorious over the sheering pain and when he blinked again the shield was gone, smothered by a shadow, someone leaning over him, he could have sworn that the silhouette belonged to his Master Sato.

"M-master..." He murmured as a warm hand touched his forehead and he felt a memory from his days spent in China creep back into his blurry mind's eye. He was still young and lay on a bed that was very low down to the floor, the room was dark and only lit by several candles scattered throughout. The warm candle light caressed Sato's ancient face as he held his wrinkled hand on his fevered brow.

"Be still Thomas." Sato said gently, "The fever has taken ahold of you, it will eat away at you if you allow it too."

"What should I do Master?" Whimpered a young tearful Thomas.

"Do not allow it to." Sato lit a strange looking candle.

"What is that?"

"This is a very special candle, Thomas. It contains the herbs and spices that grow here on the mountain. All of which have been very beneficial to us when illness comes."

The scent in the air stung Thomas' nostrils and then it slowly made him feel woozy.

"I did tell you an Xing that it was a mistake to go swimming in the lagoon at this time of year, did I not warn you this would happen?"

Thomas nodded gingerly.

"I know that Xing can be quite persuasive, but you must heed my warnings." Sato stared into Thomas' young eyes, the lilac vapour rising around his withered face, "You should always heed my warnings Thomas."

The memory was gone and Sato was replaced by Jill comforting.

"Just rest up, I promise you we're nearly..." The driver slammed on the breaks and the ambulance shudder from side to side before screeching violently to a halt.

"What the hell is going on!" Jill squealed as she struggled to keep her balance.

"Better get out here, Jill." Called the other paramedic from the driver's seat.

"What is it?" Jill asked peering through the front seats and trying to see through the windscreen.

"There's some guy in the road."

Jill babbled obscenities under he breath as she headed for the doors, she swung them open and turned back to a woozy Vatican with a smile, "I won't be a moment, you gonna be okay?"

Vatican grinned a ridiculous grin at her and held his fingers up in an 'OK' gesture.

In the road there lay a man, curled up in a heap, his clothes tattered and torn, a hood pulled up over his head.

"He was just lying there!" Cried the paramedic as Jill joined her.

"Let's check him over." Jill said kneeling down the man's side, she asked his name and if he could hear her, the man grumbled a response.

"I can't see any sign of blood anywhere, I don't think he's been hit." The paramedic said.

"Sir, where does it hurt?" The man just grumbled again.

"Sir, we are going to just examine you, Okay?"

She examined him and was confident that his spine and neck was not damaged and he would be safe to move.

"We're just going to turn you over. Can you let us know if you feel any discomfort at all?"

"Yes." Came a muffled reply.

The two paramedics turned him over, there were no cries of pain nor groans of discomfort, but when they saw his face the driver gasped and held a hand to her mouth, Jill found this very annoying, she was a professional and although this poor man's face looked like it had been pushed through a mincer she had seen much worse in her time. The unprofessionalism of her partner really annoyed her and she shot her a look.

"Get a hold of yourself, Emily!"

Jill examined the man's face, the wounds were not fresh, she could see that he had recent lacerations but that they were not caused today. The frowned as the man's eyes remained closed, she ran a finger tip over his misshapen face, the old protruding scars from along time ago.

"There's nothing wrong with you is there?" Jill asked. Elliot Hays opened his and tried to smile, his split, distorted upper lip rose to touch the tip of his nose and his eyes pleaded for forgiveness.

"I'm so sorry ladies for impeding your duty."

"Angel!" Jill gasped and ran back to the rear of the ambulance and looked inside, she sighed heavily.

"What is it?" Asked Emily joining her at the gaping doors.

"He's gone."

Penny and Burt slowly helped Vatican down the manhole that lead to the sewer which no easy feat as Vatican was still under the influence of morphine.

"Is he okay?" Penny asked called down the shaft to Burt who was supporting his weight as best as he could.

"He is, but I might need some of that morphine after hiding his heavy ass."

Vatican giggled and started laughing.

"He's delirious." Penny said scaling down the metal rungs, several bags of morphine and other equipment grasped to her chest.

"Is that all you have?" Burt asked as she joined him. "It was all I could manage!" Penny snapped.

"No matter, it will have to do."

With Vatican hung between them, his limp arms draped over their shoulders they trudged slowly through the dark sewer, Burt shined a flashlight to lead their way. This was indeed a slow process, due to Vatican's chaperones being and elderly man and a young girl.

"Well done, Penny." Burt said, his voice echoing around the narrow damp tunnel.

Penny felt the crimson kiss of embarrassment on her cheeks, she wasn't used to people saying such things to her and she didn't know how to respond.

"You saved..." Burt paused still not wanting to use his real name, "Vatican's life. We will always be indebted to you for that."

"I didn't really do anything."

"You're to modest, Penny. It was you that found him, you that freed him and the trick with the ambulance and Elliot was ingenious."

"Well, erm thanks, but it was nothing really."

"One thing that I don't understand though." Burt inquired.

"Oh, what's that?" But Penny knew where he was going with this line of questioning.

"How you freed Vatican if he was being guarded by those degenerates."

Penny said nothing, their shuffling steps on the damp bricks as all that could be heard as she rummaged through her brain for a lie that she could tell that wouldn't reveal to Burt what she was capable of. She could feel Burt looking in her direction she was waiting for the next question.

"Oh look!" Penny announced almost gasping with relief. "Here we are!"

"Yes." He smiled looking at the thick metal door that had 'Out of Use' and 'Keep Out' signage smothering it, "Quite convenient having the hospital on your doorstep."

They carefully moved Vatican into the secret cellar underneath St. Vincent's church that was once used for stockpiling alcohol during prohibition. They lay Vatican down on a bedded area that Burt had made up.

"There we go... Vatican. Rest up now." Burt said as Vatican lay on the bed.

Burt and Penny stood in silence for a few moments as they both looked at him, he looked so helpless. Burt took the morphine drip and the cannula and set it all up as Penny watched on intrigued.

"Where did you learn to do that?" Penny asked.

"Nam." Burt answered sharply as he concentrated at what he was doing, hooking the bag on a nail that protruded out of the cellar wall.

"Oh." She replied.

"You know about what happed in Vietnam then?" She nodded.

"We learnt about it at school."

"So you'll now how horrendous it was."

She nodded again a little sheepishly remembering what she

said earlier about the sights she had seen and now felt like a heel for dismissing the man that stood before him.

"I too have seen things, Penny. Terrible things." Burt said solemnly and turned his attentions back to Thomas.

"Is he going to be okay? Do you have enough here to help him?"

"He'll be fine." Burt smiled, "I'll patch him up and he'll be back on his feet in no time."

"What about the streets? The city, who is going to keep the people safe?"

"My priority is Vatican's wellbeing. Besides I can't get in the outfit." He chuckled.

She smiled but looked as though she was miles away.

"Somebody has to protect this city why he's out of action."

Burt waddled over to a table that he had placed several items he knew he would need, and poured some water from a jug into a bowl and dropped a cloth into it and took it over to where Vatican lay.

"You should think of staying with us Penny. I'm sure it wouldn't be a problem. At least it would keep you off the streets." Burt said but as he turned around Penny was gone.

He sighed knowing exactly what she had in mind and he shuffled over to the door and closed it, locking the deadbolt in place.

"May God be with you Penny."

Chapter 42

Detective's Graham and Freeman left their superior's office a little flustered, the breathed a sigh of relief at exactly the same time just as they closed the door behind them.

"Well, that didn't go to bad now did it?" Freeman grinned mischievously.

"Speak for yourself." Graham scoffed, "I thought he was gonna rip me a new ass hole."

Freeman patted him on the shoulder gently, "It could have gone a lot worse. You're lucky he likes you."

"Likes me!" Graham gawped at him, "He's got a funny way of showing it."

Slowly they walked across the busy office towards Graham's office.

"Well, you got what you wanted, Vatican's identity remains a mystery and you still have your job." Freeman said, "I heard that he never even made it to the hospital. Heard he abandoned ship n route."

Graham smiled to himself.

"Yeah, I thought he might."

"Still think he's working along side someone else?"

"Definitely!" Graham nodded, "You saw the state he was in, there was no chance that he got out of that ambulance without help."

"I still don't know why you want to help the guy though."

"He's one of the good guys."

"He's still working outside of the confines of the law though, Sid. He's still a vigilante and we shouldn't tolerate vigilantism."

"Sheesh!" Graham chuckled, "I never thought I would live to see the day when Richard Freeman starts beating his SCPD handbook like a bible."

"Get out of here!" He laughed, "You know I've always got your back. Even still..."

Graham made eye contact with Nash who had just walked into the office and was being congratulated on bringing in the drug dealer Mandrillus Kalu. They stared at each other, she smiled, but Graham turned away.

"You okay Sid?" Asked Freeman who had seen Graham lose focus for a moment.

"Yeah." He nodded, "Look, what have I always told you is the first rule of being a detective?"

"Go with your..."

"Gut!" Graham interrupted, "Exactly!"

They stood in the middle of the office as officers came and went at rapid speed all around them. They paid no attention to the two dawdling detectives and manoeuvred their way around them.

"I trust him, I believe that he is good for this city. Look at the things he has accomplished so far!" "Yeah, but..."

"He's making our lives easier, remember that."

"Okay, you're the boss. Like I said I'm always gonna be in your corner when the bell rings, you know that." Graham smiled and then his face fell and he looked at his watch.

"Oh shit is that the time?" Graham groaned and charged towards his office, disappeared behind its frosted glass door and retrieved his coat.

"Oh yeah you're taking the boys to the wrestling tonight, huh?"

"Yeah and if I'm late..."

"Mae?" Freeman winced.

"Let's just say I would much rather face the Commissioner in an ass chewing battle than Mae." They laughed as Graham slipped on his jacket and started to walk towards the elevator together, ignoring a sorry looking Nash over the far side of the office.

"So what's the main event tonight?" Freeman asked.

"I'm told it's the big one for all the marbles!" Graham rolls his eyes and laughs, "Randy Rogan versus Johnny Midnight."

"Have fun, don't let them fleece you for a program." Freeman laughed as Graham slipped into the elevator.

"Oh you know they will and a couple of those ridiculous foam fingers too no doubt."

"Erm, Detective Graham!" Came the frantic call of Sergeant Richards.

Detective Graham sighed and stopped the doors from sliding shut, "I was so close. So close to getting out on time for once."

"Ah! Detective I'm so very glad I caught you." Said Sergeant Richards adjusting his glasses and scanning his clipboard.

"You always do." Sighed Graham.

"So, what's up doc?" Freeman asked winking at Graham.

Richards paid no attention to Freeman as he ran his finger down his clipboard.

"There has been a robbery..."

"Shit, Bugs!" Graham groaned, "A fucking robbery! What are you bothering me which such trivial shit when all I want to do is go home!"

Richards adjusted his glasses again as he stared at Graham who was still sandwich between the elevator doors. His teeth hung over his bottom lip and for amount he said nothing before taking a deep breath and continuing, "If you would give me the courtesy of paying attention and not interrupting me I will tell you exactly why this articular robbery may be of interest."

"Oh brother!" Graham rolled his eyes and Freeman stifled his amusement.

"May I continue?" Richards asked, his eyes flitting back and forth between the two detectives.

"By all means please do!" Freeman announced over-enthusiasm.

"Can you get on with it please."

"Our weapons facility in Hepburn has been compromised. Three officer hospitalised, but not seriously injured."

The detectives looked at each other and then back at Richards.

"The unknown assailant has stolen a non-military armoured vehicle, I believe it to be a Lenco BearCat. Along with 5 9mm Heckler & Koch MP5 submachine guns (with ammo), 3 M4 carbine automatic (with ammo), 2 Remington 870 pump- action shotguns (with ammo), 8 M1911 Pistols, 12 Beretta 92 pistols both with ammo."

Graham and Freeman's eyes widened and Graham was about to speak when Richards cleared his throat and carried on.

"A Remington 700P rifle completed with carry case and ammo. 22 Colt M16A2 Automatica rifles, complete with a crate of ammunition. 12 tasers complete with replacement cartridges. Crates of stinger grenades, flash bang grenades, tear gas, pepper spray and some Nobel 808 c4 explosives."

"Damn, someone means business." Freeman announced with a whistle.

Richards looked at him and pushed his glass back up his nose before licking the tip of his finger and flipping back the piece of aper on his clipboard and again cleared his throat.

"An MBR... A Modular Battering Ram if you didn't know, with several various head types. 4 experimental gasmasks, 4 uniforms - 1 black, 3 desert, 8 fire retardant balaclava, 5 US military helmets, 16 ballistic vests and 3 Gerber 06 automatic knives and a 16 inch tactical Bowie knife."

"What would you like us to do?" Graham asked.

"Well, I just thought you might like to know." Richards shrugged and turned around and walked away.

"Let me at him!" Growled Graham, who was playfully reaching for departing Sergeant and being restrained by Freeman.

"Easy now tiger!" Cackled Freeman, "Go and enjoy your evening, I'll look into this."

"Thanks Rich." Graham said steeping back into the elevator as the doors slowly closed, "The main event for the evening was nearly 'Grumpy Graham' versus 'Bugs the Fu…"

Chapter 43

Burt had somehow managed to escort a woozy Thomas from the cellar to the back room of the church, where he now lay drifting in and out of sleep on the pullout sofa. Burt would have preferred to see him resting in his own bed, but he was spent. The rigours of such a stressful day had taken its toll on him and he too needed to rest his weary bones. Thomas was propped up slightly by a heap of soft pillows but remained motionless, his bruised eyelids flickering as if he were fighting to open them but his body would not allow it.

Burt turned on the television and shuffled over to his favourite armchair collapsing into with an exhausted groan.

"What a day." He sighed and looked over at Thomas, who was all bandaged up, his stab wounds had been stitched and were now heavily dressed, "You've definitely been through the mill today haven't ya?"

Thomas didn't reply.

"Yeah, probably best to just sleep it off. It's gonna take you a while to get back on your feet."

Burt gave a caring smile and yawned.

"I guess we will have to tell old Lamont that those stairs need fixing." He chuckled to himself.

Burt settled back in his chair and pulled a multicoloured crocheted blanket onto his lap and turned his attention to the TV where suave news anchor Rex Redford announced the evening's news to Study City.

"...according to some eyewitnesses the masked vigilante known as Vatican was involved and taken away with severe injuries. A representative of SCPD neither confirmed nor denied this. Two of the three men that were arrested had to receive medical attention..."

The faces of Famu, Dallas and Boris flashed up on the screen.

"Known felons and former members of the now defunct Doomsday Gang, Danny Orton and Boris Zhukov have been charged with kidnapping and assault along with Famu Alofu, a former professional sumo wrestler now head of security for Devine Incorporated. Alofu made the headlines last year while his tangle with The Angel of Justice became and internet sensation..." The candid footage of Vatican and Famu fighting on the rooftop is played, before cutting to SCTV News footage of him hanging upside down from the top of the building. *"...where he was found in a most precarious position."* Redford fought back the urge to snigger at the sight of Famu hanging upside down like an angry bull shark. *"...The proprietor of Hu Meats, Mr Yao Hu was initially questioned but later released without charge..."*

Burt's eyes were too flickering now as he wandered into

dreamland until Thomas' cell phone exploded into an offbeat high pitch whine. Burt was suddenly wide awake again and pulled himself up and made it across the room to the table where the remains of an unfinished chess game remained frozen in time. He reached for the phone and looked at the screen, No Caller ID flash at him rapidly and he declined the call.

"No calls tonight thank you." Burt said to nobody in particular and took the cell with him to his chair placing it on the arm while he got comfortable again and focussed again on Rex Redford who had now started on another report.

"...Mandrillus Kalu known better as the professional wrestler 'The Masked Mandrill', was arrested on charges of distributing several illegal substances..." A photograph of Mandrillus dressed in his wrestling gear flashed up on the screen, a mugshot of him when he was brought in and booked joined it. *"...SCPD relived that the investigation to bring down Kalu had been ongoing now for three months and were finally able to bring him in, they are confident that they have enough evidence for the charges to hold up in a court of law."*

The cell phone burst into life again and Burt grumbled loudly. He glanced at the screen it still blazed with No Caller ID, so Burt declined the call again. He looked over at Thomas, he did not stir.

"...several bodies have been discovered in a cellar of a house on Cecil Avenue in the Bertram part of the city. All the victims are believe to have been shot dead, a head of

329

black male was also found but no trance of the body. SCPD released a statement that the bodies have been there for sometime and had started to decompose. Their identity have not been made public at this time..."

The phone rang again, Burt growled and declined, turning the phone off and dropping it to the floor unceremoniously. Thomas stirred and opened his eyes.

"B-Burt?" He murmured sleepily.

"Shh!" Burt hissed rising and stopping Thomas' attempt to sit up, "Did I wake you Thomas? I'm sorry, you go back to sleep now."

"But..." Thomas spluttered, "...But I can't..."

"I know, Thomas, I know."

"No... It's the..." Thomas said before falling to sleep again. Burt patted his head with a damp cloth and looked at him with all the love and care of a parent for a small child.

"...this brutal scene has not been ruled out of being part of the recent murders that have taken place recently. The killer has been christened 'The Crucifix Killer' by the tabloids who had initially speculated that Vatican could be responsible, but a statement from SCPD's own Detective Richard Freeman revealed that they are following up leads linking the murders to Nicholas Smith who escaped from Oakland Institute..." a photograph of Smith of him looking intoxicated flashed up on the screen, *"...Smith is said to be extremely dangerous and should not be approached, If sighted please call..."*

Thomas sat bolt up right and growled incoherently through gritted teeth which scared Burt.

"The light is golden and the crane is black!" Thomas said and then lay back down. Burt looked at him concerned.

"What did you say, Thomas?"

"The light is golden and the crane is black. The light is golden and the crane is black. The light is golden and the crane is black." He muttered relentlessly as Burt joined him at his bedside again, soothing him with the damp cloth again.

"Delirious." Burt sighed shaking his head.

Chapter 44

The television blared loudly in the dark backroom of St. Jospeh's Church, the flickering screen washed over the room with a vibrant array of colours. Father Harrison sat on his makeshift bed, surrounded by his own filth as the screen flashed rapidly before him, working hard to keep the pixelated flurries of snow that attacked the obsolete television set.

"...The World Games governing body has come under scrutiny for its tackling of performance enhancement drugs as yet another athlete has failed a test for a banned type of steroid Polish gymnast, Yugo Putski, took the gold medal at the games in Canada last week for placing first in the Rings event..."

The conclusion of Putski's winning routine was then shown on the screen, as Putski then broke into tears of elation as he was jumped on by his coaching staff and held aloft on their shoulders.

"Cheating bastard!" Came the slur of words from the drunken figure swaying back and forth with his cell phone in his hand. The screen flashed up at him and illuminated his gait face, covered with an unkept nest of facial hair with bits of food concealed inside. He prodded at the touch screen slowly as Rex Redford continued to drone on.

"...Putski was obviously stripped of the gold medal, but refused to leave the stadium quietly and had to be escorted from the building..." Video footage of him being forcibly removed was then shown as he raged angrily in Polish. *"...He was heard yelling, 'I will have that medal. It belongs to me', before being ejected..."*

"Stupid phone..." He grumbled, holding the screen hope close to his face, eyes red and weary, "It's the right fucking number you piece of shit!" He growled as he jabbed at the digits again with his dirty fingers.

"...Some good news has come out of today's events though with Canada's own Holly Harris, the 15 year old took gold on The Beam..." Jubilant celebrations of Harris finishing her routine and then standing with her new gold medal around her neck beaming. *"....And now for sports..."* Father Harrison stared through murky vision to read the card clenched in his fingertips, The name Father Thomas Gabriel was apparent followed by his phone number running beneath it.

"That's gotta be the number, damn it!" Harrison spluttered, but all he got when he dialled was a robotic voice informing him that the number was unavailable and to try again later. Harrison screamed at the top of his lungs, laughing the cellphone across the room and cracking the screen, Redford quivered behind the cracked screen but still seemed adamant that he would bring the sports news to Father Harrison whether he wanted it or not.

"...S-studd...City A-angels fell again tonight, this time to a shocking d-defeat at the hands of the Sanctuary City Huskies 63 to..." Redford disappeared in an explosion of sparks and glass at Harrison's bare foot came crashing through it. An act that he obviously regretted as soon as it was over, he howled in pain as he fell back onto his bed, shards of glass protruding from his foot.

"Son of a whore!" He shrieked and then started to sob.

"What was the point of giving that card, you fuck! Why tell me you will be there if I need you if you won't be?" Tears ran down his face as he looked at his television that still fluttered with flames and emitted thick grey smoke in plumes. "Why?" He cried, clear mucus seeping out of his nostrils and settling into his beard, "You're just another liar aren't you? A Goddamn liar like all the rest of them!" His moist face sunk into the palms of his hands and he mumbled and grumbled through his sobs before peeling his face away, now wearing a face of intense malice as he spat, "I' don't need you, Gabriel!" He found the card again and crumpled it up in his hand and discarded it into the flickering flames within the demolished television set. He watched as the name burned up in the card until only black flakes of ashes dissolved into nothingness.

"I'll show them all I don't need anyone to help me!"

Chapter 45

The carriages of Forge City's subway train rattled as it hurtled through the tunnels underneath the city. The lights flickered and flashed spasmodically, diving into darkness for several seconds. Several people sat bored or dozing, some reading, some scanning monotonously through social media on their cellphones. A door slid open from a rear carriage and Nicholas Smith strode in, spear in hand, its silver tip drenched in blood. His face wore a sadistic smile, his thin face flickered with speckles of blood. Those not immersed in the pages of their books, screens of there phones or the inside of their eyelids quickly stood up and left for the safety of the next carriage along. Nicholas sat down in the middle of the carriage and looked around, holding his spear between his legs as blood dripped at his feet and started to create a puddle. The lights flickered again as the screeching of metal on metal erupted from below as the worn wheels continued to spin with reckless abandon. Nicholas stared at the man curled up sleeping on the seat opposite him, he stirred and woke up suddenly and wiped at his eyes, and asked through blurred vision, "Hey guy, did we reach Monsoon yet?"

"**Not yet my Friend.**" Nicholas replied as the man retrieved his glasses from and inside pocket and wiped at them.

We've stopped at Vigo, Tully and Valiant I believe."

"Oh that's good then, I usually miss it at this time of night." He yawned and then smiled at the blurred silhouette in front of him, in shades of red and black.

"**Easily done.**" Nicholas smiled. With the man's glasses now in place, his eyes became magnified behind them as he finally saw the bizarre and somewhat frightening sight that sat in front of him.

"What the hell..." He murmured.

"**Is hell on this line ?**" Nicholas asked "**A nice place to visit I hear, humidity is a bitch though.**"

"I..."

"**Listen...**" Nicholas whispered as he leaned in closer, clutching the golden shaft of the spear, "**I can take you there if you wish.**" And then smiled sadistically.

"W-what?" The man stuttered as he squirmed uncomfortably in his seat.

"**The Anti Christ is your saviour.**" Nicholas smiled as the lights flickered again and darkness consumed the carriage. The was an horrendous sound of the spear goring the man's chest and a gurgling sound as rising blood clogged up his throat and he died. The lights flickered and it was once again illuminated by the strip lights above.

Nicholas sat smiling unfazed by the man lolling in his seat with a gigantic spear protruding out of his chest and blood cascading down like he were a man shaped waterfall. Nicholas placed his hands in his lap and began twiddling his thumbs as he whistled *'Entrance of the Gladiators'* cheerfully. Screams erupted around him as the other passengers realised what had taken place and head for the next carriage in a chaotic stampede.

"Salvation awaits." He smiled as the lights flickered on and off again.

Chapter 46

Detective Graham's Ford County Squire turned onto Willows Lane, either side of him tall maple trees stretched up to the night sky as if tying to touch the moon.

"Well, boys I hope you enjoyed that?" Graham asked as he looked over his shoulder, Billy and Todd sat fast asleep, immersed in a of pro wrestling merchandise. Graham smiled to himself, "Lightweights! Anyone think you just took on The Rhino Brothers."

Graham's cell phone flashed at him from the passenger's seat, indicating that he had received yet another missed call. He glanced at it and picked it up, making sure that he counting to roll slowly down the lane due to his precious cargo. He activated the phone and the notification of 16 missed calls situated itself on top of a family photograph.

The cell informed him that the calls had all been from Valerie Nash and he sighed, dropping the cell back on the passenger seat.

"It's over." He said "I have to tell her its over now."

The Graham family house was in total darkness as Graham approached.

"Look's like Mommy is in the land of nod." Graham said aloud, the boys snored loudly in reply.

Mae's maroon Chrysler Pacifica remained in the driveway in front of the closed garage.

"She must have forgot to tuck the minivan in for the night." He scoffed almost annoyed, so he slowly pulled up behind it on the edge of the driveway the headlights bathing the lifeless house for amount before turning off the engine.

Graham turned to see that the boys were still asleep and exited the vehicle, quietly shutting the door behind him.

"Best open her up first, if I've got to carry you two sandbags in." So he approaches the house and opens up the front door, as he does Charlie, the family Labrador bolts out of the house with a yelp and heads for the car.

"Charlie!" Graham cries, "What the hell has gotten into you boy?" He says lowering his voice to a whisper as he approaches him. Charlie scratches at the back door trying to get in, this stirs the boys from their sleep as Graham returns to the car.

"What's up boy?" He asked stroking him on the head gently, he could feel the dog quivering under his touch and whining loudly. Charlie's eyes seemed to want to tell Graham something and he stared into them inquisitively, the dog's brow contorted causing his eyes to look somber.

"Is there something wrong, boy?" Graham asked and turned to look at the house that still stood in darkness, motionless with no signs of life. Graham opened the car door and immediately Charlie joined the boys in the back , cowering between them. Graham reached into the glovebox to retrieve his revolver.

"Everything okay Dad?" Todd asked now fully awake. "I think so, kid." Graham looked again at the house and then back at his eldest son, "Just stay in the car and look after your brother, okay?"

Todd nodded as Graham walked up the path towards the house before stopping in his tracks as his nostrils picked up the unmistakable smell of almonds, which is was notorious in Nobel 808 C4 explosive.

"No." Graham whispered.

There was a defining explosion and the house erupted, the impact of the blast sent Graham hurtling backwards where he landed unceremoniously on the front lawn. He gazed up at where he house once stood and was now replaced by a raging inferno that flick the dark sky with its amber tongues. Graham tried to shake away the ringing in his ears as he looked up in shock, the heat immense melting away any rational thought he had he leap to his feet and charged towards the house screaming "Mae!" At the top of his voice, only to be met by a second explosion that sent him back where he came from. He clambered to his feet again It was then that he heard Charlie barking and Todd and Billy's crying. He turned to face them and watched as they were

340

pressed up against the window with tears flowing from their little eyes. It was an image that would stay with Graham for a long time as he looked back at the house helpless and fell to his knees sobbing.

The Angel of Justice will return in...

VATICAN
FOUR SUNDAYS

Follow author Daniel J.Barnes on social media
@DJBWriter on Facebook, Instagram & Twitter.

Printed in Great Britain
by Amazon